EVA

WITCHES' MASQUERADE

THE VAMPIRES OF EMBERBURY BOOK 3

To Bori
Thank You for the Unicorns.
Eva

Other books in this series:

THE VAMPIRES OF EMBERBURY

You can visit the author's website at:
www.evaalton.com

WITCHES' MASQUERADE

"So be it, let me die:
but to save yourself long memories,
listen awhile.

King's daughter,
my life is not only in your power
but is yours of right.

My life is yours
because you returned it to me twice."

Tristan

The Romance of Tristan and Iseult, M. Joseph Bdier

Chapter 1

Alba

As soon as I saw the vampire queen waiting for me by the arrival gate at Emberbury International Airport, I knew the rest of the evening was going to be much less pleasant than the long transatlantic flight itself—which was no small feat, considering I hated those with a passion.

My plane had landed after 3:00 a.m., and I was one of the first passengers to disembark. Being the only one without a suitcase had certain drawbacks, but it made my trip extremely quick and breezy. It should be pointed out that my travel minimalism hadn't happened by choice: most of my stuff had burned down in a hotel fire back in Italy, while I tried—and failed—to take a relaxing vacation… all with the very respectable purpose of finding myself and not killing anyone in the process. I hadn't achieved any of the latter, and things had kept snowballing since then.

Elizabeth followed me silently to the taxi stand, not even bothering to offer me a lousy *hello*.

Things must have been dire for a woman of her status to take the trouble to show herself in a crowded, public place. Elizabeth Swamp rarely left The Cloister, unless to rapidly quench her thirst, and even when she did, she took great care to help everyone forget they had ever met her. Something told me that this evening was a first for her in many respects.

"May I share your ride?" she asked, untangling her Victorian frock from the wheels of an abandoned baggage trolley.

"Hi, Elizabeth… long time no see." I forced myself to smile, opening the door of the taxi for her. "Of course you can. Please get in."

She gathered her skirts, filling all the space in the back with a mass of pine green velvet and tulle which made the taxi look like the van of a clandestine fabric dealer. Seeing there would be no room for me to travel beside her, I took a seat in the front and started to give the driver directions to get us to The Cloister.

"Excuse me," Elizabeth said, lifting a finger from behind the fabric bundle hiding half of her face, "that's not the right address. We are staying at Westside Avenue."

"Are we?" I asked, perplexed. Last time I had checked, there was a rundown property at that address, the majority of its furnishings consisting of cobwebs and worm-eaten grand pianos. Besides, all my things were in The Cloister, and I had absolutely no personal items with me apart from the filthy clothes I was wearing and a half-empty backpack with my passport.

"How did you know about my flight?" I asked, reclining against the headrest and stifling an exhausted yawn. The past weeks in Italy had been taxing, and I had hoped for a good night's sleep at last—sadly, my humble dream seemed to be drifting further and further away.

"You sent a communication," she replied in a calm voice, and it took me a second to understand she meant *an email*, "and you also taught us how to use the information highway. I was always a scholarly woman."

I nodded in admiration. I hadn't thought her able to read my emails, but I had sent one from Tuscany anyway, just in case. Apparently, I had created a monster with my teachings; or better said, enhanced the monster she already was with a sprinkle of useful technology.

***

The rest of the car ride took place in silence; the matters we needed to discuss were all too sensitive to be tackled in front of a stranger.

By the time the driver pulled over and announced our destination, I had dozed off. The sudden lack of movement woke me up just in time to see Elizabeth extending him a tip which would have been enough to cover a round trip to Vegas. *In a limo. With champagne.*

Elizabeth and I got out of the car avoiding each other's gaze, while she dug up the keys to the main door. They were, as usual, buried in a planter. She closed the door behind us, leaving the space around us in complete darkness.

"Please, take a seat," Elizabeth said, disappearing into the depths of the old townhouse. She might have forgotten that I didn't share her superb vampire sight and wouldn't be able to find a chair in total blackness.

A match hissed on the other side of the room, and soon a soft orange light illuminated the space. I looked around, but I still couldn't find anything to sit on, so I let myself flop on the floor, using my backpack as a cushion. The place smelled of mildew and old memories, many of them involving Clarence.

"I can't believe I didn't foresee this," Elizabeth spat, dragging an antique armchair out of nowhere and sitting down on it with royal flair. So they did have furniture after all, but she wasn't going to offer me any. I shrugged, sprawled out at her feet like the sworn vassal I was, and lowered my gaze as I waited for her imminent accusations. "My entire life's endeavors falling to pieces because of a witch... *larva*."

She tapped her long, sharp nails on the gilded arms of the chair and studied me with half-closed eyes. Exhaustion had made me drowsy, and that might have been the reason Elizabeth suddenly didn't seem as formidable as she usually did. In the dimly lit house, with her skirts oddly crumpled around her knees, she looked like a very tired middle-aged lady after a Halloween party which had gone on for too long.

"I should kill you," she said. "I should have eliminated you as soon as I saw you."

She motioned for me to stand up, and I grimaced. If she really wanted to kill me right there and right then, there wasn't much I could do to prevent it. Hopefully, she would kill me fast, at the very least. As she approached me, I wondered what would become of my daughters after I was gone, and I got a knot in my stomach.

Luckily for me, she changed her mind and sat back again. I sighed in relief, but it lasted only until she formulated her next question.

"Where is Clarence?" she enquired, her lips a thin, accusatory line. "Why didn't he come with you?"

"He's still in Italy, but he'll be here soon, I hope. He wasn't feeling well enough to fly on his own, and traveling by plane wouldn't have been safe for him. Lots of security cameras and mirrors, and perhaps sunlight too."

A ladder of fine lines covered Elizabeth's forehead. "He shouldn't have gone to Italy after you," she said. "None of you should have left The Cloister without my permission."

"It was all my fault. I caused all this mess. I'm so sorry, Elizabeth."

I was. *I truly was.*

"He's like a son to me. I saved every single member of The Cloister from a horrible fate. I found them when they were lost: most were outcasts, crazed with bloodlust; others were blinded by their thirst for revenge… but all of them had one thing in common: they were worthy despite their dire circumstances. I saw their value and worked to bring their true selves back to the surface."

"You've been very kind to us all," I said, hoping to appease her. At that point, keeping the vampire queen in a good mood seemed like a great step toward surviving the night.

"Kind?" she growled. "Kind! You know what would have been *kind*? Telling me in that *communication* of yours that Francesca wasn't coming to Emberbury and why. Tell me, Alba, why? Why isn't she here either?"

I remained silent. It wasn't accidental that I hadn't given her too many details in my email. First of all, I didn't even expect her to read it, and I was also worried about strangers trying to spy upon us. And second, I hadn't decided whether to reveal the truth about Julia. As far as Elizabeth knew, Julia had died thirty years ago. Telling her the whole story would have compromised Francesca's safety, as she had betrayed Elizabeth's rules to help the previous witch of The Cloister. But then again… Francesca might be dead for all I knew. I closed my eyes and held my head between my knees, still shaken by the very real possibility of never seeing Francesca again.

"You owe me an explanation, and don't you dare lie to me," Elizabeth warned me, "I want to know exactly what happened while you were away and where Francesca is. And remember, I can hear your heartbeat. I can smell your fear polluting the air of this room. If you think you can lie to an old vampire and get away with it, you are more naïve than I thought."

"Okay." I slumped closer to the floor, trying to become invisible, and Elizabeth's eyes shone red and menacing. "Maybe I should start by telling you that Julia is still alive." I waited for her reaction, but she remained deceivingly stoic. I swallowed and continued, "She's alive, or at least she still was when I met her. She asked me to go to Italy so she could teach me magic, but in truth, she wanted me to help her rescue her lover… I mean husband… from vampire hunters. Francesca was there too, and well, the hunters…"

"Julia." Elizabeth nodded, realization sinking in. "Julia is still alive… because they turned her into a vampire… of course." She stood up and started to pace, her footsteps inaudible in the drafty room. "So Ludovic was with her all this time." She shook her head. "I was such a fool. And Francesca knew everything but hid it from me, didn't she? Of course, she would do anything for her brother."

I nodded in silence, allowing Elizabeth to figure everything out by herself.

"I still can't believe they succeeded. Most witches die, go insane or self-destruct when turned into vampires. Our customs don't sit well with their… *Goddess,*" she pronounced the last word with a mocking tone. "I suppose Julia told you I'm evil to enforce the Five Rules… but look at the chaos she caused with her *little* disruption: it proves

I was right all along. There's a reason everyone under my watch is asked to swear under The Five Rules. *Just five.* They protect all of us from the hostile world outside. But you witches are always smarter, aren't you?" She lifted my chin, forcing me to look into her glimmering eyes. "What have you done, Alba? What have you done?"

"I'm sorry," I muttered. Her fingers dug into my skin painfully, but I didn't dare move. "I… I'll fix it," I added in a shaky voice, even though I wasn't sure that what I had started was fixable.

"Hunters," she snarled. "We managed to remain invisible for two centuries, but this is what you get if you mingle with witches. Who were they? What did they want?"

I told Elizabeth about Natasha Grabnar and her underwater laboratory full of moribund vampires and how we had escaped the secret prison under the Venice channels, losing Francesca in the process.

"You had better bring them back," she ordered. "Bring my children back to me. I didn't spend half a century mending their souls just for you to turn them into a wreck once again."

"I didn't turn anyone into a wreck."

"You have absolutely no idea what you are meddling with. You can't even imagine what Francesca was like when she came to me, let alone Clarence. He was broken, a self-destructing fireball of hatred. He will never completely overcome what he did to his father. What they did to each other."

"He killed him, didn't he?" I asked,

although I thought I knew the answer.

Elizabeth raised her eyebrows. "He didn't tell you? Interesting."

"He told me part of the story, but I don't know what happened in the end."

"Maybe you aren't supposed to know."

Her almond eyes were still an inch away from mine, her face a perfect, ageless slate, and her fangs shone between her slightly parted lips.

"So… you are not going to kill me, are you?" I managed to keep my voice firm, despite the turmoil inside.

She glared at me, her eyes glowing slightly golden now, and sighed. "If I were to kill you… would that solve my problem?"

I shook my head very slowly, cowering against the wall behind me. "You know I didn't mean to cause any harm."

She huffed. "Yes, I'd love to be rid of you, but no, I'm not going to kill you *today*. I should have never allowed any witches under our roof. I regret the day I gave in to Francesca's wishes to take Julia in. It was a mistake."

"So… am I fired then?"

Her bitter laughter took me by surprise. "You took a blood oath, for all that is wicked and unholy! That's not a human contract you can just terminate. It's a bond for life, and only death can break it. As long as you are alive, it's still valid, and you will honor it." The smirk vanished from her blood-red lips, and she produced a small envelope out of the depths of her corset. "These are

Clarence and Francesca's documents. They might need them for travel if they were injured. Bring them back or die trying. If not, I will kill you myself, and it will *not* be a merciful death."

I nodded, taking the envelope with shaky hands.

"I'm glad we can agree on this," Elizabeth said, turning her back to me and heading to the door. "You can't come back to The Cloister with me. The hunters might be following you. You are allowed to stay here, but don't you dare come near Saint Anne's."

"I will bring Clarence back," I assured her. "As for Francesca, I'm not sure I can promise you anything because, for all I know, she might be…"

"Don't you dare say the word," Elizabeth warned me. "If anything happened to her because of you, you shall be sentenced to death. And this time, not even Clarence's pleas will be enough to save you."

"I… I understand. I'll do my best to find her. I swear." I swallowed. "Please have mercy, Elizabeth. I'll do anything. Just… don't kill me… please?"

"Isn't it fascinating," she said, curiosity illuminating her face, "how mortals get so attached to their brief, worthless existence. I wonder if you could enlighten me, Alba… why exactly are all of you so afraid of dying?"

Chapter 2

Alba

After Elizabeth left, I remained alone in the empty house in the disturbing company of my growing troubles. Soon it would be morning, and I decided it wasn't worth the effort to go out and find a hotel for just a couple of hours. Instead, I walked upstairs, candle in hand, and found a dusty bed with linens in one of the moldy bedrooms. Sleep eluded me, though, so I stared at the ceiling thinking about Elizabeth's threats until morning crept through the thin slits of the blinds and announced it was time to get up and start getting things done.

I was crawling around the floor, searching for my shoe—which had got lost in a massive nest of dust bunnies under the bed—when a flapping of wings blew away the dust and revealed my lost piece of footwear.

A large raven, its feathers sprinkled with white and gray, fluttered its way out of the bedroom fireplace and shook its wings to get rid of the soot and ash covering it. After that, a puff of white smoke hid the bird for a couple of seconds, and out of it came a dusty Jean-Pierre, his white hair and eyebrows covered in a light layer of ashes. He was carrying a blanket and a brown paper bag clutched against his coal-black waistcoat.

"*Ma Cherie*," he said with a bow as he rushed to hug me. "I'm so pleased to see you again. Elizabeth forbade us to come, but of course, I needed to check on our lovely little witch!"

We remained joined in a silent embrace for a few moments with our eyes closed, until he tilted his head back and started to sniff me with clear disgust. "Why do you smell like Roquefort cheese?" he asked. "Have you bathed lately?"

I smelled my clothes, and sure enough, I detected the musty scent Jean-Pierre was talking about. "Last time I showered it was in another continent, but I also think these bedsheets are a bit moldy. Sorry." I grinned in apology. "Let's go downstairs. The smell is worse here in the bedroom."

Jean-Pierre offered his elbow and escorted me gallantly down the stairs, then led me to the same armchair where Elizabeth had been sitting the night before. Once he had made sure I was comfortably seated, he kissed the back of my hand. "You are colder than I," he commented with concern, then handed me the blanket he had been carrying and glanced at the large fireplace in the corner. "Let me light a fire for you."

After that, he disappeared into a dark

doorway and came back balancing a pile of logs taller than him. Patiently, he stacked the logs in neat rows, kneeling by the fireplace. "Everything here is so damp," he complained, wiping his hand on his trousers. Using a match, he tried to kindle a wilted bunch of pine needles, but after many failed attempts and half a box of matches, there wasn't even the slightest trace of a fire, although I had learned plenty of swearwords in French. "Damned tinder… all useless!" Jean-Pierre shouted in frustration.

"Yeah, I hear all guys there are players," I mumbled, my mind too busy evaluating Elizabeth's threats and the impossible task I had been entrusted with. "Loss of time, all that swiping. One could do better sweeping chimneys. Or so they say."

"Excuse me?" Jean-Pierre arched his eyebrows, rolling up an old, musty newspaper to use instead of the pine needles. He inspected the inside of the fireplace, making sure the chimney wasn't blocked.

I shook my head, forcing myself to return to the present moment. "I'm sorry, sometimes I don't even know what I'm saying. It's been a crazy couple of weeks, and my head is a mess." Noticing his frustration with the fire, I got my backpack and found a lighter and a few old receipts: perhaps not the best tools, but at least they were dry. I handed them to Jean-Pierre, who turned the lighter in his fingers with puzzlement, pressing on the base instead of the spark wheel. It was obvious he had never seen one before. "Here, let me do it," I said, getting impatient.

He was right—everything in that house was too damp. But I was starting to feel edgy, as it was clear that Jean-Pierre wouldn't give up until he made sure it was warm enough for me. All I wanted was him to sit down already and update me on the current situation in The Cloister.

I clicked my fingers with annoyance, trying to think of an alternative. As I did it, purple sparks came out of my fingertips, lighting the room for a second.

"*Uh-huh*!" Jean-Pierre clapped and pointed at the fading sparks with admiration. "Very nice. Do it again!"

I repeated the clicking motion, and the sparkling intensified, creating a soft purple glow around us. With a wave of my hand, I directed it toward the logs in the fireplace: a thin purple fog came out of them and disappeared into the chimney, but nothing else happened. I tried to generate more sparks, but the trick had stopped working.

"Pure luck," I said with a sigh. "As usual, I don't know how I did it."

Jean-Pierre inspected the firewood, rubbing a stick with his fingers and smelling it.

"Good job anyway," he said with an appreciative nod, lighting one of the thinnest twigs, "looks quite dry now."

"So, why are you here?" I asked him, hauling Elizabeth's armchair next to the fireplace and rubbing my hands to warm them up. "Aren't you worried Elizabeth will find out you came to see me?"

Jean-Pierre shrugged, reclining against the fireplace. He was dressed in black from head to toe, and his snowy hair shone slightly golden and orange by the first flames of the fire.

"I am, but I wanted to make sure you were alright. Also, it worries me that you will not be able to solve all this on your own."

I plopped into the armchair again. He was so right. I had no idea how I was going to bring Francesca back to The Cloister. "So, you heard the news."

Jean-Pierre nodded. Elizabeth must have told everyone about my failed vacation while I was tossing and turning in a moldy bed till the wee hours of the morning.

"I know about Francesca, but tell me, *ma belle*, what's wrong with Clarence?" he asked cautiously, crouching to poke at the fire.

"Nothing is wrong with him. He's just recovering from a curse, but he should be here soon. He was tired, that's it."

"A curse?" Jean-Pierre raised an eyebrow. "Well, that's interesting. Not many modern curses could make a vampire… *tired*. Do you, by any chance, know its name?"

"I think it was called *The Silver Cast*. Have you heard about it? Francesca mentioned the name, but I didn't have the chance to ask her for details. I think it's supposed to encase the heart in a thin layer of silver, which seeps slowly into a vampire's blood…"

"…and kills them slowly but relentlessly," Jean-Pierre finished the sentence for me with a gloomy nod.

"Yes," I said calmly, "but we managed to reverse the curse, so he should be fine soon." I tried to sound reassuring.

"Did you? How?" His tone was skeptical and curious at the same time.

"Well, you know… Carlo…" No, he probably didn't know him. "He's a former vampire hunter I met on the plane. He suggested we could reverse the curse the way vampires usually solve everything… if you know what I mean." I was feeling suddenly coy for some absurd reason, overwhelmed by the memories of Clarence's bites and kisses in Venice after fleeing Natasha's prison. I knew I had no reason to blush in front of Jean-Pierre: as much as he enjoyed playing the role of an innocent monk, everyone in The Cloister knew he was one of the least innocent vampires to walk on Earth.

Jean-Pierre's mouth curved in a cunning, delighted smile. "Oh. Glad to hear he finally saw reason. I was starting to think there was something wrong with him."

"What are you talking about?"

He caressed the top of my head. "Nothing, nothing. I'm just pleased you two are getting along again. I remember you had fallen out a little when you left The Cloister. The only problem is…" His expression turned somber, and he remained suddenly silent.

"Yes?" I invited him to continue.

"I'm not sure you want to hear this."

"Hear what?"

He fidgeted with the buttons of his waistcoat, staring at the floor, and I puffed with impatience, about to pull out my hair. "What's wrong? What's the problem?"

"It's about the Silver Cast," he said, his smile completely vanished. "If what you are saying is true… I know about this curse. It was very popular a few centuries ago, when we were forced to battle against witches."

"Finally! I've been having a hard time finding information about it. Clarence doesn't seem to know much, and…"

"Oh, Clarence does know," Jean-Pierre interrupted me, rolling his eyes, "we fought together back then. He saw many of our kind succumb to the curse. But I can understand why he would hide this piece of information from you."

"Hide what? Will you tell me already?"

"I don't want to worry you, *ma belle*," Jean-Pierre said ominously, taking my hand in his, "and I'm sorry to be the bearer of bad news… but someone should have told you that The Silver Cast is not a reversible curse."

Chapter 3

Alba

"What do you mean it's not reversible?" I shouted, jumping up from the armchair to look straight into Jean-Pierre's eyes.

Jean-Pierre put his hands on my shoulders and sighed. "It used to be a well-known vampire slaughtering spell. Deadly, but extremely hard to cast. I am surprised there are witches out there who still remember it."

"But Clarence said he was feeling better," I said, crossing my arms. "He would have told me if he wasn't!"

Jean-Pierre raised an eyebrow. "Would he?"

I held my breath, realization sinking in. Had he known the truth all this time? Did he know the curse was not reversible? Why had he sent me away then?

I growled, pulling at the ends of my hair. *"That. Stupid. Vampire!"*

"Yes… as you know, the curse creates a cast around the heart." Jean-Pierre looked at me, expectant, and I invited him to continue. "What you might not know is that this silver cast later extends to the rest of the body, consuming the life energy of the victim. And once all their energy is gone, they slowly turn translucent until they vanish forever, turning into dust."

"Oh my God," I gasped. "That's horrible."

Jean-Pierre hugged me. "I'm sorry, Alba. I am sure his intention was not to worry you unnecessarily."

"Unnecessarily?" I shouted, kicking the heavy armchair.

"Calm down, will you please?" he said. "There might be a way. I'll look into it and get back to you. Don't lose hope just yet." He reached for the brown paper bag he had been carrying on his arrival, now forgotten on a dresser, and handed it to me. "Here, have a croissant. Croissants always make everything better."

***

Jean-Pierre flew away, promising to research more about The Silver Cast and leaving me with a still-warm French pastry I didn't feel like eating. After a while holding the poor croissant and staring at it with disdain, I followed Jean-Pierre's advice and ate half of it.

I was considering what to do with the other half, when my phone rang, and Carlo Lombardi's voice greeted me from the other side.

"I hear you are back in Emberbury," he

said. It was early—too early to call anyone but your own mother in an emergency—but Carlo Lombardi was one of those people who thought his attention was always the most wonderful gift anyone could receive. I had texted him my new phone number and informed him of my arrival; perhaps not the smartest thing to do, but I couldn't think of anyone else. It was good to have someone know I had returned, in case Elizabeth decided to kill me and get rid of my body.

"I'm back, yes," I said.

"Where are you staying?"

Good question. Even though I had come to trust Carlo, to some extent, there was no way on earth I would have shared with him the location of The Cloister, nor the one of the house which the vampires used as their official address.

"I'm staying at a friend's house." *Not a lie.*

"Are you busy today?" he asked. "I think we should talk."

"Actually, I am. I need to pick up my daughters. I hope they still remember me."

As soon as I said it, I realized that this dark and cold house wouldn't be suitable for Katie and Iris to stay. If they were to live with me again, I needed to find a better place until Elizabeth allowed me to go back to The Cloister.

"Okay, then let's have dinner tonight," Carlo suggested. "Do you like Mexican food?"

I grumbled, hesitating. "I do, but..."

"It's not a date," he clarified, sounding offended. "I don't care about you and whatever you have with the bloodsucker. But we need to talk. Meet me at eight o'clock at Taco Hell, on Queen Street."

"Such a perfect name," I said, exhaling with relief. "Okay, see you there tonight."

Chapter 4

Alba

I took a bus to Mark's new apartment, which was very close to the courthouse: a place filled with unpleasant memories of my ex-husband, who I was about to see. In need of courage to survive the encounter, unavoidable if I was to pick up my daughters, I grabbed a takeaway espresso by the bus stop and drank it in one single gulp. It didn't make me braver right away, but it helped appease the confusion and tiredness caused by jet lag.

It was Saturday, a week or so away from Valentine's Day. The whole city had gone crazy with perfume ads, red hearts and pink garlands everywhere: funny how stores started celebrating V-Day a bit sooner each year. My thoughts drifted to Clarence, and I wondered what he might be up to, alone in Carlo's villa in Italy. I wished he was here with me in Emberbury. I couldn't remember ever going on a proper date on Valentine's Day, and I was sure the company of a handsome vampire would have made it an exciting experience.

Definitely more exciting than meeting grumpy Mark before caffeine kicked in.

He caught me yawning as he opened the door and greeted me with a growl. "I didn't expect you so early," he complained, chewing a piece of toast with avocado. His blond hair was tousled, like he had just got out of bed, and he was wearing an expensive, though understated, t-shirt with matching sweatpants.

"That life-coach of yours from London seems to be working wonders on your manners, Mark," I commented. I meant it—it was a clear improvement compared to the last time. No death-threats, for a start. "What was his name again?"

"Vladimir," he answered. *He answered!* Yes, there was visible improvement going on. "Minnie will make you coffee," he added then, perhaps exhausted after refraining from insulting me for a whole sixty seconds, "I have things to do."

Mark disappeared into one of the rooms, leaving me in the middle of his new, open-plan kitchen, which was as empty and sterile as everything of his. High-pitched voices came out of the bathroom, mingled with Minnie's posh accent, and I heard my daughters and Mark's new girlfriend singing a cartoon tune and laughing together. I felt a pang of jealousy and sadness, suddenly aware of the shared experiences I must have missed during the last weeks, including most of the Christmas holidays. I shook my head. No, no. *Wrong attitude.* I should be happy they were having so much fun with Minnie. Yes, Minnie was a blessing in disguise, and she was kind to them. If it hadn't been for her, I wouldn't have trusted volatile Mark with the girls for longer than two hours.

Two golden-haired elves emerged from the bathroom and ran straight into my arms like tiny, effervescent bath bombs of happiness.

"Mommy!" they cheered and danced around me, still singing the same silly song and clad in horrid, glitter-ridden tutus.

I had missed them so much.

"Did you have fun in Italy?" Minnie asked. Even in her too-short silk robe, she was as spotless as usual, with perfect make-up and shiny ironed hair. I didn't want to look at myself in the mirror—I hadn't had time to exchange my unflattering t-shirt and jeans from the plane, which were some spare clothes I had found in Carlo's Tuscany guesthouse, the ones forgotten or discarded by tourists on their way home. I was quite certain my coat had a hole too, right behind my elbow, so I flattened myself against a wall to prevent Minnie from seeing it.

"The trip was…" I paused, wondering how to explain I had almost died twice, been held prisoner by witches, caused an explosion and lost a vampire friend under a collapsing building. "It was great, thanks!"

"Venice is so charming, isn't it?" Minnie nodded. "It's one of my favorite cities. I remember the last time I was there…" She hesitated before continuing. "With my parents." She finished the sentence in a surprisingly unsteady voice, which made me wonder whether she had been there with Mark, perhaps during one of his business trips, as they had been together while we were still married. I didn't care. She was welcome to keep Mark forever, as far as I was concerned.

"Nice," I said, hugging Katie and Iris. "So, Minnie… we're going out for the day, but I must bring them back here this evening."

Minnie gaped at me, incredulity apparent in her eyes. "You mean *this* evening? No way. They can't stay here tonight. We have things to do, too. This was supposed to be two weeks and here we are, early February and still baby-sitting for you. Why on earth did you ask for full custody if you never have time to take care of them?"

I died a little inside listening to the truth in her words. If only she knew how I wished to take these two girls with me. But where was I supposed to take them? The house in Westside Avenue was a moldy hole, and if I didn't find Francesca soon enough, they would soon be motherless anyway.

"My place has leaks," I said in apology. "Also, my boss wants me to go on a business trip for a couple of weeks… it's been a series of… unforeseen circumstances." Minnie raised an eyebrow, and I grinned in desperation. "I'm so sorry."

"That's impossible," Minnie retorted in an icy tone. "Then at least tell your nanny to come here. I just dismissed ours, and I can't find a new one with such short notice. We have jobs, you know."

Francesca... I missed her too. Had she been there, I wouldn't have had to beg Minnie to take care of my kids, when that was nearly the last thing I wanted in the world.

"I'm really sorry, but Minnie, please, can you find a babysitter on your own? Mine is out of town. I don't know who else to ask. I need your help," I pleaded, holding my breath. "I'll find a way to make up for all your troubles, I promise."

Minnie sighed with impatience and started to browse on her phone. "Yeah, okay. I'll do it. But two weeks, max. One more day, and I will make sure that Mark starts getting ideas to fan the flames of your rocky separation. And then you won't need to pick the girls up ever again."

"Thank you," I said, swallowing my sadness and frustration.

Taking the hands of Katie and Iris, I grabbed their coats from the rack by the door and threw a last look at their little suitcases, neatly stacked in Mark's hallway. They remained there, behind us, like a gloomy reminder that they wouldn't spend the night with me for many days to come.

***

After such a long absence, I wanted to take the girls to a special place. The Butterfly House had always been one of my favorite places in Emberbury, and it was the ideal day trip during the winter months, thanks to the constant warm temperatures inside. Within its tall glass walls, it was easy to get lost and imagine being on a remote tropical island, covered in lush vegetation. The air in the conservatory was always thick, balmy and damp, brimming with the scent of orchids and other exotic flowers, and best of all, rainbow clouds of butterflies filled the air with fluttering colors. If you remained still for long enough, one of them might take a seat on your shoulder, or even kiss the tip of your nose.

My heart melted a little as I watched Katie and Iris run after the swarms of butterflies, trying to catch them and glowing with glee and childlike happiness. A group of visitors gathered around a bubbly tour guide with bouncing, blond ponytails, and I chased my kids to get them into the circle. Hopefully, we would be able to learn something new from the visit, apart from jumping over benches while attempting to catch a monarch butterfly.

"Welcome to Emberbury's Butterfly House," the guide said, swiveling to point at a particularly large specimen. "Follow me on a thirty-minute visit, where we'll find out about the fifty-seven butterfly species living in our conservatory. This enclosure mimics their natural tropical environment almost perfectly. Even when it's snowing outside, the temperature inside our glass house remains constant throughout the year…"

I squinted at her, my arms full with three heavy winter coats. *Oh really, I hadn't noticed.*

We walked at the tail end of the group, admiring the many butterfly species and listening to stories about their favorite flowers to drink nectar from and places to live.

Toward the end of the visit, the guide stopped in front of an informative panel showing the different life stages of butterflies.

"Butterflies have an exoskeleton," she explained. "That means they don't have bones like humans do, but instead, they have a hard shield protecting their bodies from the outside. As all insects, they are invertebrates. Any questions so far?"

Little Katie started to hop like a hare, as if about to implode with all the questions bubbling inside her. She had always been a bit nerdy and advanced for her age.

"Yes?" the guide pointed at her, inviting her to speak.

"Hi, I'm Katie… I… I have a question…" she stammered. "I hope it's not silly."

"No such thing as a silly question," the guide encouraged her.

"Okay! So, butterflies are *invert… um*, in-ver-te-brates?"

"Yes, that's right," the guide answered.

"And people? What are people?"

The guide glanced at her watch and sighed. "Vertebrates."

"So…" Katie bit her lip with deep concentration. "What about ghosts? Are ghosts vertebrates or invertebrates?"

The guide gaped at her as if struck by lightning. "*Uhh…*" she muttered, open-mouthed. "Good question."

People laughed in the background, and I turned around to throw the offenders a steely glance to make them shut up.

"To tell the truth, I have absolutely no idea," the guide apologized. "Maybe you can ask your mom? I only know about insects, sorry! Anyone else?"

Katie sulked and slumped against my hip with disappointment. I stared at my clever little humans, and for the first time ever, I wondered what kind of effect growing up surrounded by vampires would have on their views of the world when they were adults.

Meanwhile, the guide continued with the visit. "As you can see," she was saying, her voice steady and neutral, like a recording, "all butterflies start their life as caterpillars, which hatch from tiny eggs like this." She pointed at an enlarged picture of something looking like a semitransparent water droplet. "We call them *larvae.* After a while, the caterpillar builds a chrysalis around it. Inside the chrysalis, the caterpillar goes dormant, and all its organs melt into some sort of soup…"

A few younger members of the audience let out appalled gasps, and the guide smirked with visible pleasure as her discourse achieved its expected effect.

"*Ew,*" groaned a little boy nearby, disgusted by the concept of caterpillar soup. "Gross."

"*Uh-huh*, as you heard, they dissolve into caterpillar goo! But then, everything comes into place, just in a different order, creating their colorful wings. And when the time is right, a gorgeous butterfly emerges from the cocoon!"

She pointed at the last picture of the sequence, and Katie raised her hand, stirring nervously on her feet as she waited for her turn to ask yet another question.

"Yes?" the guide said, a bit more skeptical than the first time.

"*Uh*..." Katie stammered, and I prodded her softly, for courage. She swallowed and continued. "So, the caterpillar..." she paused and stared at her feet.

"Yes...?"

"Isn't the caterpillar afraid?"

"Why would it be?" The guide blinked, scrunching her nose.

"Because she has to go into that cocoon and melt, and she doesn't know what will happen to her. What if it hurts, or she dies, or she doesn't remember her mommy when she comes out?"

The guide gave her a sweet, amused smile. "Of course not! Metamorphosis is a magical transformation. It's a beautiful thing. They have no reason to fear it. They say butterflies still remember their caterpillar days when they come out of the cocoon. And there's not much they can do to stop nature from taking its course anyways. They just go with the flow. A caterpillar is happy to go to sleep with a full belly and wait for her wings to grow inside the chrysalis. They trust the process, and it usually ends beautifully. And I'm sure it's really cozy in there!"

"Yes, but… what if someone eats them while they are sleeping in their cozy cocoon?"

"It could happen, but as the saying goes… *nothing risked, nothing gained!*"

"I think caterpillars are pretty," little Iris said, with the endearing matter-of-factness of a four-year-old.

"I think caterpillars and worms are disgusting, but butterflies *are* pretty," Katie pointed out.

"I wish I could fly like they do," her sister continued. "Will I grow butterfly wings when I grow up?"

The guide turned off the lights over the panels with a remote. She seemed eager to leave and flee my daughters' interrogation. "No, I don't think you will."

The tour was over, and people started to leave the conservatory, chattering with amusement about Katie's debate on the existential dilemmas of caterpillars. Yet that little girl was persistent, and she tried to slip in one more question before the guide was gone. "But Francesca has wings sometimes. And a beak. She showed me. Why can't I have them too?"

I hushed my overtalkative kid before someone started to ask *us* uncomfortable questions. "We don't talk about such things in places full of people, remember?" I whispered, thankful the guide was dealing with a lost tourist and hadn't heard her.

"Sorry, mommy." She stared at her tiny trainers. "Minnie is nice, but I miss Francesca. When will we see her again?"

I flinched and steered them toward the exit, following the other visitors. It was almost dinnertime, and I thought it better not to anger Mark by bringing them back too late.

"I don't know, darling," I said, helping her get into her coat. "I don't know where she is." Willing to be honest with my children, I added, "Maybe she won't come back at all."

Katie pushed me away, determined to do up her buttons herself. "Oh, no. I'm sure she will. She likes us too much to not come back."

Nodding, I held back the tears as we stepped on the cold asphalt of the street. "Yes, that's true. Maybe you're right."

I kissed the top of her head, marveling at the intensity and persistence of children's innocence and hope.

How I wished I still had some of it myself.

How I wished it hadn't been gone for so, so long.

Chapter 5

Clarence

London, 1807

I clearly remember the day I lost the last trace of my ephemeral, infantile innocence. Even though it was dead long before it was gone, I still held onto it for a while, flimsy and transparent as it was. Its loss turned me into someone else, harder and wiser, but more bitter too. I was still a child, not long past my ninth birthday, when my father, deeming me old enough for such endeavors, took me to an operation theatre at St. Thomas Hospital with the intention of introducing me to his peers and ascertaining whether I was to become a man worthy of his consideration: a man strong enough to stare death in the face without flinching.

As we alighted from the carriage, he took my hand in his and showed me the way. He was always cold, despite the impeccable leather gloves. The stench of the hospital was noticeable even from the outside, and I swallowed, holding my breath before entering the crowded operation theatre.

Father holding my hand was never a gesture of affection: it was either a practical matter or a sign of possession. On that morning, I was thankful for it and held onto his arm like a castaway, fighting to avoid being crushed by the compact human mass which kept crowding tighter and tighter to get a better glimpse of the spectacle about to start. My height limited my range of sight to belts and armpits and regaled me with all sorts of unpleasant smells which added up to the rancid odor of the theatre itself.

Father navigated the stairs down the semicircular wooden stands toward the front rows, which were reserved for medical professionals like him and his colleagues. The populace would have to be content with a place in the background, their line of sight constantly blocked by taller individuals. They swore and protested, pushing each other, but I envied their luck. From our privileged spot, the view of the milky white naked corpse was agleam as a cloudless morning sky.

The scalpel went in, slicing the dead woman's abdomen like butter. A horrid stench reached me when the anatomist pulled out her innards. They scattered all over the dissection table, under the entranced stares of the onlookers. Someone vomited in the back, and people kicked him away from them, taking advantage of the weakling to secure a better spot.

A small, warm creature scurried between my

feet, making me stumble.

A rat.

The rodent had looted a fleshy leftover and started to chew on it, right beside me.

My stomach churned, followed by a strong taste of rising bile.

"Sir…" I whispered with a hoarse throat, pulling at Father's sleeve, "can I wait outside, please? I am feeling… unwell."

"Nonsense. Of course not." Father's upper lip twisted with disdain. I silently pleaded for mercy, but he threw me a glacial glance in response. "Do not dare humiliate me in front of my peers, boy, or you shall pay dearly for it later."

I held onto his coat, fighting the stale air which reeked of maggots, vomit and death.

"But Father…"

The world started to spin and faded to black. Father did not turn around, purposely ignoring my pleas. He wasn't even looking when I collapsed on the floor, right next to the feeding rat, oblivious to Father's peers and their opinion of me.

***

The empty sockets of a black skull were staring at me, creeping up and down the wall of my childhood bedroom while a woman screamed for help.

I blinked awake, realizing I was still dressed, lying in my bed. Father must have brought me back home, and the ghostly shapes were no more than the shadows cast by the single candlestick on the bedside table; the screams solely part of the nightmare I had been having while unconscious.

Or perhaps not.

Father's voice boomed downstairs, and a shiver ran down my spine.

"That boy is a disgrace," he was shouting.

"He is but a child," Mother answered. Her voice sounded brave and steady; a rare occurrence these days. She never fought for herself anymore, but she always found the odd scrap of courage to stand up for me when needed. "Give him time, Victor."

"I was leeching patients at his age," he continued. "You made a girl out of him, encouraging his whining and teaching him skills suited for a lady's maid, not a man."

I tiptoed down the stairs, taking in the scene from above. Father was still wearing a suit, standing with his waistcoat half unbuttoned and his cravat undone. Mother, on the other hand, was already in her shift and sitting on the divan, her golden locks falling down her shoulders and gleaming in the candlelight.

"Let the child be a child a little longer. He will be a good man one day, Victor. I can assure you of that."

"What would you know, woman?" Father snorted. "You have not even left the house for months, so fragile you are. You cannot even stand on your own feet most days. What do you know of the real world? It is a tough life out there. There's no place for weakness if a man is to thrive and support a family with integrity."

"It is not weakness that afflicts him." She placed a hand over her heart. "He just feels things too deeply." Her eyes paused for a second too long on Father's empty bottle of Port wine, almost accusing. "Each of us deals with life's troubles the best we know."

"That's ridiculous," Father puffed and dismissed her words with a wave of his hand. "You can retire now, Rose. This conversation is over."

Mother stood up to leave, but her knees failed her, and she had to sit down again. Father seemed cross that she was still there despite being dismissed, and I had to step in to protect her in my childish way.

"I am sorry, Father," I muttered, peeking from behind the door frame. "Please forgive me. It was not on purpose."

"No, I know it was not. It was your mother's fault for coddling you."

"No, Father! Mother did nothing wrong! It was the rats…"

"How dare you contradict me like that, boy?" His voice shook with barely contained rage. I knew that tone, and I knew what it portended.

"But Father…!"

Father exhaled slowly with his eyes closed.

"He is trying to explain to you what happened. Why not listen to him?" Mother interrupted.

"Silence, Rose! This boy needs to see reason

once and for all. Go upstairs before I do something I will regret."

"Don't you dare threaten me," she retorted with her hands on her hips, still too weak to stand up.

"Rose. Go. Upstairs!"

I stared at Father in horror, knowing what would come next.

"P-please, Father," I stuttered, "chastise me if you must, but leave Mother alone."

Father stood up, his eyes half-closed. "I did not ask for your opinion, boy."

"Leave the child. Talk to me, Victor," Mother pleaded, taking Father's hand. "Do not touch him. I beg you."

Father shook off her hand and took the poker which hung by the fireplace, then sat on the divan and gestured at me. "Come on here, boy. Let's get this done with quickly."

I remained still in front of him, my eyes narrowed, hoping that would make the whole room, and especially Father, disappear. Perhaps if I pressed them together hard enough, I might travel somewhere else, somewhere far, far away, where Mother and I would be safe from him.

Mother held onto the arm of the divan, stood up and set herself between us. "Leave the boy. He did nothing wrong."

"Step aside, Rose," Father commanded without glancing at her.

Yet Mother, small and reedy as she was, stood between us, steady as a mountain. But her body was frail as glass, and the slightest gust of wind could have blown her away.

"I said step aside!" Father shouted.

When Mother still did not budge, I closed my eyes even tighter.

I muttered a prayer.

And waited… waited for my nightmare to be a mere nightmare; but just like most times, it ended up being a premonition and not a bad dream after all.

***

Tuscany, present day

A hard slap on the face woke me up.

I opened my eyes to find a dead bird lying on my chest, right on the spot which hurt with that cold, metallic pain radiating from the center of my heart.

Judging by the look and smell, that bird must have been dead for days. It had fallen from the ceiling, straight on my face, while I was trying to slumber inside an open trunk, in a vain attempt to fight the exhaustion and pain. Its flesh was crawling with maggots, its rotten stench so foul that I jumped out of the wooden chest to escape it.

Tuscany.

I was still in Tuscany.

I checked the small device Alba had bought me in the village before leaving. There was a message stating she had arrived safely.

I was hungry, but the cold fire of the curse kept burning my insides, steadily extending to my fingertips and arms. I needed to quench my thirst, but that would mean leaving the small winemakers' hamlet and risking being discovered. I hadn't tried to fly for a long time. Perhaps I should walk, if it was dark enough.

Taking the stylus Alba had carefully left by the telephone, I typed a message for her, like she had taught me, telling her I wasn't fit for travel *just yet*.

"I'm going out to have dinner," I finished it, adding an affectionate goodbye to dispel her worries.

I took the dead bird outside and buried it. I would be better off slumbering with the lid closed from then on.

After that, I attempted to turn into a bird myself. I tried many times, and each time I failed. My anger escalated with each unsuccessful attempt. Finally, I surrendered to my new reality. I let out a frustrated sigh and started to walk among the vineyards, hoping to catch at least a mouse to survive the night.

Chapter 6

Alba

Eating tacos in Carlo Lombardi's company was far from a pleasant experience, and I should have anticipated that before agreeing to the stomach-wrenching horror I currently found myself part of. Dismayed by the sight of many green lettuce tendrils dangling from his greasy fingers, I pushed the monstrous marigold bouquet toward the middle of the table, hoping to block the hideous view.

"So… what brings you here, Carlo?" I asked, staring down at my plate to spare myself the still discernible sight of Carlo's half-eaten tortillas.

"Protecting and serving you, what else?" he scoffed.

I snorted. "Yeah, right."

"Can I tell you something personal first?" His eyes brimmed with mischief as he wiped his mouth with a checkered napkin.

"No," I said, knowing he would do it anyway.

He did.

"If you need money for clothes, don't hesitate to ask me. I'll be glad to help."

I rolled my eyes and tugged at the fringed tablecloth which adorned the solid wood table. I had spent the day entertaining the girls, so I hadn't had any time to go shopping. Which meant I was *still* wearing whatever the guests had forgotten in the closets of Carlo's Tuscany villa, just dirtier than in the morning. But Taco Hell wasn't the fanciest restaurant in Emberbury, and I wasn't particularly interested in impressing Carlo Lombardi either.

I squinted, trying to comprehend Carlo's words over the ridiculously loud mariachis, and a bunting of Mexican flags swayed over our heads as if dancing to the music. Carlo was talkative and looking like his old self again, fully recovered from his little tryst with Clarence around Christmastime. He had been on duty that day but had exchanged his uniform for civilian casual: namely jeans and a nicely ironed blue shirt. He didn't look bad at all—shame he couldn't keep his mouth shut.

"So how was your first night back home?" he asked conversationally, waving at the waiter.

"Wonderful. I slept in an abandoned house, in a damp, moldy bed covered in dust, and I didn't get pneumonia."

"Well, my dog caught fleas in the doggy hotel while I was in Italy, and now they are probably all over my house. Can you beat that?"

"Not really. All bedbugs long dead where I was staying. Nobody had slept there for decades."

"You can sleep in my house tonight if you prefer. I have central heating and no mold. The fleas are friendly too."

I pictured sharing Carlo's non-moldy apartment while being attacked by hordes of fleas. *Not very enticing.* I shook my head. "No, thanks, it's fine. I have enough friends, and I got a new blanket."

"No, really, I think you should come. Dog fleas don't bite humans. At least I think they don't. They just tickle a little."

"Forget it," I said.

"Think about it." He shrugged. "And in the meantime, tell me, how is my best friend?"

"If by your *best friend* you mean Clarence, he's still in Italy. Thanks for allowing us to stay in your house, by the way. But I don't think you called me to discuss my boyfriend's wellbeing, or did you?"

"So, he's officially your boyfriend now?"

Come on. Vampires didn't think in terms of labels. They were above such human trivialities. I took a deep breath and pushed my plate away, trying to dispel the discomfort his question had stirred. "Okay. What did you want to tell me, Carlo?"

"I found something you might want to check out. Something related to Natasha."

Now, this was interesting.

Last time I had seen Natasha Grabnar, the scientist working for vampire hunters, she had jailed me in the basement of her Venetian house,

43

and I had escaped thanks to a sheer miracle… with the help of an explosion and a teleporting, magic mirror. No victims had been found in the rubble, according to the news: not Francesca, not Natasha, nor any of her minions. My logical conclusion was that Natasha must have found a way to get out before the house blew up in the air. She must have fled somewhere else, probably to the same place where she held captive Julia and her husband, if they were still alive. Perhaps Francesca too, unless she had remained trapped under the crumbling building and been reduced to dust by the first rays of sunlight.

But no. Of course, that wasn't an option.

I was going to find Francesca, Julia and her husband Ludovic, and earn Elizabeth's favors back so I could resume my peaceful existence as a glorified vampire secretary in The Cloister. Anything else was out of the question.

"I'd definitely like to hear whatever you found out," I answered, studying Carlo's expression in search of deception. He seemed sincere. "But why, Carlo? Why would you help me… again?"

"Because you have pretty eyes?"

I laughed at the audacity. "Good try. But no. Seriously."

"You know I have my reasons. Some I told you already in Venice. Some I don't feel like sharing because they have nothing to do with you."

"Fair enough, I guess."

Carlo smirked and turned to the young waiter. "Pedro, will you bring us a bottle of that special homemade mezcal of your mother's? I think my friend here could do with a glass or two."

Pedro nodded knowingly and disappeared into the kitchen, only to be back two minutes later with a bottle wrapped in a checkered towel. He glanced left and right before setting it on our table, like he was about to present us with some rare, illegal, smuggled goods.

"Just because it's you, *Carlos*," he said before retiring back behind the bar. "But don't tell Papi I gave it to you. There were only two left."

Carlo unwrapped the bottle which had no label and looked a bit filthy. It contained a pale golden liquid, and he poured a bit in each of our glasses, raising his for a toast.

"What should we drink to…?" he asked with a smirk. "Oh, I know! To life, and may we keep ours for many years!"

I frowned at his sense of humor. After my conversation with Elizabeth, joking about such matters didn't seem funny at all.

"Fine," I conceded, raising my glass to his, "*to life*." I was about to sample a little of the suspicious liquor when Carlo stopped me.

"No, no. You must drink it all at once. Like this." He swallowed the whole glass in one gulp and shook like a wet dog. "See? This is how it's done. Otherwise you won't be able to drink it up."

I raised an eyebrow but did as told, out of sheer curiosity. I almost choked with the extremely strong liquid and controlled the urge to spit everything back into the glass. "This is disgusting!"

I shouted, slamming it back with no intention of ever trying mezcal again. "What have you given me?"

I grabbed the bottle and turned it in my hands. It smelled of alcohol, smoke and herbs. I was about to set it aside when I noticed a thing, no, *a creature*, lurking at the bottom of the bottle.

"Oh my God," I shrieked, about to throw up, "there's a worm inside the bottle!"

The creature was fleshy and soft and horridly *real*. Carlo took the bottle from my hands, as if scared I would smash it on the floor. "Don't be silly. This is a delicacy. It's an *edible* worm, and nowadays it's almost impossible to find mezcal with a real agave moth larva. People pay good money for these! And it's very common to fight for the worm. Everyone wants it!"

"Well, I'm definitely not fighting you to eat a dead worm."

"Great. More for me." He shrugged and fiddled with the back of his fork, trying to get the revolting dead creature through the neck of the bottle. I looked away to keep my dinner inside my stomach. "Also, I forgot to tell you," Carlo said, "I don't think it'll happen to you, but just in case, you should know homemade mezcal can cause hallucinations in some people, especially if you aren't used to it. So if you see anything strange tonight, stay calm: it's probably the liquor and nothing to worry about."

***

I didn't have any hallucinations, at least not during dinner, but I was in the middle of dessert when the sight of Carlo sinking his spoon into a wobbly mass of caramel flan sent me running to the bathroom. I threw up noisily with the door open, under the judgmental gaze of two elderly women who needed a surprisingly long time to wash their hands.

"What?" I said to them, wiping my mouth on a piece of toilet paper. "I had to choose between locking the door and throwing up all over the floor. What would you have done?"

They looked away and pretended I was invisible as I made my way out of the bathroom and back to my seat, trying to walk in a straight line and failing.

"What the hell was that drink you gave me?" I growled at Carlo, drinking two glasses of water in a row in a vain attempt to settle my stomach.

"It's not what I gave you, it's what you didn't eat," he replied, pointing at my untouched dessert.

"I'm going home," I said, standing up and heading to the bar to pay for my half. "Talk tomorrow."

***

A thump of heavy, rushed steps made the air tremble behind me.

Someone's going to miss the bus, I thought vaguely, still absorbed in my musings as bus number twelve passed by. The stop was a few steps away, but I knew mine wouldn't arrive for at least ten minutes, so I took out my phone and googled Natasha Grabnar's name. Even though she was supposed to be a scientist, there was nothing to be found about her: no pictures, no scientific papers or research. She was probably using a fake name.

There was one lonely metal bench at the bus stop, and I collapsed on it with a sigh, allowing the tiredness of the last days to slowly swim to the surface. My stomach was growling, and I could have lain on the seat and fallen asleep in the middle of the street, had I wanted to.

A man approached and stood by the bus timetables, then sat next to me. I slid silently to the other side of the bench, annoyed by the excessive closeness of the stranger.

"Where are you going?" he asked, grabbing my shoulder with disgusting familiarity.

I tried to shake him off me, but he got a small knife out of his pocket and pressed it lightly against my side, cornering me against the bus stop. "I can drive you, honey. No drama, please."

I looked around, trying to find an amicable face to help me, but there was nobody around. A couple in love appeared in the distance but passed by, their arms linked in a romantic embrace, and ignored me like I was nothing more than street furniture.

"I said no drama," the thug warned, following the direction of my gaze and sinking the blade slightly deeper, enough for it to sting but not to draw blood.

He tried to drag me away from the bench and toward a black SUV with tinted back windows, but I fought with all my strength, kicking and biting: being killed before dawn, particularly by someone who *wasn't Elizabeth*, wasn't on my to-do list.

I closed my eyes, willing the familiar electric flow of magic to start rushing down my arms. The tingling was very weak, and my arms felt heavy. The trip had been challenging, and I was exhausted after a whole day out and about. When I felt the surge, I released it on the man's chest, but he dodged my attack like he had been expecting it. The ray of light landed on a nearby trash can, blowing its contents up in the air and dying off with weak, tiny flashes like a lighter out of fuel.

With a last pull, the man lifted me off the sidewalk and carried me to the car, where another one was waiting with the trunk open. Then the lid fell, and darkness ensued.

***

I frantically searched the inside of the trunk for a lever, a button, or any other way to open it from the inside. The trunk light had gone off as soon as they had closed the lid, and now I could only feel many small, pointy things inside, similar to gardening tools… or vampire hunter stakes. The air was stale and stank of cigarette smoke.

A loud bang shook the vehicle. I had heard

both front doors closing, but the SUV hadn't started.

The trunk lid opened again, and right in front of me stood Carlo, with a steaming gun in his hand and a deep frown marking his forehead.

"Get out. You are coming home with me."

I had never been so thankful to see someone in my life; even if it was Lombardi, the most conceited human being on the planet.

"You should have agreed to sleep in my apartment," he growled.

I was tipsy and about to throw up again, so I didn't even answer. Thinking clearly was becoming harder and harder.

"Come," he said, grabbing my arm, "it's not safe here."

We walked for a few blocks while I tried to process what had just happened. I was still in a state of shock when we reached an old, but neat, apartment building and he threw me an apologizing look.

"Elevator out of order," he said, pointing at the long and steep staircase. "Sorry. I hope that's okay."

I dragged my feet after him, holding on to the handrail. He was faster and didn't wait for me, but I found an open door on the fourth floor and stepped in without thinking, hoping that was Carlo's apartment and not someone else's.

Carlo was standing next to a coat hanger, tapping his foot with impatience.

"Do you usually walk around armed?" I

asked wearily, throwing my coat at him and scanning the space for couches. I detected a green, battered one nearby, and slumped into it, too tired to ask for permission.

"Do you usually get kidnapped?" he quipped. "And yes, the answer to your question is yes. I feel safer that way."

I was exhausted but not sleepy. As soon as I lay on the couch, the room started to spin like a helicopter over my head. I could almost hear the propellers.

"At this rate, your bloodsucking friend is going to try to kill me again in no time. Can you please text him and make sure to tell him I had nothing to do with the kidnappers, in case they come back?"

"*Hmm*," I mumbled, too tired to form any words. I should really text Clarence, but I was drained, and my brain was muddled.

Carlo's place was warm and dry as he had promised, and it wasn't a car trunk. *Progress*, said a deep, dark part of my mind.

"The guys from the bus stop ran away," Carlo was saying. "I really didn't feel like killing them and having to explain that to my boss. But I jotted down the registration number, and I'll look into it tomorrow at the office."

"*Hmm*," I repeated, the sound of the helicopter propellers getting louder and louder. The couch smelled of cheese and old socks, but it was warm and velvety, like a soft cocoon. I couldn't even feel any flea bites. Yet. "Why do you have antennae?" I asked, noticing with shock the two long, shiny appendages sprouting out of Carlo's head. They seemed to be made of pure light. How wonderfully odd.

"Remind me never to offer you homemade spirits again." He let out an exaggerated sigh and disappeared into a nearby room. When he came back, I was almost asleep despite the spinning walls. He threw a pillow at me, and it landed on my face. "There. Keep the couch," he grunted, his voice sounding farther and farther away. "I'll be in the bedroom if you need me. "Sleep tight, you drunken lunatic."

***

I blinked awake in need of a toilet. Propping myself to a sitting position, I scanned the room. Carlo's living room was dirty and cluttered, and a dining table stood in a corner, covered in food leftovers and boxes. Crouching over a laptop, a tall figure appeared blue behind the soft light of the screen.

"Where is the bathroom?" I asked him.

He raised his eyes from the keyboard, and I gasped when instead of Carlo's blue gaze, I spotted Clarence's crimson irises glinting in the darkness.

I rubbed my eyes and took a deep breath, struggling to wake up. No, this had to be a dream. How else could Clarence appear in Carlo's apartment in the middle of the night?

"The bathroom is over there. Just down the

hall," Clarence said, as if his presence in Carlo's apartment was the most normal thing in the world.

"What are you doing here?" I asked, standing up on my unsteady feet. I rushed to hug him, but a foul smell made me stop a few steps away from him. "What's that smell?" I scrunched my nose and tried to pinpoint the source of the stench. It was him, no doubt.

"I don't know what you are talking about, my dear," he answered with a shrug, closing the laptop, then stood up and opened his arms. "Come here. Have you not missed me?"

"You know I have…"

Clarence hugged me, his solid arms calming my nerves with their steady embrace. "There. Better?"

"Why are you here, Clarence? Weren't you in Italy?"

"I needed to tell you something… a confession, shall we say."

I nodded, circling around him. Something was amiss, but what? His hair was slightly ruffled, the mischievous smile warm as usual. But there was something… something which didn't seem right.

"Tell me…"

"I killed someone," he said, leaning his head to one side and extending one hand in my direction. "Someone very dear to me."

"Oh, Clarence, no…"

I faltered and stepped away from him. *Fear.* His words had scared me, and he knew it. I could see it in his eyes. I studied his face and noticed it was covered in tiny holes which resembled pox marks. I had never seen those before.

"Yes. He was my best friend," he confessed with a trembling exhale. "But there was someone else, too. And that was even worse because…"

While he was talking, a worm peeked out the corner of his eye, and I screamed, stumbling backwards against the sofa behind me.

"This is not real," I said, my voice weakening.

"I wish it weren't." He sighed, and as he did, slight ripples started to form under the surface of his skin, with tiny bumps crawling under it.

"Clarence, your face…" I gasped.

Suddenly, dozens of worms burst out of his darkened pores, covering him in a gruesome, moving mass of white, glow-in-the-dark creatures.

I shrieked, and a myriad of fleshy maggots devoured Clarence right in front of me, until there was nothing left of him.

***

"Why are you staring at me like that?" Carlo said, lifting his gaze from the laptop. He looked a bit like an ant, but I attributed it to the liquor. "Are you going to use the bathroom or not? Would you like me to go with you?"

I blinked and shook my head, then held it with both hands, trying to get rid of the disturbing visions of Clarence. What the hell had that been?

"I think I just had another hallucination," I

said with an exhausted sigh. "Unless you have grown antennae for real."

"Really? Well, that sucks." Carlo stood up and poured me a glass of water. "Drink, and let's hope you'll be all right tomorrow so we can discuss what I found out about Natasha."

I sipped some water, and Carlo's antennae slowly vanished.

"Yes, thank you, I hope so too." I closed my eyes, imagining how the water flushed out the remains of that wicked Mexican liquor. Two ghostly figures, one larger and one smaller, crossed the room and flew out the window. *Yet another hallucination.* I stumbled back to the sofa, making sure my feet were up to help with my spinning head.

"I think I really need to sleep," I said, my eyelids heavy. "Good night, Carlo. See you in the morning."

Chapter 7

Alba

Carlo went off to work very early in the morning, leaving behind a pleasant caffeine-scented cloud which made the apartment warm and cozy; at least much more so than my previous accommodations. He even left some coffee for me in the kitchen, and I drank it directly from the pot, staring at my disheveled reflection on the window panes. The windows were nearly opaque, covered by a thick layer of dust and grime, not unlike me. He had also left a stack of printed documents by the sink, and I started to flip through them while nibbling on a stale cookie I found under a heap of greasy takeaway boxes.

A raven shrieked outside the windowsill, and I struggled with the rusty locks to open the window and let him in.

"Hi, Jean-Pierre," I greeted him, quickly closing the window again to ward off the chilly draft. The raven hit the glass repeatedly with his beak, and I stared at him blankly, trying to figure out what he was trying to tell me.

"Oh, yes, sorry!" I pulled down the shades to darken the interior of the kitchen and turned on the lights, then backed off to avoid the burst of thick fog I knew was coming. Vampire mist was unpleasant to get caught in: it felt cold and wet to the touch, but also thick and grainy, like being battered with handfuls of wet sand on a frosty winter day. Clarence had invited me to stay in it once, and I didn't wish to repeat such an eerie experience ever again.

"*Bonjour!*" The gray haze vanished, and Jean-Pierre materialized in the kitchen, a wide smile on his face. "Your daily croissant delivery just arrived!" He presented me with a brown paper bag and gave me a genteel bow.

"I could get used to this." I nodded approvingly as I bit into the still warm croissant with a sigh of pleasure. So much better than Carlo's stale cookies. Also, the bag was covered in tiny red Valentine's hearts. "How did you find me?"

He wiggled his nose, glancing sideways at my dirty sweater. "I'm not sure you would be too pleased to hear the answer. Let's say I happened to fly by and…"

Witch smell, of course. Extremely off-putting to most vampires, except for Clarence perhaps. I sighed. "I see… well, thanks for coming. It's nice to see you again."

"I brought you something else. Apart from croissants," he said.

I leaned against the kitchen counter, but my

palms got stuck on its sticky surface. Maybe I should get Carlo a set of microfiber cloths for Valentine's Day?

Meanwhile, Jean-Pierre took a ring out of the pocket of his waistcoat and extended it to me. It was a vintage-looking gold band with what appeared to be a tiny butterfly encrusted with jewels. It looked old, out of fashion, the kind of jewelry nobody would wear nowadays.

"When you see Clarence, would you be so kind as to give him this from me?" he said mysteriously.

I took the ring, which was cold to the touch, and scrutinized it for a while.

"Looks like something one would find on the Titanic," I commented. It was a beautiful piece of jewelry but very much démodé.

"You aren't entirely wrong," he agreed.

"Why does Clarence need this? Does it have magic powers or something?"

Jean-Pierre smiled. "I think so. It was forged by witches, and it might help you find Francesca… if she can be found, that is."

"Ah, so it's Francesca's!" Yes, it was definitely her style. Even though I had never seen her wearing it, the intricate, old fashioned design suited her well. Interesting she would own a ring made by witches.

"It was hers, and it wasn't," he answered cryptically. "Just give it to Clarence when you see him, will you? He will know what to do with it."

I popped the ring in my pocket, and Jean-

Pierre took out a fountain pen and a piece of paper and started to draw at the kitchen table. An oily stain formed under the paper, and he cursed in French, taking another one and starting anew.

"What's that?" I asked, staring as he retraced the symbol, which reminded me of a round, large head with long stickman legs and slumping arms and shoulders.

"This is the Knot of Isis," he clarified, leaning back to scrutinize his creation before handing it to me. "The *Tyet*." I took the drawing. It wasn't very pretty, but I refrained from commenting in hopes he would continue. "As promised, I looked into the Silver Cast curse. I found out a couple of interesting things."

A smothered gasp got stuck in my lungs.

"Ah… and…?" I stammered.

"The Silver Cast curse dates back to Egyptian times. Back then, priests and priestesses with powerful magic walked the earth. They were experts in dealing with death and the dead, and they found many ways to guard themselves from the evils lurking at night." He chuckled grimly, making it clear what kind of nightly *evils* he was referring to. "Isis was the Mother Goddess, a Healer. She could be invoked for the hardest healing spells and was said to be able to even resurrect the dead. She brought back her husband, Osiris, from death."

"From death…" I repeated, starting to see where his discourse was heading and wondering whether such a healing spell would work on the undead.

"Yes, from death. When I was living in Marseille, I came across The Daughters of Isis." He paused, as if trying to put his memories in order. "No, in truth it was they who sought me, for I was the only one who could translate an ancient text for them. Funny how witches are willing to be forgiving toward our kind when they need assistance and nobody else can provide it…"

"You can read Egyptian hieroglyphs?" I interrupted him. The man was a walking Rosetta Stone! No wonder witches had turned a blind eye to his blood-sucking habits.

"There are many things I can do, *ma chérie*. Casting spells is not one of them. But translating and transcribing most human languages, that poses no challenge to me. And I have an excellent memory too." He sauntered toward me, his presence becoming denser around me. His hair and short beard were completely white and spotless, not a single gray strand marring them, and they contrasted starkly against his dark velvet outfit. Jean-Pierre wasn't conventionally attractive, but his charm stemmed from his sharp intellect: he had lived long and acquired enough knowledge to keep a listener entertained for all eternity. Combined with his exotic accent, I could see how some women might find him irresistible, even though Clarence never missed an opportunity to smirk at his complacency.

"That's impressive," I conceded.

"It is, I agree," he said with a smug smile.

"And that's why I was hired by the Daughters of Isis, the mightiest witch coven in Europe…"

"Hah! So now we know who took the first place from those Italian snobs!" I couldn't help myself from interrupting him, remembering the sulky attitude of the Witches of the Lake in Como when I had asked them why they called themselves the *second* most powerful coven in Europe.

"Oh, yes," Jean-Pierre agreed, "the Italians were never happy about it. The Daughters of Isis are powerful. Very powerful. And if you could summon their help, you might be able to reverse that curse. Although I'm not sure it has ever been done before."

Mingling with witch covens was always a scary prospect, especially after my last experience in Italy, but I would jump straight into a boiling cauldron if that could help rid Clarence of the mortal curse that was threatening to kill him.

"I'll do anything," I assured him. "Just tell me where to start."

"The Daughters of Isis are the keepers of the Alcazar Grimoire, a manuscript which contains the only counterspell suitable to reverse the Silver Cast. Remember that *Fulminatio* spell I gifted you? That was a discarded page from the same book. I was commissioned to transcribe it… but I sneezed while working, and ink bled everywhere… I am proud to always deliver a spotless piece of work, not like these modern scribes today." He rolled his eyes. "Anyhow, it proved lucky for you that I had to re-do it, don't you think? Otherwise, I would have never kept that copy in the library for several hundred years."

"Very lucky indeed," I agreed, thinking of the many times the *Fulminatio* spell had got me out of trouble in the past months. "And if I understand correctly, this grimoire is now in Marseille?"

Jean-Pierre's forehead furrowed for a second. "No, I was living in Marseille when the Daughters of Isis found me, but they took the grimoire to Alcazar Abbey, in the French Pyrenees. I suppose they keep it in a secret vault somewhere in the abbey."

"Doesn't sound very secret if you know where it is."

"Yes, I may know its whereabouts, but it's not going to be easy to get the manuscript out of there," he clarified, pulling out yet another piece of blank paper. "I'll write everything down for you, so you don't forget."

"Thank you so much, Jean-Pierre," I said, hugging him. In normal circumstances, he would have taken advantage of my hug to bring me closer, but this time he remained tense, a deep frown forming between his eyebrows.

"Only…" he paused, his voice an anguished whisper. "Alba… do you remember that day, when we were alone in the library?"

I stared at him, puzzled. We had spent many hours in the library of The Cloister, although not usually alone. There was always someone else, mostly Francesca. *Although… wait a second.* "The Green Fairy?" I ventured, remembering with a shiver the time Jean-Pierre had lost control and almost bitten me with the excuse of being under the influence of an absinthe spell.

"The Green Fairy, yes," he repeated, gloomily. "Do you remember her prophecy?"

I nodded slowly. I did remember, even though I had seemingly buried it in the deepest crooks of my mind.

"*The Green Fairy wants you to know…*" I started, echoing a message I had heard through his lips a long time ago, but my voice broke before reaching the end as realization sank in.

"…*that Clarence Auberon will be your death,*" Jean-Pierre finished the sentence for me, taking my hands.

"And what am I supposed to do with this information?" I asked with annoyance. "Why is it more relevant now than it was two months ago?"

"High magic spells can be dangerous, *ma belle…*" he said, his eyes glowing softly with something akin to fondness. "Promise me you will be careful and won't take on more than you can handle, agreed? You must seek help from other witches. Don't try to do it alone."

"Oh, I see…" I sighed, then forced myself to smile at him with self-assurance as I placed a chaste kiss on his beardy cheek. "No, I would never do such a thing. I'm aware of my limitations. So yes, of course, Jean-Pierre: I promise. I'll be careful. You have nothing to worry about."

Chapter 8

Alba

I spent the morning with Katie and Iris and bought myself a few warm sweaters and two pairs of jeans. Everything I owned was still waiting for me in The Cloister, so it was a choice between shopping and walking around looking homeless. I wanted to get a pair of warm shoes too, but the kids were getting cranky, so I decided my current ballet flats would have to do. After lunch, I dropped the kids back at Mark and Minnie's. Saying goodbye once again made me sad, but there was no way I could take them with me to freeze in Westside Avenue, and family camping in Carlo's living room didn't sound like a very promising alternative.

Carlo had promised to come back home straight after work so we could discuss his findings, but when I knocked on the door nobody answered. Not even the dog, whose main function seemed to be sleeping all day, ignoring everything and everyone around him. Thankfully, Carlo had left me a spare key, so I let myself in. While I waited, I had a look at Carlo's documents while trying to make myself a sandwich. In a place that messy, the task wasn't much different from hunting wild gazelles in the jungle: there was trash and leftovers piled everywhere, threatening to bury you forever if you weren't skilled enough to evade them. Once my mission to feed myself was accomplished, and seeing Carlo hadn't returned yet, I went to the bathroom to try my new clothes on.

I was still there when the main door slammed closed, and Carlo called to me from the living room, "Anybody home?"

"Yes, give me a second!" I shouted back at him, struggling to get out of a pair of supposedly elastic jeans. *Why didn't I try them on in the store? Oh yes, because my kids had the habit of whining loudly when dragged to stores, and they often amused themselves by opening the curtain of whatever changing room I might be using and flashing my underwear to the whole store.*

"Did you have a chance to read Natasha's emails?" Carlo asked, his steps approaching down the hallway. "The ones I printed for you this morning?"

Still trapped in the new jeans, I hopped on one foot, trying to reach the bathroom door and close it before Carlo found me in such an undignified predicament.

"Yes! Yes, I did!" I yelled, tripping on a set of cast-iron dumbbells in my vain attempt to kick the bathroom door closed. I fell and flew straight into Carlo's open arms just as he was about to come in. He caught me with a surprised grin.

"Well, thanks for the warm welcome," he said, hugging me with nonchalance as if half-naked women jumping into his lap was the most common occurrence in the world. "I see you are happy about my findings." He blinked in a clear come-hither gesture, holding me by the armpits. My toes hurt after their brief encounter with Carlo's weightlifting equipment, and I groaned.

"There's a reason those are called *dumb* bells," I mumbled, motioning to kick my leg out of the hellish jeans but then changing my mind and trying to pull them up again. "I think it's related to the people who use them."

"So, what do you think?" Carlo asked, ignoring my rudeness.

"I think it would be nice if you could wait outside while I get changed," I said grumpily.

He obeyed with a shrug and left. The jeans had decided to stay stuck around my mid-thighs, so I wrapped myself in the least filthy towel I could find before coming out once again and answering, "As for the emails, I didn't understand much, but they often mention a Natasha Dupont."

"Exactly. And I'm almost sure Natasha Grabnar and Natasha Dupont are the same person. There are several people with that name in France, but if you keep reading…" Carlo went to the kitchen and peeled off the wrapper of a protein bar while he was talking. I hopped after him and cleared a stack of fitness magazines from a chair in order to sit down and listen. "They mention a laboratory in Paris and a contact in London."

"I noticed that. But when I googled the name, I found dozens of people called Natasha Dupont."

"Yes! But…" Carlo opened a can of soda, and the fizzing sound made me thirsty. I grabbed another one for myself while he kept talking and followed him to the living room. The dog woke up, sniffed my towel and tagged along lazily. "Today, at work, I checked the plates of the car of those men who tried to kidnap you last night. And, who knew? The owner's name is Natasha Wilson, a biologist from Boston. Ms. Natasha Wilson owns an apartment in the center of Paris, and today, I found that address, too."

"Good job," I said, impressed, "so, I guess I should go to Paris. Do you think that's where she took the vampires?"

"I don't know, but I think that's your best bet, unless you have a better lead."

I didn't, so that would have to do. I took a sip of my coke and sighed. "I don't even know how to thank you for all the research you have done. This is going to be so helpful, I really appreciate your efforts…"

"Actually," he interrupted me, "I'm coming with you. I have a few questions for Natasha myself."

I stared at him blankly. *He was coming with me? To Paris?* Some children in the apartment above us started to jump, making the ceiling tremble, and one of the photo frames hanging on the wall tilted abruptly, offering a tacit answer to my question.

"This is about Eleanor, isn't it?" I asked. The tilted picture was Carlo's wedding photo, with his red-haired bride smiling and holding a delicate bouquet of white roses. According to Carlo's story, Eleanor had been murdered around the age of twenty-five, not long after they got married.

"It is," he said curtly.

"What would Natasha know about that? I thought it was vampires who…" *Killed her*, I wanted to say, but I couldn't bring myself to say the word in front of Carlo.

"Let's say I have a hunch she was connected to Eleanor's death. I met Natasha one day after Eleanor's funeral, and she offered me a job to work for her as a vampire hunter. Such a nice coincidence, don't you think?"

I sank back into the couch, hoping the fleas were asleep during the day. "I don't know what to say. Maybe. But it sounds unlikely."

"I have a few reasons to believe she, or someone above her, was involved in Eleanor's murder. They wanted me on their side; an insider in the police who would have access to useful information—things that are out of reach for ordinary citizens. They also knew I wouldn't be weirded out when they told me about the nature of their supernatural-hunting business, since I come from a family of vampire hunters. But after all the horror stories I had heard from my grandfather, I never wanted to become one. All I ever wanted was to live a normal life, and Natasha took that away from me."

His voice faltered, and I looked away, overwhelmed by Carlo's sudden vulnerability. "I'm sorry, Carlo. I understand. Of course, you can come with me. But… I'm going to need to add a few stops to our route."

"Okay. No problem. Where?"

"I was thinking Tuscany and Southern France."

Carlo blinked, the protein bar falling off his hands onto the coffee table. "Sorry, what?"

"Yes," I said firmly. "We are picking up Clarence in Italy first, and then I must drive to borrow a book in the Pyrenees, and well, he can't board a plane…"

"Maybe I wasn't the best student at school, but I don't think you were paying much attention during geography class either, were you? Do you know how far Tuscany is from Paris? This is not like picking up your kids from soccer training and dropping them off at Grandma's."

I nodded. *Yes, I knew.* But as much as I wanted to find Julia and the others as soon as possible, I also needed to make sure Clarence was safe. If saving him from that deadly curse implied driving thousands of miles, I would do it, with or without Carlo. "I know it's far, but I'm determined to do anything in my power to help Clarence. He's my priority right now."

"Why can't he go to Paris on his own and meet us there? I thought he could grow wings or something?"

"Why? Oh wait. He can't walk in daylight. And, oh yes! Your witch friends poisoned him and he's too weak," I growled, referring to the Italian coven Carlo had been collaborating with. *The ones who had cursed Clarence with The Silver Cast.* "He's not well, and he needs me."

"I don't care. It's too far, and I'm running out of vacation days. Also, nobody in their right mind…"

"Fine. Then I'll go alone. You invited yourself anyway."

Carlo grumbled under his breath and threw me a narrow glance. "Look. I like you and all, but I'm not going on a Eurotrip with a freaking vampire. That's asking a bit too much from me."

"No problem," I said, crossing my arms. "Is that your last word? If it is, I'm going to pick up Clarence first on my own, and I will see you in Paris."

"You are a stubborn little witch, did you know?"

I shrugged. I had heard that before.

"Okay." He rolled his eyes, then pointed at his laptop. "See if you can find us plane tickets for this weekend, will you?"

Chapter 9

Alba

Never in my wildest fantasies had I imagined I would be sharing yet another transatlantic flight to Italy with Carlo Lombardi. And yet, here we were, sitting side by side and shooting through the clouds together as the vast ocean blue glimmered thousands of feet below us; all while I scratched the dozens of flea bites I had acquired during my brief stay in his apartment.

I had managed to book two last-minute tickets to Italy, and Carlo had found a spot for his dog back in Flea Hotel. This gave me enough time to re-read all the printed correspondence between Carlo, Natasha and the rest of people related to her, in hopes of finding more useful clues.

Even though Carlo had volunteered to come along, my request of doing a stopover in Italy had made him extremely grumpy. He kept mumbling things under his breath, which more or less could be summarized as, *"What kind of idiot books a flight to Italy when their end destination is France?*

Are you aware those are two different countries?" Most of the time I ignored him or reminded him politely that I hadn't asked for his company in the first place. If we were going to team up, he needed to accept that Clarence was coming too, whether he liked it or not. True, I had no idea how this was going to work—hopefully, they wouldn't turn the trip into open warfare, but if they did, I knew for a fact who was going to leave our mismatched team first.

I hadn't heard much from Clarence since my departure. Still, I knew the scarce messaging wasn't a big deal for him, accustomed as he was to communicating through letters, or carrier pigeons, or whatever he had been using a couple of centuries ago. For me, on the other hand, the scarce dripping of news was a source of stress, particularly while he was away and sick. Hopefully, he would wait for us in Italy. I had sent a text informing him we were on our way, but I had no idea whether he had read it because, as usual, he was taking his sweet time to reply.

Carlo and I rented a car after landing and reached his ancestors' residence just as early sunset was starting to paint the Tuscanian village a warm shade of apricot. The isolated, classic villa sat among hundreds of grapevines, now turned into a rental property for tourists with the help of a kind local lady who took care of all the housekeeping. The place was empty during the current low season, save for the hungry vampire hiding in the cellar… or so I hoped.

When Carlo unlocked the door of the villa, everything inside was dark, silent and overall, exactly as I had left it at my departure. All the shutters were down, and not even one chair stood out of place. Carlo opened the windows and turned on the lights, and I waited by the entrance, in the large farmhouse room which served as a kitchen, living room and entryway at the same time. He checked every single room from the basement to the upper floor and came back after a couple of minutes with a satisfied expression on his face.

"All clear," he declared, heading to the kitchen to turn on the fridge.

I left my bags on the kitchen island and crossed my arms. "What do you mean, 'all clear'? Where's Clarence?"

Carlo shrugged, not one bit concerned. It was strange that Clarence wouldn't come to greet us. He must have heard the car engine from miles away. Also, it wasn't dark yet, so it was unlikely that he might have gone off hunting.

"I have no idea, but he's not in the house," Carlo said. "I can't say I will miss him if he never comes back, but I doubt I'll be all that lucky." He whistled a tune as he took out an iron pan and covered it with a thick layer of olive oil. "I'm going to make some food. Are you hungry? How do you like your eggs?"

I squinted at him, annoyed by his indifference.

"*Deviled*," I answered tautly.

"Bit grumpy, aren't we?"

Ignoring his comment, I rushed upstairs and checked all the bedrooms, including the closets. A growing heaviness clutched my chest as I realized Clarence hadn't touched a single thing: it was as if he hadn't been there at all. A horror movie started to play in my head, regaling me with all the possible things which might have gone wrong in my absence. What if Carlo had sent a team of hunters the moment I had left? What if Natasha had found Clarence and taken him away? What if he had fallen unconscious in the forest, and the sun had burned him to ashes?

Okay. I needed to stop that train of thought right away before I went insane.

I headed to the storage room and the garage, which were vacant too, just like the rest of the ground floor. I was about to give up when I remembered I still hadn't checked the wine cellar. Carlo had been there already, but what better place for a vampire to spend his days in blissful darkness?

I ambled under the red brick arcades that held the low, vaulted ceiling of the cellar. Dark wood shelves covered the walls, bent under the weight of hundreds of dusty wine bottles. Several barrels occupied one side of the room, and in a corner stood a large wooden chest with vintage forge ornaments. It was big enough to accommodate several blankets... or a human body.

My hands were shaking as I tried to lift the lid; but it was too heavy for me, and in the end, I had to give up.

"Clarence?" I said, knocking on the chest. "Are you in there?"

There was no answer, but I could feel his presence, nonetheless. We shared an uncanny connection which made both his presence and his absence clearly perceptible when he was nearby.

A throat-clearing sound echoed in the staircase, and I turned around to find Carlo leaning against a wall behind me. Judging by his bored expression, he must have been watching me for a while. I gave him a "what?" look, and he walked in, strolling around the basement with a careless grimace, pretending to search the room. Finally, he stopped by the closed trunk and puffed.

"So you found him?" he said, not looking pleased in the least.

"Can you open the trunk? It's too heavy for me," I asked, striving to sound nice.

Carlo glanced at his watch, then pointed at the slight glow coming from upstairs.

"He's probably day-slumbering. Bloodsuckers do that. Just wait for a few minutes for the sun to set, and he will open the lid himself."

"Clarence doesn't usually slumber," I said but then changed my mind. As far as I knew, most vampires slept seldom: to recover from injuries, survive famine or more rarely, just to pass the time. And all options sounded quite likely for a cursed vampire left alone for days in a remote Tuscanian villa, particularly while suffering from a nasty curse.

Carlo scoffed. "If he's not slumbering, why did he lock himself in our largest wine crate? To play hide-and-seek with the bats?"

"Okay, maybe he is," I said. "So, are you helping me open this or not?" I pushed the lid with all my weight, in a vain attempt to open it.

Carlo's eye roll was so pronounced that I could almost hear his eyeballs rubbing against their sockets. He pushed me aside with a hip bump and flexed his knees in a sumo pose. After some grunting and plenty of complaining, the wooden plank gave way and moved aside, creaking under its own weight.

I peeked into the trunk, wringing my hands with uncertainty. Clarence lay inside it, with his eyes closed and a deathly pallor washing over his cheeks. He looked dead, but I could still feel his presence in the room. I caressed his forehead, cold and hard under my fingers, and wiped away a wisp of black and silver hair. It felt so much silkier to the touch than one would have thought just by looking at those unruly waves.

"Hi," I whispered, nudging him softly. "I'm back."

Carlo hovered over my shoulder, studying Clarence's inert form with apathy. "I can't believe I have a slumbering vampire in my house, and I'm not going to stake him," he commented. "There must be something wrong with me because it's actually the *second* time I'm missing a chance like this. My grandfather would be livid."

"Come on. I know you wouldn't do that. You didn't kill him in Venice, so no reason to do it now," I said, more to reassure myself than anything else. "He looks so… still, doesn't he?"

"Give him three minutes," he said grumpily. "I bet it won't take him much longer. But sometimes they wake up hungry, so I would step back if I were you."

Carlo stepped on a stool and started to unbolt one of the cellar windows, which were all shut and darkened with blinds.

"No!" I shouted, forcing him to step down. "What are you doing?"

"Just airing out the place?" he snapped at me. "There's a dead man in my cellar! Can't I open the windows to get rid of the stench? It's dark enough outside. Stop being so protective of that corpse, will you?"

"That was rude," I said, offended.

"No, it wasn't rude. It's a fact. The guy is dead, so he's officially a corpse. How many stages of death can there be?"

"Seemingly, a few! Also, he doesn't *stink*! You say you know vampires well, but it's clear you don't understand *anything*."

"And you do?" His tone turned defiant; he leaned forward, bringing his face so close to mine that I could see the specks of brown in his blue irises. "I don't think you do either. Because if you did, you would ditch the parasite and find yourself someone who could make your life—and your bed—warmer, not colder than it already is."

"Someone like you, you mean?" I sneered. I was about to punch him when two icy, sturdy hands grabbed my waist from behind, lifted me off the floor and set me aside with utmost care. Neither Carlo nor I had heard Clarence rise. He must have taken one single, silent leap to reach the corner where we had been arguing.

Clarence pushed Carlo against the wall and held him by the neck, squinting at him with red-glowing eyes which didn't foretell anything pleasant for my cheeky travel companion.

"Clarence!" I shouted, placing my hands on his shoulders. I flinched at the haze of madness marring his glowing maroon eyes but tried to keep my voice steady nevertheless. "Stop!"

Carlo was strong but no match for a demented vampire who had decided to make him his dinner. Clarence didn't seem to hear me; I wasn't even sure he was awake at all.

"Well done, Auberon," Carlo spat, sinking his hand in a pocket. "Why don't you bite me again? Bleed me dry and let her watch. Show her who you really are. Do both of us a favor."

Clarence faltered for a second, as a fleeting flash of recognition passed over his face, then it vanished as quickly as it had appeared. Despite the precarious situation, Carlo remained calm.

"No!" I growled, throwing myself at Clarence in an attempt to come between both men. "Clarence. It's me! Alba! Leave him alone; he's our ally! He's here to help! Clarence, please!"

Carlo remained calm. I thought it was odd until I realized he had been in control of the situation from the very beginning.

Carlo's hand flew out of the pocket, holding

a small silver gun. He shot Clarence from a distance of a few inches, and the projectile wheezed as it came out through Clarence's back and left a dark notch in the wall behind him, its sound lost in my shocked scream. Clarence stumbled back and bent to press his hand against the wound, letting go of Carlo with a pained roar.

"I missed the heart on purpose," Carlo gasped, regaining his breath. "Consider this a friendly, cautionary shot."

"Alba…" Clarence said in a raspy voice, rubbing his eyes like a barely awake child. A dark red stain had started to flourish under his sleeve, and he exhaled, collapsing on the floor with his back against the wall. Carlo panted and watched him warily from a distance but clearly without fear.

"Please forgive me," Clarence said to me, staring at his ruined shirt with sadness. "I tend to wake up moody when I sleep for too long."

I knelt to hug him, squinting angrily at Carlo, but the latter just shrugged, rubbing his neck where Clarence had almost bit him—again.

"Don't worry, darling," Carlo spat, putting the gun back into his pocket. "He will be fine before you know it. The devil takes care of his own."

After that he left, slamming the door behind him, and we remained alone in the cellar in a reunion that was far from what I had imagined.

Chapter 10

Clarence

The half-Italian scoundrel had left the premises with the excuse of having a drink in the nearby village, as if the cellar of the villa was not full to the brim with all sorts of alcoholic beverages. Even so, it was perfectly fine by me if he wished to drown to death in a spirits barrel, perish on his way there, or at the very least, lay inebriated on the floor of a seedy countryside tavern for the rest of the night... or for all eternity.

But it was obvious none of that was going to happen.

Shame.

I stared at the night, pleasant and silent on the other side of the basement windows. An onyx umbrella sheltered us, burrowed in the bowels of the remote Tuscany villa which had been my home during the past weeks.

"It's a nice place, isn't it?" Alba said, her voice drowsy after the long trip. I was sitting on a wooden bench, and she lay on it on her back, her head resting on my lap as I drew butterfly shapes on her forehead.

"It is," I agreed, unwilling to break the flawless silence with trivial conversation. It was a perfect moment just as it was, and I told myself that as long as we remained still, we could avoid the reality surrounding us, the steep slopes looming over the house, covered in deceivingly dead vineyards, now invisible to her eyes in the moonless night—but not to mine—reminding us that one day, very soon, we would be forced to face reality once again.

My senses captured even the smallest details. I barely remembered being human, unable to hear the dormouse snoring under a floorboard, or the cobwebs swinging on the ceiling, or seeing that minute beginning of a teardrop, threatening to seep out of the corner of Alba's eye as she held it back with all her will. No, nowadays nothing escaped me. A blessing most of the time but a curse too.

I cradled her head in one arm, leaning down and inching toward her face, holding her gaze. She smiled, expectant, but I kissed the side of her nose instead, chuckling softly against her cheek. The tears dissolved as her heartbeat quickened, and a rush of desire overcame me as I devised every little thing I would like to do to her next. She squirmed in my arms in protest, clearly disapproving of my chaste kiss. She fought my grip, her lips seeking mine, but I kept teasing her, kissing her hair, her cheek and the tip of her nose, until her heartbeat was racing so fast that it became deafening.

"Clarence!" she scolded me, propping up against the bench. She grabbed the front of my shirt, impatient, and pushed me against her.

"What?" I said, laughing and kissing her at the same time.

She glanced away for a second, "You know *what*."

Feigning innocence, I nuzzled her nose, smelling her delicious excitement as it clouded the air.

"What about that bullet wound?" she asked all of a sudden, inspecting my torn, bloodied shirt with apprehension.

"I will be fine," I whispered, biting her earlobe playfully. "But your obnoxious friend might come back any minute."

"Then we should make the most of our time alone…"

"Should we, now…?" I smiled. Her pulse sped up even more as my fingers drew a path down the side of her neck, and she nodded knowingly. "Fine," I said, fighting back my grin, "I'll see what I can do."

***

We sat snuggled in each other's arms, drowsy and blissfully drained. She closed her eyes and took a deep breath, mumbling into my hair.

"So, is it true?" she whispered, still breathless.

"What?" I asked, enthralled by her warmth radiating through my arms, an illusion of life creeping back for a second.

"The curse. What Jean-Pierre said." Her voice was calm, but I knew better.

I shrugged. I had seen a few of our kind meet their end that way. Some weathered the curse for decades, while others were gone in a matter of weeks. When I contemplated my options, the first one sounded perfect: being granted a human lifespan to spend by her side, to be ultimately gone together, erased forever into eternal silence and darkness, just like all earthly creatures were meant to be. I found the idea oddly appeasing. Immortality was meaningless if you were to spend it alone, watching all your loved ones die before you.

"He might be right," I conceded, "but it's hard to guess how long it might take. Hopefully, years. It could be one month, in theory," I said, but seeing her despairing expression I added quickly, "Although most probably a century. This might come as a surprise, but I used to be a doctor… I suppose I would know if I were on the verge of death."

"You, a doctor?" She raised her eyebrows. "Why haven't I heard that before?"

"Maybe because I was a terrible one."

She puffed, and I could almost hear the hundreds of questions bubbling in her mind.

"Also," I continued, "we cannot know whether she cast the Silver Cast curse on me." The poisonous cold inside my chest left little doubt as to what else it could have been, but I decided not to tell her that. "Those texts were lost and forgotten centuries ago."

"No." She sat up, burrowing herself into my chest like a mouse. "They weren't lost nor forgotten. Jean-Pierre knows about a grimoire in the French Pyrenees, and that's one of the reasons I traveled all the way back here."

"But... Francesca? Julia...?" I protested. I was skeptical of Alba being able to retrieve a secret grimoire, let alone put it to use on her own. As much as I believed in her dormant abilities, I knew that a curse cast by someone else was virtually impossible to reverse. Meanwhile, there were people we might be able to save, if only we could find them soon enough.

"Oh, yes," she said, standing up and squeezing my hand before walking away and up the stairs. "Wait here. I almost forgot."

When she came back, there was a small object inside her tightly closed first. I could see it twinkle between her fingers, covering the darkened walls of the cellar in kaleidoscopic sparkles.

"Jean-Pierre asked me to give you this," she said, her eyes narrowing in a silent question. She opened her hand, and I drowned a gasp.

Francesca's ring.

My ring.

I hadn't seen it for a very long time. Once, many moons ago, I had sworn to protect Francesca from any harm which might come her way. Her brother was gone, and I was infatuated with her, as I often was with most beautiful creatures and particularly her. Ours was a whirlwind romance that kept going on and off throughout the decades, and neither of us dared take it too seriously. She had brushed off my chivalry when I presented her with the jewel, as she always did. She never needed me. Or anyone.

I slid the ring Alba had brought onto my little finger, knowing exactly why Jean-Pierre had sent it my way: he knew I might be beyond saving, but there was still hope for Francesca and the others. It was his genteel reminder of life's priorities.

"Thank you," I said. "You were talking about that grimoire…"

"Yes," Alba agreed, "we must get it as soon as possible. It's in a place called Alcazar. I know it's a bit of a detour, but I think it's worth the effort if we can get hold of the counterspell."

"Forgive my saying so, but I think we should go to Paris first and try to track Natasha's steps with the clues you and Lombardi found. For once, I see eye to eye with that half-witted friend of yours. This curse is not going anywhere. We will be able to tackle it later, when everyone is safe."

"Will we?" She crossed her arms, standing in front of me with a challenging expression.

"Of course. With a mighty sorceress like you by my side, what have I to fear?"

Her eyes narrowed into thin, dark lines.

"You aren't mocking me, are you, Clarence? This is not funny at all."

"I would never do such a thing!"

"Sure."

She was cross, but I did not want her reservations to ruin what still had the potential to become a perfect evening.

"Did you know I have magic powers too?" I teased her.

She rolled her eyes. "You do?"

"Allow me to show you…" I pulled her closer and extended both hands toward her stiff figure. "It is called—" I waved my hands in S-patterns along her sides, wiggling my fingers in the air over her body. She squirmed. "—*The Magic Tickling Touch*."

She giggled, wriggling and ticklish even though I wasn't touching her. "See?" I said, nodding as I enjoyed her cheery misery. "Magic!"

"That was silly," she puffed, pushing me away, but her mood had improved.

"Do you think so? Then, please, show me a better example of *magic*," I defied her. "Could you, perhaps…" I looked around, searching for a suitable subject. Finally, I picked a random wine bottle from a shelf and two glasses. "…open this bottle for me?" She shrugged and tried to take it from my hands, but I hid the bottle behind my back and lifted a finger. "*Uh-uh*. No touching."

"You know I can't do that," she protested.

"Well, you could at least try. Why deprive

me of a deserved, though brief, goodbye party?" I told her with a wink.

"What are you talking about? I know for a fact you despise wine."

"The time I have spent in this cellar has been so memorable… I shall be saddened to bid farewell to all the lovely mice and cockroaches who kept me company in your absence. Why not indulge me with a toast, if nothing else? If only Lombardi did not keep his corkscrews so well hidden…"

She let out a sigh, but a soft glow swirled around her, unbeknownst to her: a clear sign that she had accepted the challenge.

"Please. Humor me," I said, stealing a brief kiss on her forehead. "Just try. What's the worst that could happen?"

"Okay." A sudden glow illuminated her eyes with mischief. "But on one condition."

"Do tell," I encouraged her, intrigued. I placed the bottle on a table in front of us, then sat with an ankle on my knee and waited.

"If I manage to open that bottle, we go to Alcazar first. No whining. And above all, no trying to make me change my mind."

"And if you don't?"

She dismissed the thought with a curt hand wave, perhaps a little bit too confident. "I don't know—" Her mind must have been somewhere else, her eyes fixed on a distant point in the empty space before us. "—just pick whatever you want."

"*Whatever* I want?" I repeated, blinking back

a smirk as I crept closer, just enough to feel her sunny warmth. I had not expected our game to turn into such a pleasing enterprise so quickly.

She dismissed my mischievous question with a huff and concentrated on the dark, sleek bottle on the table. Her eyes were closed; her eyelashes trembling like feeble butterfly wings. A bright radiance grew around her and turned from a faint lilac into a rich, velvety purple.

The little witch didn't seem so small anymore.

Plop.

The muffled sound of the cork flying out of the neck of the bottle and hitting the ceiling startled me. I clapped my hands quietly, nodding at her in amazement.

"Very nice, my dear..." I congratulated her. I started to pour some wine into the glasses, but another loud *plop* interrupted me. And then another. And another.

The entire cellar room shook, and in a matter of seconds, all the bottles started to tremble. With a loud bang, they all exploded at once, in a violent display of wine fireworks. A shard of glass cut my eyebrow, and I brushed it off with oblivion, my eyes stuck on Alba, who had wine dripping all over her damp hair and shirt.

Silence ensued, only broken by the tiny scarlet rivers flowing down the shelves and down our faces, pooling in crimson puddles around us.

Drip, drip, drip.

I threw her a sideways glance and grimaced.

She stared back, and we snorted simultaneously, taking in the ridiculous scene surrounding us.

"You wanted a party," she grunted. "Here's your party." Her words were smothered by hardly contained amusement.

"Looks more like a murder scene," I pointed out.

"That's because it's a vampire party," she said.

I burst into laughter, and my chuckles swept away the tightness which had lived inside me for weeks. Her eyes were teary as she, too, gave in to a cascade of roaring laughter, bracing her middle with abandon.

She leaned against one of the red-stained walls to catch her breath, and her arms clutched me, as if to avoid toppling over.

Even drenched in wine, she was absolutely beautiful, and I had to use all my self-control to avoid pinning her against that very wall once again and kissing her senseless. *Biting* her senseless.

"I am the worst witch ever," she panted, still breathing heavily after the laughing fit.

I silenced her with a finger over her lips and shook my head. "That's not true," I whispered. "One day, you will unveil the true wonders you are capable of and surprise everyone around you… and yourself. But not me, because I believed in you from the very first moment I met you." *And hopefully, I shall live to see that day.*

She smiled weakly, and I showered her in an unhurried rain of tiny kisses. I explored the narrow, delicious space behind her ears, burying myself in her hair, which was soaked in expensive red *chianti*. The scent of old smoke still lingered underneath, even though she had escaped that fire many weeks ago. I traveled down her shoulder, following the invisible path which led down to her wrist, where her veins pulsated with deafening expectation. Glass shards had scratched her forearms, and a single pearl of blood was forming on her pale skin, almost indistinguishable from the hundreds of wine drops which covered both of us like liquefied confetti. Indistinguishable… for a human. But not for me. Elated, I licked off the pearls of blood, relishing her surrendering moans. Her eyes were oddly glassy, and I put it down at first to exhilaration. But then I noticed the sudden weakness of her stance, barely holding herself on the bench. I let go of her hand and leaned back to look at her.

"Is anything wrong?" I asked.

"Just a bit tired," she mumbled, the words garbled. "Don't worry."

She tried to bring me closer, but she seemed unwell and about to pass out.

"Let me take you to bed," I offered instead, holding her hand.

She shook her head, dismissing my help, and tried to get up from the bench, but she fainted and collapsed. I caught her right before she hit the floor, her eyes still open and staring into the emptiness.

We stayed there for the rest of the night,

and I held her unconscious body in my arms until I heard a car parking in the driveway, announcing the return of the owner of the villa.

Chapter 11

Alba

My roaring stomach announced it must be past lunchtime, and the bright slits of sunlight filtering through the embroidered curtains of the bedroom confirmed it. I didn't remember getting into bed, and the last thing in my memory was kissing Clarence before everything had started to spin and faded to black. The night had been long and dreamless, and I was sore all over; I felt as if someone had stolen a few days of my life.

I got up and followed the enticing smell of melted cheese that pervaded the whole house and led me to the large country kitchen, where Carlo was chopping tomatoes with an irked expression and much more verve than strictly necessary.

"Good morning?" I said, trying to sample his humor and the time of day in one single greeting. If he didn't stop slaughtering those poor vegetables, his salad was soon going to turn into marinara sauce.

"What makes you think it's a good one?" he

answered. The knife left a deep cleave on the cutting board, but he kept beating it. "Not my business, but I've seen sloths that sleep less than you two. Also, who is going to pay for all those bottles in my cellar?"

"Ah, yes, about those bottles… look, Carlo, I'm sorry, I…" I rubbed my eyes and held onto the edge of the table, still feeling like I had spent the night weightlifting. *How on earth had I managed to break a thousand bottles in one single second?*

Clarence's voice interrupted us, booming from the depths of the staircase. "You said you would take her to see a doctor when she woke up," he said. "What are you waiting for?"

"What?" Carlo said, pretending he didn't hear him. "I don't remember saying that. Why don't you come up here and talk, like normal people do? Or, even better, why don't you take your… *girlfriend* to a doctor *yourself?*"

Sunlight was bathing the whole kitchen, and it was obvious why Clarence would be yelling from the cellar instead of coming up to discuss the issue or simply driving me wherever he wanted to.

"I don't need a doctor," I said, although I wasn't entirely sure. I felt dizzy, and my stomach was in knots, but perhaps a plate of Carlo's lasagna would help with that. I peeked into the oven; the lasagna looked and smelled heavenly, with a layer of golden cheese on top and tomato sauce bubbling nicely around the corners.

Carlo wiped his hands on a kitchen towel and poured some beer into a glass, spilling half of it over the counter. Then he shoved it in my direction brusquely, avoiding my eyes.

"Thanks," I said, taking the beer with hesitation. It was cold and bitter, and I didn't particularly like beer, especially not on an empty stomach. "I'm sorry about yesterday. We'll pay for all the damage."

"Make yourself useful and chop these carrots," Carlo grumbled, passing me a board and a knife.

I took the knife and started to trim off the tops of the carrots, then focused on grounding myself in the present moment so I could cut them into even slices without having an accident. As I was working, my thoughts drifted to Francesca, who had been emaciated when I last saw her in Natasha's prison in Venice. I shook my head and concentrated again on the task, but the carrots turned to fingers on the board, and when I lifted my eyes, I found Julia's gazing at me, purple and terrified, her hand on the wooden plank, her fingers bleeding and partially chopped under my knife.

"I will never tell you where they are," Julia growled. "Never."

I screamed and let the knife fall to the floor with a loud clunk, missing my foot by an inch.

Julia disappeared, her fingers turning back into innocent carrots.

Carlo huffed and pushed me away with impatience. "Maybe it's better if you go and wait on the couch. I'll do it. Just take your beer and go."

"Could you perhaps come down here for a minute, Alba?" called Clarence from the basement.

I set the beer back on the counter. I didn't feel like drinking anymore. I headed downstairs where I found Clarence standing among piles of glass shards from the previous night. His shirt—the one he had borrowed from Carlo's closet—was completely ruined and covered in stains.

"You look so poorly, my dear," he said, squeezing me into a firm, comforting hug. "What you did yesterday must have been too much for you. You need to rest more. I don't think you should travel anywhere without seeing a doctor first."

He was paler than usual too, his lips nearly blue. It was hard to guess whether it was due to the curse or insufficient feeding, but he certainly wasn't his usual self. "Says who? Have you looked at yourself?"

Clarence raised an eyebrow, reminding me he had no way of checking himself in a mirror. Then he leaned down, his head tilted sideways as he stared at his reflection in my eyes. "No, but I'm sure I look absolutely dashing, as always," he stated with a smirk, running his fingers through his raven black hair with visible delight.

I puffed. "I'm fine. I don't need anything but food. If someone is sick here and needs urgent care, it's not me. Also, didn't you say you used to be a doctor? Feel free to examine me."

Clarence's eyes glinted with mischief, but Carlo's annoyed voice rumbled from upstairs.

"Look, both of you are sick and annoying as hell, and if I'm forced to listen to your cooing for much longer, I might throw up and ruin lunch. Just tell me whether I should go pack the car while the lasagna is in the oven."

"Yes, I think we should leave as soon as possible," I said pensively as Carlo's head peeked into the cellar, frowning with disgust at the sight of his ruined wine collection and Clarence's hands around my waist.

"Okay," Carlo agreed. "Then we can leave in an hour. We eat and go."

I stared at the weak gleam coming from upstairs. It was too early for Clarence to travel by car. Too sunny. "No, we'll have to wait till dusk," I said, pointing at the darkened windows of the cellar.

"No. I have a better idea." Carlo retrieved a small, rusty rabbit cage stowed in a corner, then set it on the floor with a triumphant grin. "Your carriage, sir," he sneered, bowing to Clarence as he imitated his accent.

Clarence eyed the cage with incredulity: the bottom was filthy and covered in dry rabbit droppings. "Excuse me?" he said, looming menacingly over Carlo.

"No, no, no," I said, trying to put some distance between both men. "Don't start again, you two. Of course he isn't going to get in that cage. Are you crazy, Carlo?"

"I don't see why he can't just turn into a bird and travel comfortably in the cage," Carlo said.

"I'm not going to drive only at night. That would slow us down too much. Also, does he even have a passport? I bet he doesn't, and that's going to cause trouble at the border."

"As a matter of fact, I do," Clarence answered, straightening his back with dignity. "It's just unfortunate that I didn't bring it with me, as I flew all the way here with my own wings."

"Sorry, man, but that's the same as having none," Carlo pointed out. "You walk into that cage now, or you are not riding in my car. End of story."

"He does have a passport," I said, lifting a finger to stop Carlo's cocky discourse. "I have it upstairs." I could feel Clarence fuming silently at the other man's arrogant tone, but I ignored the tension in the air and hoped they didn't kill each other in my absence. "Wait a minute."

I went to my room and found the envelope containing Clarence's passport in my suitcase, then rushed back to where both men were waiting, engaged in a stare duel of sorts... but alive.

"See?" I said, waving the brown booklet triumphantly. "Here it is."

Carlo snatched the passport and opened it to the first page. After a couple of seconds, he started to laugh hysterically.

"Who the hell is this?" he asked, giving it back. "*Tristan?*" He was holding his belly, his whole body shaking with laughter.

I took it, confused. Was that Clarence's passport at all? I hadn't even checked it out when Elizabeth gave it to me, just thrown it into my baggage without opening the envelope. When I opened the small booklet under Clarence's apologetical gaze, I quickly understood what Carlo was talking about.

The photograph showed a thirty-something man with dark hair and brown eyes, and a nicely defined jaw which offered a vague resemblance to Clarence's. But the similarities ended there; that was *not* Clarence, and there was no doubt about that.

"Who is this?" I asked, handing Clarence his alleged documents. "Tristan? Really?"

"Well…" He shrugged. "I thought you would appreciate my name choice. Besides, you know how it is with mirrors… photographs are no different."

"Oh, no." I held my forehead on my hands to process the situation. That passport was useless for travel.

"It's the best match we could find," he apologized. "Nobody has ever noticed anywhere. And those who did… usually forgot it quickly."

I blinked with disbelief. "So, you coaxed a random man to have his picture taken, then stole it from him and impersonated him?"

"Well… it's a complex matter…" Clarence stared at his shoes with innocence.

I sighed. I had been filing plenty of paperwork for Elizabeth but never came across Clarence's current passport before. "Maybe you should really consider the cage… we don't want to attract more attention than necessary."

"I'm really sorry, but that will not be possible," Clarence said brusquely, crossing his arms.

"I'll clean it well. There's a hose in the garden. We can fix it to the back seat with the seat belt, and you will be fine. It's just a few hours until dark."

"No, you do not understand," he replied, rubbing his temples.

"So what's the problem then?"

"I thought I had told you…" He lowered his voice, watching Carlo warily. It was obvious from his tone that whatever it was, he *hadn't* told me. "I can't shift anymore. I haven't been able to since we returned from Venice."

***

"He can travel in the trunk then," Carlo said. "It's a big car."

"No, I don't like that," I protested. "We will leave after sunset."

Clarence stood silent behind me, feigning disinterest, but the fiery glint in his eyes served as a small reminder that he could just decide to dismember Carlo if he got on his nerves. Such a long silence, especially coming from a vampire, could either mean that his mind was elsewhere or that he was deciding which side of Carlo's throat might be easier to access from his position.

"It's a very long drive, and we are supposed to travel in the Pyrenees," Carlo said, staring at the route on his phone. "The GPS is showing snow, roadblocks, and who knows what else we'll find on the way. I have two weeks to solve this mess if I don't want to lose my job, and I already lost a few days coming all the way here to pick up—" He nodded toward Clarence, avoiding looking at him directly. "—your boyfriend."

"He's not my…" I started to say, but Clarence placed his hands softly on my shoulders and interrupted me.

"It's fine. I will travel in the boot until sunset. I'm very tired anyway. Just help me find a thick blanket to block sunlight."

***

After eating Carlo's lasagna under Clarence's bored gaze, we packed our bags and left the keys with Maria, the housekeeper, who promised to clean everything and get it ready for the first tourists of the season.

I was distressed after hearing Clarence's confession. Not only wasn't he able to turn into a raven anymore, but also, he mentioned he was having lots of trouble staying awake during the day, instead surrendering to the pull of slumber. All those difficulties could only mean one thing: he wasn't getting better, and the curse was stronger than he had cared to admit the previous day.

Carlo brought the car into the garage, and I kissed Clarence goodnight, or whatever one was supposed to tell a vampire who was about to have a nap in the trunk of a car. I felt bad for him but couldn't think of a better solution. We agreed to take the fastest route and stop after dark so he could at least stretch his legs for a while.

"It's a twelve-hour drive," Carlo announced, "possibly more, given the weather forecast. I suggest we try to reach the French border today, and then we can decide whether we find a place to sleep or keep going."

I sat next to Carlo, watching the anodyne landscape through the passenger window and thinking about Alcazar and whether we would find the grimoire there. Meanwhile, I texted Minnie, who had barely woken up five thousand miles away in Emberbury, and we were chatting about the girls and whether they had eaten and slept enough. Eventually, Minnie had to log off, and I kept myself busy counting the trucks coming from the opposite direction, a lingering habit after many years of entertaining kids during car rides. The highway wasn't particularly busy, and evening was closing in on the road to the Italian-French border. It was odd because almost all the cars on the opposite lanes were red. I had been thinking about Carlo's anger while he chopped those tomatoes for lunch, so I smiled at the coincidence. The radio kept blabbering in Italian, but I had long ago tuned it out because it required too much effort to follow whatever they were saying. Seemingly, Carlo had been listening because he lowered the volume and said, "See? It's going to snow."

"When?" I asked, wondering what I had

been thinking when I packed only a pair of ballet flats.

"Probably tomorrow."

I nodded, now worried about my feet freezing on top of all my other concerns. The cars around us were all white, and I stared at them in disbelief. Another coincidence? Or was I attracting cars of a certain color somehow? I tried to think of a ridiculous color as a test. *Purple,* I told myself. There were hardly any purple cars. I pictured Miss Jilly's eyes, or better said, Julia's eyes when she had followed me around as a black cat, before I knew about The Cloister and the otherworldly creatures its vaults guarded.

A dozen purple trucks appeared in the distance, some of them covered in a dusty layer of thin snow.

"Carlo, look!" I shouted with excitement, shaking his shoulder. "Look what I can do!"

Carlo twisted his lip and blinked at the crazed woman sitting next to him. "What? I can't see anything."

"Look at those trucks! I… made them appear!"

"No, you didn't. Those are just ordinary fruit trucks. That brand uses only purple trucks."

"I swear it was me! Let me show you! Pick a color, and you'll see!" I needed to share my excitement with someone, and Carlo happened to be the only available candidate.

"Yeah, okay," he said with disinterest. "Blue."

I took a deep inhale and thought about the ocean; about those lazy summer afternoons on Revere Beach with my student friends, building castles in the sand and dreaming about a future which had turned out to be completely different from my wildest youth fantasies. Sure enough, a dozen cerulean blue vans materialized behind us and started to overtake us like an eerie tide.

"Hah! I told you!" I started to laugh and clap my hands like a child, delighted with my newfound skill.

But Carlo just puffed and rolled his eyes. "That's the most stupidly useless ability a witch could have," he declared, sliding right to avoid one of the demented blue vans, which breezed by at a dangerously short distance from our car.

I slumped in my seat, angry at his lack of enthusiasm. "Thanks for the encouragement," I grunted, squinting at the speeding blue dots as they disappeared in the distance. The beach in my mind turned into a raging sea storm, and I shook my head to dispel it as quickly as I could.

"Do you enjoy reading?" I asked Carlo without much hope, trying to start a conversation.

"Nah," he answered.

"So, what's the last book you read?"

"No idea. I think I read *Moby Dick* in high school. And that one where they burned all books so people couldn't read anything. Smart move, if you ask me."

I rolled my eyes at his joke—had it been a joke?—and remained quiet, once again haunted by visions of rampant sea tempests at the mention of *Moby Dick*. I couldn't wait for night to fall so Clarence could finally get out of that trunk and free me from the frustration of sitting for hours on end next to someone who considered the events in *Fahrenheit 451* a perfectly valid social measure.

The traffic in front of us started to slow down, emergency flashers staining the darkening horizon with blood red sparks.

"Seems something happened further down the road," Carlo commented, stating the obvious as we slowly joined a trudging queue of cars turtling their way down the highway.

I nodded, glancing at the clock with sadness. Hopefully, this wouldn't slow us down too much. Our destination was far enough as it was, and I really wanted Clarence to get out of the trunk already.

We came to a halt and saw a man walking on the emergency lane while he talked on his mobile phone. Carlo waved at him and asked him what was going on. The man answered something in quick, garbled Italian and waved toward a highway exit to our right.

"He says there has been a really bad accident. A heap of snow fell off the roof of a truck and blinded the driver behind it. There was a chain crash. He's suggesting we get out of here while we can and take the state road instead. The exit is right there." Carlo steered the car toward the emergency lane to escape the traffic jam. "Can you see anything?" he asked, his eyes fixed on the road as we made our sneaky escape.

I caught a brief glimpse of several blue vans squeezed into a battered metal mess, lying like toy cars forgotten by a toddler and blocking all the lanes from one side to the other of the highway. Sirens wailed behind us, and horror clutched my stomach as I remembered my previous visions of ocean gales and sinking ships, when Carlo had angered me. "No. I can't see anything," I lied.

"Oh well. Shit happens," he said dismissively, concentrating on the road signs to exit the highway. "We'll take the local roads for a few miles. I need a bathroom anyways."

Chapter 12

Alba

"Wait here," Carlo said, pulling over in the middle of a very questionable-looking and narrow mountain road. For the past fifteen minutes after leaving the last village behind, I had suspected we were lost; the fact that we were now climbing up a very steep and holey path overlooking a sleepy valley was a betraying sign that we were definitely not where we should have been on our quest to get back on the highway.

While Carlo disappeared into the trees, I got out of the car and pondered whether to wake Clarence up or not. The sky was indigo blue, but there were still broad stripes of pink and purple in the horizon. How much sunlight was too much for a vampire? I sighed and decided to let him sleep a little longer, just to be on the safe side.

"Hello," a female voice whispered in the trees. It came from the opposite side from the one Carlo had disappeared into, and it startled me. I wrapped my woolen cardigan tighter around myself and hesitated between trying to find out who was there or locking myself in the car until Carlo returned.

"Alba," the voice said, and this time, there was no doubt it was calling *me*.

I stepped back, terrified that this stranger hidden in the trees knew my name. That couldn't be a good sign when lost in a remote place south of Modena. I fumbled with the door handle and realized the door had been locked from the inside. Carlo had taken the key with him, and I didn't have any.

"Please, come here, we need your help," the woman said. *We?* So there was more than one? Her voice was but a hiss, almost like the trees themselves whispering into my ear.

"Who's there?" I asked, wondering why Carlo was taking so long.

"Help us, Alba. We need you."

I couldn't see anyone, and despite the sharp, cold air, a wave of heat washed over me. I took a few steps toward the trees, unwilling to leave the relative safety of the car.

"Please…" the voice pleaded. "Someone has to fix this. We cannot."

"I can't see you," I said with a trembling voice. "Who are you and what do you want from me? Show yourself!"

"My name is Laura… my daughter and I need help… if you help us, we can help you in exchange."

"Where are you?" I asked out of

desperation.

"We have been following you… turn around," she whispered softly, "I am right behind you. But please, do not scream."

Taking a deep breath, I braced myself and did as told.

Behind me stood a middle-aged lady holding a grimy little girl's hand, and all would have been well and good had she not been carrying her own head in the other one. It was dangling by a long tuft of matted, bloodied hair.

"*Maman*, is that the Angel of Death looming over this lady?" the little girl asked sweetly, bending over to talk to her mom's head and glowing against the tree trunks like a firefly.

My shriek was probably heard beyond the French border, wherever it was.

Carlo's steps crushed the frosty leaves in the darkness, and he appeared behind the lady and her child, then proceeded to walk right through them and throw his hands in the air with annoyance.

"Woman! Why the hell did you have to yelp like that? I thought you were being murdered!"

The ghostly lady frowned, and the little girl combed her mother's hair with her fingers. "Should we show ourselves to this gentleman, *Maman*?"

"Not now, darling," the mother said with a sad smile, "perhaps some other day."

Both vanished into the ground, leaving thin tendrils of white steam behind them.

"Carlo…" I said, my voice unsteady. "I just saw a… a…" I took a deep breath. "A ghost." He rolled his eyes, but I insisted, "No, seriously. Actually, two. You walked right through them. I swear."

"You keep seeing weird things. Antennae, hordes of blue cars and now ghosts? Isn't there a way to get that witchy side of yours under control? Because it doesn't seem healthy to me."

I shrugged and waited for him to unlock the car. Just as I was about to get in, a set of blue lights flashed behind the last bend of the road, and a police car parked right behind us.

"Shit!" Carlo groaned.

I wondered which god or goddess it would be more suitable to pray to in such a situation. Perhaps Shiva, protector of outcasts?

"*Buona sera*," the policemen greeted us, shining their flashlights on us. "Why is your vehicle blocking the road?"

I pretended not to understand, but they repeated their question in English.

"I needed to find a bathroom," Carlo said abruptly.

"I see," the officer said. "Also, we heard screams. Was it you, madam? Everything alright?"

"Oh, there was a—" I scratched my head. *A what?* "—a spider. A really big one."

They stared at each other, their faces revealing they didn't believe my story. "Can we have a look at your documents, please?"

Carlo handed them his passport, and I rummaged into my bag for mine, just to realize with concern that I must have left it in my travel bag. *Which was in the trunk. Being used by Clarence as a makeshift pillow.*

"I don't know where it is," I mumbled. I glanced at Carlo with sheer desperation, hoping he would know what to do. Should I say I had lost it? Or should I open the trunk and risk the policemen seeing Clarence?

"What do you mean you don't know where it is?" Carlo growled, oblivious to my hints. "You had it at the airport. Things don't just vanish. Search for it."

"Yes, but…" I nodded toward the back of the car, hoping he would get the message. He didn't, but the policemen did notice my strange behavior.

"Can you please open the trunk, sir?" one of them asked, his fingers tapping with impatience on the hilt of his gun.

I leaned against the car, desperate to come up with some sort of spell to make them go away and leave us alone before something horrible happened.

"Of course," Carlo said, and his throat bobbed as he started to open the lid very slowly.

The small side lights inside the trunk revealed a dark, daunting fabric bundle, which greatly resembled a dead body wrapped in a blanket.

"What are you transporting here, sir?" The policeman leaned down but avoided touching the blanket. "Can you please open the parcel?"

I swore under my breath and waited for

disaster. From where I was, leaning against the driver's door, I didn't have a great view of the scene, but the faces of the policemen were clearly visible, and their expressions were enough to unveil the exact moment when Carlo uncovered *what he was transporting*, as they had put it.

"*Che cazzo...?*" one of them muttered. I took a couple of steps toward them, hoping for my erratic magic to solve the situation on its own. "Nobody moves!" the policeman shouted, pointing his gun at me.

I raised my hands, feigning innocence.

"Hands against the car," the other one said. "You too," he added, pushing Carlo to the other side. Carlo obliged, raising his eyebrows at me, a mute question in his eyes. *Is the vampire going to wake up or what?*

"Is this man dead?" the policeman asked, to no one in particular. They seemed convinced he was, so the question was superfluous.

"He's just having a nap," I answered with a tight, all-teeth grin.

"A nap, *huh*? In the trunk? And his lips are *blue*. Must have been a *really* long nap. Paolo, call a medical examiner."

Paolo eyed the contents of the trunk with a weary grimace, then turned on his radio monitor and muttered something into it while the other one handcuffed us.

"They'll be here soon," he reassured his companion. Both men stood side to side, watching us warily while they waited for reinforcements to arrive.

The other one hmphed with frustration. "And to think, tonight Isabella is making pizza. It's going to get cold before I get home... I hate being late for dinner."

An arm sprouted out of the trunk, followed by a pair of long legs in a pair of borrowed, ill-fitting jeans.

Clarence stood up and bowed politely to the policemen, who stared at him with wide-eyed bewilderment. "Good evening, sirs. Did someone say dinner?"

***

"This is *bad*," Carlo grunted, crouching over the unconscious officers and turning his back toward them to search their belts. It had taken Clarence two-and-a-half seconds to knock both of them out in one single, almost lazy blow. Despite his mention of dinner, he had spared us the uncomfortable sight of a vampire doing what vampires usually did and left the agents untouched right where they had fallen.

"Where the hell are the keys to these handcuffs?" Carlo grumbled, fumbling in the darkness with his hands tied to his back.

"I could help you with that," Clarence offered, pointing quietly at Carlo's tied hands, but the other man scowled at him and kept contorting, trying—quite unsuccessfully—to fit the key he had just found into the tiny lock. Clarence had set me free as soon as he had knocked out the poor agents, but Carlo had refused any assistance from him and insisted on doing everything himself.

"What are we going to do when they wake up?" I asked, rubbing my wrists to restore the blood circulation. I stifled a yawn, exhausted after causing car accidents, meeting headless people, and all the other crazy things which seemed to follow me wherever I went.

Clarence glanced at me with worry, ignoring my question. "It's been a long day for you. You must be tired," he said, rubbing my back.

I smiled at him with affection. It was cute he thought he could help me warm up with his ice-cold touch. I nudged him away and knelt in front of the policemen, who were immersed in a peaceful sleep, faint smiles on their lips. "I am. But we can't just leave them here. It's too risky."

Carlo kept twisting and trying to get rid of the cuffs. "What do you mean?" he asked. "I don't know about you, but I don't usually kill people, particularly not unconscious people," he muttered.

"Neither do I," Clarence said, offended, but after a brief pause, he quietly added, "most of the time."

"I wasn't talking about killing anyone!" I whisper-shouted, appalled at their interpretation of my words. "I just meant it's cold, and they'll freeze to death here, or they could be eaten by wild animals. But yes, we don't want them to follow us either. I agree on that. It's risky for all of us."

"We leave now as fast as we can, and we

hope they don't catch us again?" Carlo suggested. His cheeks were cherry red due to his struggles to free himself, but his hands remained tied behind his back.

"In my opinion, that's not a very clever plan," Clarence said, then took a stride toward Carlo, grabbed the handcuffs and broke the chain without even flinching. Looking at his effortless moves, one would have thought the handcuffs were made of play dough. "There. Stop torturing yourself," he said, ignoring Carlo's fierce look of hatred. "I have a better idea," he continued impassively. "Allow me to take care of this mess. Lombardi, please drive yourself and Alba to the nearest hotel along this road and get a room. In fact, no. Get two, please," he warned him, holding the man's gaze. "I shall join you in a minute, when I am done with the cleaning up."

Chapter 13

Alba

Carlo threw the broken handcuffs at Clarence's feet and got into the car with a puff. "Good luck getting rid of all the evidence," he sneered. "Because they also called reinforcements, and they must be on their way."

I kissed Clarence hurriedly and followed Carlo to the car. My pinky toes were numb with cold. "Please be careful," I told Clarence, watching in awe as he folded the discarded cuffs like fresh clay and rolled them into a shiny, silver ball. "Will you be okay on your own? Are you sure you don't want us to wait here?"

"Don't worry," he answered, handing me the metal ball he had modelled out of the broken handcuffs. "You are tired, and I could benefit from a brisk walk. I don't mind. And it's safer if you leave."

Taking a seat in the warm vehicle, I nodded; he was right. I held the metal ball he had given me, mute proof that, sick or not, he still had the upper hand when dealing with ordinary humans. Sometimes it was easy to forget the things he was able to do.

Carlo turned on the engine, and we drove in silence. The road became steep and narrow in front of us, with no villages in sight, let alone hotels. I couldn't stop thinking about the cop whose wife had promised to make a pizza, and I finally voiced the question which had been lingering like static electricity in the air. "What do you think he's going to do?"

Carlo put an arm around the passenger seat and turned to look into my eyes with disgust. "What do you think, love?" he spat, "What do *you* think?"

I sighed, turning the metal ball in my hands and allowing the dim light of the moon to reflect on it. Of course. What was a hungry vampire supposed to do with two unconscious victims?

"I guess you are right," I said and kept silent the rest of the way.

***

A pink neon sign with the words *"Camere, rooms, Zimmer"* greeted us from a distance, a couple of letters flickering in a near-death last cry. The whole place seemed to have been scrapped from a 1966 photo album, with a grey cement façade that must have been screaming for new paint for at least half a century.

We parked in front of the main entrance

and rang the bell. To my surprise, a lady came to open it and showed us two humble—but clean—rooms on the first floor. Carlo booked both of them, honoring Clarence's request. Thanking him for the ride, I rushed to my room and left the window ajar in case Clarence didn't feel like bothering the receptionist.

I found some cookies, an energy bar and an apple in my bag and decided they would be enough to survive until morning. After a brief, mismatched picnic on the bed, I went to brush my teeth. Even in the badly lit bathroom, I could distinguish the many wrinkles spidering over my forehead and around my eyes like eerie cobwebs. Some were more like mountain ridges. Most hadn't been there a couple of months ago, and a wave of panic took hold of me when I tried and failed to smooth them out with some cream. The stress and jet lag definitely weren't helping. Moody, I searched in my toiletries bag and pulled out a moisturizing mask. I spread a thick layer of white paste over my whole face and checked the text on the box, which promised to "*return youth and freshness to tired, mature skin*".

Excellent. Just what I needed.

"I think you overdid your vampire make-up a little," Clarence greeted me, stepping over the windowsill and sitting on the bedspread. He nodded smugly as he admired the white and greasy paste which covered my whole face, except my eyes.

I ran to the bathroom to wash my face, as

quick as if chased by ghosts. Wouldn't have been the first time anyway.

"Very funny," I growled, wiping my face dry with a towel as soft as a saguaro cactus. "Vampire make-up, huh?"

"You are beautiful either way. But I think your normal shade suits you better. Unless you are practicing for the future?"

"The future?" I asked. "What future exactly?"

"Well, I know you said you weren't interested, but…" he smirked, letting his fangs show. "You know, in case you change your mind."

"Oh, stop that, Clarence. I'm serious. This is depressing. I'm starting to look like a raisin," I whined, but he just chuckled at my words. The color had returned to his lips and cheeks, a clear clue of what he had done with the two policemen after we left. "A wrinkled, old raisin."

"Don't be silly," he said, brushing damp wisps of hair away from my forehead with fondness. "Wrinkles are maps of memories. Just make sure yours are happy ones."

I sighed with exhaustion and let myself slump on the bed next to him. "You don't understand," I said quietly, handing him the metal ball he had given me by the car.

He let the ball roll to the other side of the bed, and it dropped on the carpet with a soft thud as he took my hands in his. They were cold as snow. Then he sought my eyes before saying, "Believe me, I do."

"You're freezing," I said, shrinking into a tight knot of arms and legs as the chill traveled from his hands to mine. It didn't help that the room was damp and had no heating whatsoever.

"Breaking news," he answered, then his smile faded, and he recoiled with a worried expression. "Oh, I'm sorry, does it bother you? Please forgive me. I tend to forget."

"No, I mean... you are colder than usual. Are you okay?"

He seemed to be colder with each day that passed, colder even than the air around us, and that had started to worry me.

"Oh, yes, I'm perfectly fine. I'll take a shower to warm up a little. Give me a second."

He skipped gracefully and disappeared into the bathroom. Once I heard the water running, I decided to go have a little peek through the shower door.

"Do you need a towel?" I shouted from the door, knowing that it was pointless to tiptoe around him. He would hear me no matter what.

"I have everything I need," he answered, his voice more mischievous than usual. "Particularly now that you have come."

I wiped the steam off the screen, only to see him standing under the shower fully dressed, still wearing Carlo's borrowed clothes, which were filthy through and through with mud and blood.

"What are you doing?" I asked, hardly

containing my laughter. "Why are you dressed?"

He grinned. "I needed to wash them anyway. I'm saving water, I suppose?" The water had soaked the fabric, making the white t-shirt completely see-through and offering a magnificent glimpse of his perfectly shaped torso. "Care to join me?" he asked, his smile growing wider and wider.

Glossy charcoal strands of wet hair fell down his neck, and steam flooded the tiny bathroom, giving him, and the whole space, an ethereal, mysterious aura: like a place out of this world. I took off my watch and left it on the shelf by the mirror. The mirror showed my reflection, but not his: a reminder that any inkling of normalcy in our lives was but an illusion. An illusion I was eager to keep, at least for the night.

"I hope the water is warm," I warned him. I was skeptical of Clarence's judgment regarding normal, human temperatures. After all, he could sit on a block of ice without flinching.

"I don't know what you would consider warm enough," he said, confirming my suspicions. He turned the tap left a few times and shrugged. "Perhaps try it first?" He wiggled his fingers and smirked. "Do you need help undressing?"

"I'm fine, thanks," I answered with a defiant glance. Fully dressed, I stepped boldly under the abundant cascade of water, but a shriek escaped my lips as soon as the scalding stream hit my shoulders. "Gosh, Clarence, are you trying to boil yourself alive like a lobster?"

I glued myself to the damp, cold tiles in the

corner, dodging the steaming hell of a shower he was still standing under, unfazed.

Clarence shook his head with amusement and turned the tap towards the other side, chuckling at my dismay as he rubbed my scalded back softly. "Sorry, Isolde." He was chuckling, but I wasn't. I wouldn't be surprised to find a third-degree burn by next morning. "My bones are so cold. I miss the warmth of being alive. Let me remedy this awful mistake."

"No living creature on this planet would survive such molten lava of a shower," I grunted, still cranky. He raised an eyebrow, leaving it clear that he wasn't included in that statement. "Yes, I know, I know. But if you were trying to burn this witch, you almost succeeded."

"Never. You are my favorite witch." He pushed me gently back under the gushing water, which was—finally—warm and pleasant.

"That's better," I groaned, closing my eyes and letting the water massage my nape and upper arms under the thin fabric of my shirt.

"You look so beautiful right now that it hurts," Clarence whispered in a raspy voice, his touch over my backside becoming needier, stronger. "If I could freeze this feeling forever, I would, so I would have you forever like this, in my arms, where you belong." He sighed. "If you ever forget how to go back home, remember this feeling, and call it back. The memories will take you to the place where you belong, and that is… with me."

I shuddered as his fingers ran through my soaked hair behind me, and his lips found that perfect spot behind my earlobes. His breath, usually inaudible, was rushed and heavy, echoing in my ear as he licked the reddened skin, turning the aching into bliss. I swiveled to meet him, and he bit the side of my neck gently; just a soft nibble, but enough to melt any rational thoughts I might have had.

His body poured over mine like a waterfall, washing over me like a warm, wet, unstoppable surge of energy. Droplets got into my eyes, blocking my view of him, and I wiped them out with a wave of my hand. Following the direction of my gesture, the stream started to swirl around us, spiraling in circles of silver and azure that started to glisten and sparkle like a coiling blue rainbow.

"Queen of Water," Clarence murmured, echoing a name I had already been called before.

"Kiss me," I commanded, indifferent to the magical water show around us.

Kissing him was like breathing.

Just more urgent.

More essential.

The only thing necessary to keep me alive in that moment.

Our soaked clothes had become a maddening barrier, preventing me from touching him. I waved my hand, repeating what I had done with the bothersome water stream getting into my eyes, and willed our clothes to dissolve and disappear.

And so, they did.

"Finally," he sighed, kneeling in front of me to kiss the long scar under my navel. The one I loathed so much. Then he stood up and lifted me in the air as I laced my bare legs around his back.

I didn't know how long his energy would last—how long until the curse got the best of him—but I had this moment, and I was going to seize it before it slipped through my fingers like the streams of water washing our entangled bodies. As the water got colder and our bodies warmer, we kissed more passionately than ever before, with the urgency only known by those who might not live to see another day.

Chapter 14

Clarence

I carried her to the bed and covered her with a coarse linen sheet. Her hair was still dripping, and she was shivering, wrapped in the only dry towel I had been able to find after the rainbow swirls of water had languished and plunged onto the floor with a magnificent last splash. However, she seemed oblivious to the cold and dampness. She kept smiling, a wistful expression clouding her drowsy eyes, perhaps on the brim of the land of dreams as she recalled her last magical feat.

I stood by the window, framing her soft, small shape in the middle of the rundown room, reminiscent of Goya's Nude Maja reclining on a pile of pillows. I wanted to imprint her forever in my mind's eye, with her messy, damp hair and misty, alluring eyes. I wished I had oil and canvas to paint her, for how many more times would I have her like that? How many joyful moments did we have left, before one of us was gone forever?

She smiled and patted the bed, silently inviting me to sit by her side.

"Come here, *Doctor*," she cooed, but her eyelids were visibly drooping with weariness. I complied and took a seat, ignoring the naughty nuances in her tone.

"Go to sleep, my dear," I told her, kissing her forehead. "It has been a long day." There was a foreign bible in the nightstand drawer, and I pulled it out without much enthusiasm. "I'll read while you rest."

She shook her head and snuggled next to me. "I could do with some cuddling. I can't turn off my thoughts."

"I understand," I said. My mind was racing too. So many uncertainties and so few answers.

"Why are you so moody all of a sudden?" she asked, the mischievous smile still shining. She pulled at the sheet over her bare legs and lifted a foot, wiggling her toes in the air. "You weren't like that five minutes ago."

Her boldness made me grin. "That's because I was too astonished to think clearly. I didn't know witches had such a peculiar way of… *washing*," I answered, tickling her sides and causing her to twist with delight. "Forgive me if I need a minute to process this fascinating, new information."

A sparkle of glee danced in her eyes. "That thing with the water swirling around was crazy, wasn't it? I have no idea how I did it!"

"You never seem to," I observed. Her hair

had started to drip over the pillows, so I handed her the towel.

"It actually worries me," she confessed with a sigh. "I'm afraid I'll end up harming someone. It's getting out of control."

"I don't think you will. But you might harm *yourself* if you are not a bit more sparing with your magic. It's a basic law of the universe: you cannot create energy; just transform it. So, it's wise to ponder carefully what you are going to use yours for."

She started to braid her dark, still damp locks over her naked shoulder, covering and uncovering the twin scars on the side of her neck with distracted abandonment as she went down. Bite marks. *My* bite marks. The scar had been there for weeks, but the sight was always unnerving. Alluring too.

"It just keeps happening," she whispered with a tinge of sadness. "It's beyond my control... I don't know what to do. But I'm not worried about myself. I think I'll be fine. The people around me though..."

"Well, you should be," I insisted, pushing her loosely braided hair aside. The floor wobbled as soon as my eyes fell once again on those tempting dots on her neck. "You could even..."

"Die?" she finished the sentence for me, swaying gently; oblivious to the annihilating effect the curve of her shoulder had on my logical thinking.

"Yes." I closed my eyes and inhaled her

scent, tracing the crook of her neck with the tip of my nose.

"Would you take me with you if I did?"

Her words startled me, bringing me back to the present like a strike of lightning. I jumped back, holding her small shoulders with shock. "What do you mean?"

"If that happened. Would you… make me *like you*?"

I stared at her, trying to decipher her expression.

"Would you want me to?"

She exhaled. "I don't know. Maybe?"

We held each other in silence for a long time, until I noticed she was quivering like a leaf in my arms, and I wrapped her tighter in the blanket.

"Does it hurt?" she whispered with innocence. "I mean… did it hurt for you? How was it… dying… coming back?"

I closed my eyes and sighed. "I cannot remember."

"You really can't?" She sounded surprised. She caressed my temples, a look of wonder lighting her eyes as she gazed into mine. "Maybe it's better like this."

"I am certain it is," I said, kissing her cheek.

She got up, and the towel fell at her feet. Her hair was still dripping, and the drops hit the worn hardwood floors.

Drip.

Drip.

Just like that cursed night in 1834, when a

clock of raindrops had counted down my last seconds of life.

And how could I forget?

***

London, September 1834

A dreary autumn rain was drumming outside Anne's house on the night I finished her portrait. I should not have been there that day, but there was nowhere better to be. Mother had been coughing blood since morning, and Father had determined bloodletting was imperative. I had always abhorred the practice, since it never seemed to produce any results apart from terrifying most patients. Still, Father rejected new discoveries, and my opinion was of no concern to him. *Mama* had fallen mercifully unconscious after endless hours of misery and a copious dose of laudanum, and even though Mary, her maid, had begged me to stay by her side, I had refused.

Oh, Mary. How could she know what I suffered in not being by Mother's side at the darkest of moments, how I loathed myself for my weakness? But despite her pleas, I could not bring myself to stay. I loved Rose Auberon too much to watch helplessly as life escaped her lungs like rainwater seeping into the earth, like the drops washing down my fingers when I knocked on Anne Zugrabescu's door that evening.

Anne was pleased to see me and did not

mention I was several days early to our weekly rendezvous. She received me in a draped black dress which enhanced her striking figure and also matched her luscious onyx hair, contrasting with lips so red that they did not seem to belong to this world.

Perhaps because they did not.

"Welcome," she greeted me, offering me a drink and a seat by her side on the narrow velvet divan. I accepted both, sipping her exclusive brandy and exhaling gradually in the hopes that my troubles would dissolve into the air and vanish. When they did not, I refilled my glass, encouraged by Anne's usual half-smirk. She enjoyed our game and was always eager to help me go astray. She found it exceedingly entertaining, and I did not care anymore.

"Shall we start?" she asked, unpinning her hair so it fell loosely beyond her shoulders, just like in the nearly-finished canvas.

I nodded and dipped the thinnest paintbrush into the darkest carmine of my palette, then slithered it around the delicate silhouette of her lips on the canvas.

I lost count of the minutes. All I knew was that we were halfway through the second bottle when I added the very last touch: that maddening, rounded black mole by the side of her mouth.

It felt so final.

Like the period at the end of the very last sentence of a book.

Like a wax seal on a death sentence.

"Your commission is done," I whispered, sorrow oozing off my words. "I hope it is to your taste."

Anne shrugged, a devilish smirk adorning her perfect countenance. "It is just as I expected it to be. But posing for it was highly entertaining. I think this calls for a celebration… of our last night together."

Last. I could not bear the sound of that word.

"Please, tell me I will see you again," I pleaded, reluctant to accept her final farewell. "Tell me this is not our last night. Otherwise, I do not know what I shall do with myself. I would miss you too much."

"Very true, my dear, I daresay you would." She laughed, pulling at my lapels with her accustomed boldness and dragging me toward her. This sudden closeness was new and almost painful. She had always held her distance, and I had thought that was the way she wanted things to remain. "Did you think I had not noticed the way you look at me?" Her smile was dazzling; sinful. "I know just the perfect way to put an end to your sorrows," she whispered into my ear, casually undoing the clasp of her pearl necklace and watching it slide down her cleavage; it crept down her dress and emerged under her skirt, right at her feet. "But you must say the right word."

"The right… word?" I repeated in confusion, my mind blurry with a mixture of brandy and desire as my eyes retraced the invisible path followed by the pearls as they had slid down her svelte figure, "What word?"

"Just say yes."

I inhaled slowly, trying to clear my mind. At that point I, just like any mortal man on earth, would have said yes to virtually anything she would have asked of me. And so, I did. "Yes," I gasped, kissing her tomb-cold lips, "yes."

"Your wish is my command," she sneered, stepping out of her dress like a snake shedding her skin. I let out a ragged breath, taking in her magnificent naked figure, but I could not relish the sight for too long because Anne started to tear off my clothes with ferocious abandonment, leaving a trail of shredded fabric in her wake. She did not bother to undo any buttons or laces, and I did not care, for she was finally mine. Or was I hers? I did not think the distinction mattered, although it ultimately did. She perched on my chest like a gargoyle and clawed at my bare skin with nails of iron, pleasure and agony intermingling in an inextricable blend as she rode me with a delicious recklessness I had never experienced before.

I surrendered to the pleasure of being one with the woman I had craved for weeks on end. Only three words: *Anne. Mine. Finally.* When I thought I was about to shatter into a million pieces, she leaned down, never letting go, and a sharp pain gripped the crook of my neck, piercing an artery as her crystal laugh filled the air, an air already brimming with the scent of alcohol, paint solvents and blood.

She rose to face me, and the frail, delicate traits I had known up to that day twisted into a grotesque, horrific grimace. Bloody traces stained the corners of her mouth, leaving a thin trail down the sides of her chin.

"Now the most enjoyable part begins," she said, cackling, and a bloody set of fangs glinted in the dim lights of the room.

"Anne, what are you doing?" I tried to escape her grip, but it was too strong, and I could not move. I felt the wound pulsating and my blood spilling over the upholstery. "That hurt. Stop, please. I do not want this. Not like this."

"But you said yes," she said sweetly, licking the blood on her chin with an unnaturally long and rosy tongue. "It is too late now."

I screamed as she bit my neck again and crippled me into a pulsing ball of agony.

Pain was all I remembered from that night.

Even though I had grown up listening to the screams of Father's patients, my screams were probably louder than any of theirs ever were.

"Let me go," I begged, feeling limp and weak as life started to leave my body.

She paused, a faint glint of humanity flickering in her eyes for a split second. But she shook her head. "No. That would be a shame now," she decided, suddenly pensive as her nail carved bloody trails on my chest, "to allow a worthy young man like you to be lost to the ruthlessness of time and fleshly decay. You deserve greater things." She let out a moan and kissed me, allowing me to taste my own blood on her lips. My eyes rolled back as I lost control of my body, and I subsided to the pleasant softness of feeling nothing. "I have come to esteem you too much, my dear. You are to stay with me, and you shall be immune to the fickleness of mortal life. You chose well when you said yes. I am so pleased with your decision."

I passed out, still inside her, wishing for death to take hold of me quickly.

But as much as I wished death upon myself, it never came. Or if it did, it did not last long.

***

I woke up contorting in pain and dying of thirst. Anne was sipping port wine on the settee, wearing the same dress and the same condescending smile, as if time had ceased to exist; as a matter of fact, it had not existed for her for a very long time.

"Welcome to Hell," she murmured as she helped me stand up for the first time, and the room started to spin. "I am certain you will enjoy your stay."

Chapter 15

Alba

The next morning, I found Carlo having breakfast in the restaurant of our motel, surrounded by enough cups of coffee to conduct a very long and exciting stuffed animal tea party. Clarence must have gone hunting or roamed back to the trunk of the car while I was sleeping because I had woken up to an empty room and the sun shining brightly through the curtains.

"What did you do with the leech?" Carlo asked, stirring sugar into his fifth espresso with the help of a long grissini. "You sent him to sleep on the couch? Lovers' quarrel?" he added with a twinkle of hope in his eye.

"No, I think he's in the car," I groaned, not in the mood to engage in an argument before coffee.

"Yeah." He nodded, eating the mushy grissini. "I don't blame you. Vampire morning breath must be something else."

I rolled my eyes and went to the bar to find

something to eat while he tried to figure out the next stops along our route.

When I came back with a tray full of fruit and pastries, he was staring at a map on his phone and frowning.

"We have deviated too much from the original route, which isn't great," he explained, pointing at the thin blue lines depicting the possible roads. "Maybe it makes no sense to try and go back to the highway anymore. I think we should continue along the smaller, local roads. What do you think?"

I studied the available options, not sure I wanted to cross the Provence-Alps in the middle of winter with high chances of being caught in a snow storm. "I don't know. You said it was going to snow?"

"But not today."

"These things aren't always super accurate, you know…"

"Nah, I think it should be fine," he said, and I shrugged.

We left the motel after breakfast, and sure enough, the first flurries started to form a gentle dusting over the windshield somewhere in the vicinity of the French border. But it stopped at that, and in the afternoon, I was surprised to note that we had almost reached France after a fairly uneventful drive. Once it got dark enough, we pulled over, and I went to check on the poor, long-legged vampire crumpled in the trunk.

"Good evening," Clarence said, popping out

of the car and stretching himself in a delightful s-motion, "thanks for letting me out. I was looking forward to sitting next to you. I don't have many opportunities to ride in a car as it is, and it does get a tiny bit uncomfortable in the trunk after a while."

Carlo was smoking by the side of the road, just a couple of steps away, and he muttered a string of curses in two languages as he put out the cigarette and trudged toward us.

"What now?" I asked, crossing my arms.

"Nothing," he snapped, "but that was not our deal. I agreed to drive a caged bird. Nobody said anything about a dangerous bloodsucker sitting behind me for hours."

"I could drive." Clarence regaled the other man with a wide and wicked smile. I was already familiar with his driving expertise, so I silenced him with a stern glance before Carlo gave him the chance to kill us all on those steep and narrow mountain roads. "Alright, alright. You can chain me if it makes you feel better," Clarence offered his wrists solemnly, standing tall against the empty road. "I am certain you own vampire hunters' chains, do you not?"

"Yeah, sure, I'm gonna drive a handcuffed guy in my back seat," Carlo scoffed. "That will definitely *not* look weird if we are stopped again. I'm sure the border control agents will have no questions at all."

"Just chill a bit, Carlo, will you?" I said, trying to make peace between the two men.

"I can't chill with a murderer in my car. I

won't allow that," he growled.

"I cannot recall at which point you became the leader of this expedition, Lombardi," Clarence said calmly, wrapping his arms around me with possessiveness, "I am trying to be gracious, but you make it exceedingly hard."

"Okay, okay, guys," I said, rolling my eyes and pushing them apart from each other. "Carlo, I think there's no harm if he rides in the back for a couple of hours. I'll take the wheel if you get sleepy, and with some luck, we'll reach Alcazar tonight. The weather is behaving, and everything should go as planned. Just stop fussing about every little detail, okay?"

We kept to local, low-traffic roads and met barely any other vehicles on the way. I considered that an advantage because it gave me fewer chances to cause accidents with my new-found magical skill. It also made it easier to stop and rest when necessary.

Both men avoided talking to each other, save for the few essential things we needed to agree on the trip. Clarence held my hand the whole time and stared out the window with endearing fascination. I stared at him in exchange, finding his reactions to the landscape much more entertaining than the monotone succession of nondescript villages and closed petrol stations I could barely see through the glass.

"I'm going to grab a coffee, and we can keep going for a couple of hours more," Carlo declared as he slowed down in front of a derelict village café. "Do you want one too?" he asked, and I shook my head no. Then he added in a mocking tone, "What about you, *Mr. Auberon*? Should I check if they have something… *someone*… for you to nibble on?"

"Thank you. That will not be necessary," Clarence replied curtly.

"Oh, of course. You brought a take-away!" Carlo continued, ostensibly committed to pushing all of the vampire's buttons. "Who will it be tonight, sir? Ms. Lumin? Or me, *again*?"

Clarence's eyes blazed red, but thankfully he didn't rise to the bait. Still, Carlo's provocations didn't get any better as the hours passed and he got sleepier and therefore grumpier.

We crossed to France through a small, local border, which ended up being vacant: nobody even looked at us, let alone asked for any documents. After that, we kept driving until dawn started to creep over the horizon and a road sign informed us that we needed to take a detour in order to reach our destination.

"Turn left!" I shouted at Carlo, who was starting to get sluggish and had almost missed it. "If all goes well, we will be there in less than an hour!"

"Really… so soon…" mumbled Clarence, seeming distracted as he eyed the orange morning glow beyond the mountains with worry.

"Yes," I said, hugging him. "And then we can reverse that curse of yours."

Chapter 16

Alba

Even though there were just a few miles left until Alcazar, the roads were winding and difficult, and soon it became obvious that we wouldn't win our race against the sunrise.

Clarence looked out the window, the sky turning purple and orange beyond the treetops. "I should retire to my—" he said and hesitated, letting out a brief sigh as he pointed toward the back of the moving car, "—sleeping quarters." He had turned extremely pale again, and a dark purple tinge had stained his lips and the circles under his eyes. I could also see a fuzzy halo around him, like his edges were turning blurry, but I wasn't sure whether it was actually there or my witchy senses were playing games again.

"You don't look very good," I said, squeezing his hand and feeling my chest constrict when I confirmed it was colder than it should have been. "And it must be so cold in that trunk. I'm sure that's not good for you."

"I will be fine. I can't feel the cold at all."

"Maybe you two should share the trunk tonight?" Carlo suggested, turning down the volume of the horrid music he had been playing for revenge. "Wrap yourselves in that blanket like a burrito and enjoy some cuddly bites?"

I blinked, and for a second, I actually considered his suggestion. After all, I had been dozing on and off on Clarence's shoulder for the last couple of hours. It couldn't be *that* different to do the same in the trunk.

"Just find a place to stop at your earliest convenience, please," Clarence told Carlo.

I closed my eyes and listened to the monotonous sound of the engine. It was still dark outside, though not for long, and the last time I had seen the headlights of another vehicle must have been at least half an hour ago. We seemed to be the only ones interested in driving along narrow Pyrenees roads on that chilly February night. So narrow, in fact, that Carlo couldn't even find a place to pull over for many miles.

I was starting to doze off when the sound of screeching brakes startled me, and a heavy jolt nearly sent me flying through the windshield. I screamed, holding onto the seat belt. Clarence kept me safe in my seat with an iron arm until a loud thump on the roof shook the vehicle and the engine stopped abruptly.

Carlo cursed and kicked the door open, while I rubbed my sleepy eyes and tried to understand what had happened.

"A deer," Carlo said, slumping back into the driver's seat and hitting the dashboard with rage. "It's gone, but the front is completely smashed."

"What now?" I asked, straightening in my seat.

"Well, we didn't kill it, so I guess we are free to continue. That is, if I manage to start this thing up again." Carlo turned the key and the engine let out a whine, then started to hum nicely. "Okay. It still works."

Clarence crept back into the trunk, accepting his fate with stoicism. As I was helping him get wrapped into the blanket, I noticed a faint glow illuminating his face in the darkness, like a saint's halo. It disappeared after a few seconds, so I dismissed it as yet another of my hallucinations and gave him a quick kiss before closing the lid. When I got back into the car, I could only think about him, forced to hide in that narrow, asphyxiating space, with his legs tucked against his chin. I was furious at Natasha and the witches who had caused all of us in The Cloister so much pain, particularly Clarence.

We kept going, and the car kept overheating. Only one of the headlights was still working, which made it hard to see the bends in the road. The town of Alcazar couldn't be too far anymore, but it was becoming apparent that our wretched car might not make it to our destination, and calling roadside assistance was probably out of the question until Clarence woke up.

"The radiator is dying," Carlo muttered, and the car chuffed awkwardly, agreeing with him.

"The *what*? What does that mean for us?" I asked in confusion.

"It means we are going to need a tow truck, and the only question is *when*."

By some miracle, after countless stops to allow the engine to cool off, we made it to the sign announcing the proximity of Alcazar, the small mountain town at the foot of the Abbey. That was exactly when our car decided to let out a loud screech signaling its dying breath, right by a small picnic area in a copse of fir trees.

"Well, it could have been worse!" I said, getting out of the car in order to help Carlo push the vehicle under the trees and out of the road.

It was early morning; too late to go find a hotel, but still too cold for leisurely touristic strolls.

"Let's go find a café or something," Carlo suggested, stifling a yawn. "Before we get frostbite out here."

"Yes, but… what about Clarence?" I asked nervously, tapping on the lid of the trunk.

"Would he walk into a café in plain daylight?" Carlo asked, rolling his eyes because he already knew the answer. "Also, can you wake him up at all?"

He had a point. Even if I could wake Clarence up, he wasn't able to shift anymore. The only viable option was to leave him where he was, tightly wrapped in his blanket until sunset.

"Maybe I should stay here with him," I

suggested without much conviction. The ground was frozen under my feet, and I was hungry. Carlo watched me with an arched eyebrow while I weighed up twelve hours outdoors versus a cup of coffee in a café, with proper heating. "Yes, you are probably right," I said, giving up. "The car is locked, so I guess he'll be fine. Let's go find something warm to drink, and we can come back to check on him in a couple of hours."

***

We lugged our worn-out selves toward the first row of houses in the village, a thin mist lifting off the ground around them as the sun started to thaw the frosty mulch. The lonely, small town had started to wake up, getting ready for an ordinary Friday morning. Alcazar was a long ride away from most large ski stations and therefore not very appealing to tourists during the winter; this was probably the reason why we could only find two open establishments: a bakery and a grimy-looking café. The only store I saw was selling everything from cutlery to boots and parkas—I eyed the latter with longing and decided to come back when it opened because I was freezing in my ridiculously chic trench coat.

"So, do we get something from the nice-smelling bakery and eat it on an ice-cold bench, or should we brace ourselves and enter that dragon's lair of a café?" I pointed at the rundown sign over the door and the tables visible through the window.

I was sure one could lay a banknote on them and expect it to stay stuck there for centuries. "It looks warm… but a bit filthy…"

"Warm and filthy sounds like my kind of place," Carlo said, nodding in approval as he grabbed the door handle and disappeared into the dark stickiness of the building.

Soon we were defrosting our limbs next to a radiator with large macchiatos in front of us, and I took out the neat piece of paper where Jean-Pierre had written down for me all he knew about the Alcazar grimoire.

"So, what now?" Carlo asked, eyeing Jean-Pierre's gothic calligraphy with skepticism. "We start with a romantic walk around this charming village while *Mr. Thirdwheel* is asleep?"

"I thought *you* were *Mr. Thirdwheel*," I mumbled, but seeing his irritated reaction I decided not to go that route and stick to business. "Never mind. Let's go to the abbey. I'm hoping they keep the grimoire in the library. It would be great if we could take some photos of the spells and continue our trip this evening."

Carlo sneered. "Why do I doubt that?"

The waiter, a big, healthy-looking man with round, red cheeks, appeared from behind me carrying an assortment of homemade jams and baguettes sliced in half. "Try this! My wife made them with fruits from our orchard. Are you enjoying your breakfast? It's so nice to see tourists around here in winter. We don't get many until t-shirt weather arrives." I smiled at him, marveling at the nicely arranged jars. They looked quite clean too. "I overheard you came to see the abbey; is that right? Or are you here because of the fair?"

"The abbey, yes," I said, leaning toward him with interest. "Can you tell us how to get there?"

"Of course!" he said proudly. "You will love it. It's wonderfully preserved, and the wedding venue is beautiful!" he paused for a second, watching us with new eyes, then nodded. "You are getting married in the abbey, aren't you? So wise to come check it out before the spring crowds arrive. It's usually booked out by March. After that, they come in droves!"

"Oh, no, no…" I started to say, but Carlo smiled with delight and cut me off, placing a hand over mine.

"No need to pretend, *honey*," he said, enjoying my suffering. He should have become an actor. It suited him better than being a corrupt cop. "Nobody knows us here. It's okay."

The man winked knowingly. "Ah, still a secret, is it? Don't worry, your secret is safe with me. You make a lovely couple, if I may say so. Oh, to be young and in love again! My wife and I got married up there too, in the seventies. It was late May. It's the best season, when everything is in bloom, and you can get pictures with the cows."

Carlo nodded, like a wedding surrounded by cows was a very normal wish to have. "That's exactly what we were looking for, isn't it, *honey bunny*?" He elbowed me, and I smiled through my teeth, making a mental note to strangle him as soon as we stepped out of the café.

The café owner dragged a chair from an empty table and parked himself beside me, armed with an herb-smelling shot glass.

"So..." I said, leaning toward him, "I've heard there's a library in the abbey. Do you think it would be possible for us to visit it?"

"Ah, a library?" He shrugged. "Who knows? Monks used to live there, yes. Or maybe they were nuns? I guess monks had books... Bibles, for sure. I'm not much of a bookworm, to be honest." He leafed through a newspaper, twisting his lip with revulsion at the tiny text. "People usually come because of the views from the top. Look." He pulled out his cell phone and started to show us photos of his grandkids surrounded by gardens and antique buildings. The sight made me miss my own daughters, and I tried to guess what time it was back home. I wished I could call Minnie, but they were probably asleep in a different time zone.

"What time do they open?" I asked the barman, hoping he would stop torturing us with photos of his grandchildren.

"I'd say around ten or so?" he answered, checking his watch. "I haven't been there for a while, but I think it's still a bit early. You can walk to the main square and ask at the tourist office; they will also tell you how to book a taxi to drive you to the top. And while you wait, there's a medieval Carnival fair going on in Alcazar this weekend. There will be jugglers, magicians, archers... and traditional food, of course!"

Food. I really liked the idea of sampling French country cuisine. Although magicians sounded interesting too.

"Yes, maybe we should get going, honey," Carlo said, throwing his arm around my shoulders with a smirk. I pinched his back in exchange, and the smirk vanished.

"I agree... *honey,*" I said, squinting at him. "Let's have a look at the fair... and the abbey."

***

The mountain village of Alcazar was much prettier than I had initially expected. Most houses were built with rustic, brown stone, all furnished with wooden shutters and steep black roofs, surrounded by greenery. The streets were narrow and winding, paved with stones so worn that they shone like silver pearls, slippery under a thin layer of melting ice.

Carlo marched silently by my side, the smug smile from the café back on.

"If you ever call me *honey bunny* again, I'll turn you into a toad," I said softly.

"I don't know why you're so pissed." He shrugged. "I thought you would find it funny."

I sighed, and I could have sworn he uttered the words *bitter sourpuss* under his breath, but I made an effort to ignore them. Instead, I followed the soft lute music coming from the main square, where a bunch of wooden stalls with curtains and flags were lined up and getting ready for the

Carnival fair.

"Look, roasted potatoes," Carlo said, pointing at a food truck disguised as a medieval tent, "and crystals!" He chuckled evilly. "Maybe we should get you an engagement ring, *honey*?"

"Give me a break," I growled, then added quietly, "*frog.*"

***

Five minutes later, I was holding a paper bag full of warm and crispy potatoes sprinkled with yoghurt sauce and parsley. Carlo had found a cozy bench in the sun and was content checking his phone, so I left him alone and strolled around the stalls on my own. Most sellers were dressed in medieval attire, complete with linen gowns, flared sleeves, and woolen capes. Seeing the women's long skirts and fitted waistlines made me miss The Cloister and the careless days drilling holes and laying cables with Clarence and Jean-Pierre. I sighed. *And I thought I had problems then.* Fascinating how things could always get worse.

The crystal stall was small, but its contents twinkled like a magical rainbow in the shy morning sun. I knew at least one sparkle-loving raven who would have lost his mind in its vicinity… but what was wrong with me? *Everything* reminded me of him. *Get a grip, Alba. He's in the car; you'll see him this evening!*

"See anything you like?" the seller asked, her long earrings tinkling like tiny bells. "All these are my own creations," she added proudly, allowing her flared sleeves to sweep over colorful stones and tiny works of art in silver, detailed and luxuriant with occult-related motives. I recognized jade and amethyst from the years spent living with Grandma, but there were many other crystals I had never seen before. "Perhaps rose quartz, for love," the seller suggested in a soft French accent, offering me a tiny pink pyramid as she glanced at Carlo, who was texting merrily on his bench. She studied him with half-closed eyes, then turned back to me, clicking her tongue, and set the pink crystal back on the table, handing me a black, rounded stone instead. "No. Black tourmaline. For protection."

"Oh, you think?" I said, taking the stone she was offering. It was extremely smooth and shiny and felt warm in my hands. "How much is it?"

"How much do you think it's worth?" Her voice was warm and sultry but slightly defiant too.

I shrugged and returned the stone. I had never enjoyed bargaining. When I asked for a price, I just wanted to be told. "*Uh*, I really don't know. It's very beautiful, but I was just looking anyway, thank you."

The woman shuddered, as if feeling chilly all of a sudden, then clutched the pendant around her neck so hard that her knuckles turned white. I looked at the pendant; it seemed very familiar. It reminded me of the Egyptian symbol Jean-Pierre had sketched for me before I had left Emberbury.

"Have we met before?" the lady asked, and

a faint aura enveloped her. Perhaps not an aura: more like a shield. Not only could I see it; I could also feel it, like a magnetic field around her.

There was *something* familiar about her, and my intuition told me she could sense exactly the same about me—thus her question. "No, I don't think we have met before. It's my first time here," I answered cautiously.

"Oh, is it?" She kept ogling me with a mixture of fascination and suspicion. "Well, I'm sure you will love Alcazar. How long are you staying?"

"Just for today. Maybe a couple of days, we'll see. I'm here to visit the abbey."

"Really? What a shame," she said, her voice more and more tense. "The abbey is closed for visitors until late March."

Her words felt like a hammer blow.
No. That couldn't be true.

"Are you okay?" she asked, noticing my distress. "I sell herbal teas. This one is good for anxiety, and that one helps with insomnia."

She showed me a black iron cauldron under the table, and a row of paper bags full of herbs, but after my experience with the Italian witches, I had learned not to drink tea brewed by strangers under any circumstances.

"No, I'm okay, thanks. Just a bit disappointed because I really wanted to see the abbey… now this whole trip feels kind of pointless."

"Well…" she whispered, leaning toward me with a mysterious smile, "there's another way to get in. Follow me… I will show you."

Chapter 17

Alba

"There's a Carnival ball in the abbey tomorrow evening," the bejeweled lady explained, "and that might be your only chance to get in before they reopen in March. Not only that, but they will also open several areas which are not accessible for visitors on a regular basis. You can get tickets at the tourist office, but you better hurry. We are expecting a horde of weekenders after lunch. Do you have a costume, perhaps? It's an entry requirement."

Of course not. Who traveled around carrying Halloween costumes in their suitcase? "No, I don't. Although I could go as a haggard-looking mom?"

The lady smiled as she came out from behind her table and walked toward a small, white van parked behind her stall. "I can help with that too. Have a look at my humble selection of second-hand gowns."

I followed her to the van, ignoring my

mom's childhood teachings and mostly hoping I wasn't about to be kidnapped again. I found the seller rummaging in an old cardboard box, and after a few grunts, she produced two tacky dresses and several carnival masks covered in glitter and feathers. "I think these two should fit you."

I stared at both dresses, each gaudier than the other. They were made of ragged and shiny synthetic fabric, and neither was particularly clean or new.

"I'm not sure…" I trailed off, inspecting the dark and worn-out rim of the skirts, which must have swept the dirty floors of one too many dens of iniquity.

"You don't like them?" she asked, offended.

"Oh, no, no, I just think I'm too old for a princess costume," I clarified.

She held one of the dresses against my shoulders. "That's nonsense. You are gorgeous, and you are going to look so pretty in it! We women are the embodiment of the Goddess, never forget that. We are all beautiful. These dresses are very versatile… you can be a princess, a fairy, whatever you desire. Perhaps a witch would suit you better?" Her eyes glinted, and I wondered if something in my expression had given away my shock at the mention of the word *witch*. I studied her face, but the funny glance had vanished. *Yes, I must have imagined it.* We were discussing Carnival costumes after all; what was she supposed to say? "This one," she declared with complete confidence, thrusting a pink satin bundle into my chest. "It's like it was made for you. I'll give you a special price."

***

"What took you so long?" Carlo complained when he saw me trotting out of the tourist info office, waving at him with the tickets I had just bought. I had followed the seller's advice and gone there straight after getting the dress, in case they were really sold out by lunch. Meanwhile, Carlo was still sunbathing on the same park bench, his arms extended over the backrest with careless confidence.

"You're going to love the news. Surprise!" I said, throwing a ticket at him. "Did you bring a formal suit by any chance?"

He caught the small piece of paper in the air and read it with growing interest, his face shifting from cynical skepticism to a smug and perplexed smile. "You are taking me to a masquerade ball? Cool!"

"Before you get your hopes up, I bought *three* tickets, not two. It's the only way to get in. Otherwise, the abbey is closed until March."

"So… are you attending in that awful sweater? Because it says here *'formal attire required,'* and you have an oil stain over your left boob." He pointed at the location of the dark blotch, and I grabbed the tip of his finger, feeling tempted to twist it.

"That's none of your business, but no. I got

154

myself a—" I sighed, waiting for the inevitable mockery. "—*princess* costume, and Clarence is going as a—" I paused for a second. "—well, as a vampire, I guess. Here, I bought a bird mask for you." I let the cheap mask fall on Carlo's lap, sprinkling pink glitter all over his clothes.

"Come on, Lumin, you got me a *pink* mask?" He lifted it with his little finger, like it was disgusting. "With butterflies?" He shook his head and tossed it on the bench, as far from himself as he could. "This is for girls. I'm not wearing it. But you can give it to Schmaltzy Bloodsucker. I think it suits him better."

"Sorry, Big Boy, they didn't have any with trucks and tractors," I said, snorting. "Do you want me to return it? I can go to the ball just with Clarence. You don't have to join us. I didn't want you to feel excluded after lending us your villa and all that."

He grunted something about not giving a damn and retrieved the mask without much enthusiasm. "Whatever," he said, hanging the mask around his arm like an elbow pad as he stood up. "I'll go. Maybe I'll get to kiss a nice... *nicer* girl. Let's go now and see that old pile of rocks from the outside. Maybe you could make something explode and get us in?"

"So funny," I said, rolling my eyes as I started to follow the rustic wooden arrows marking the path.

The signs led us out of the quaint little village and onto a steep and muddy road called

Chemin du Calvaire, which was supposed to end at the old abbey. Private cars were forbidden on the path, but there were 4x4 taxis available for those whose legs wouldn't have stood the hike up. Carlo decreed we had time to spare and a healthy walk uphill would benefit both of us after so many hours sitting on planes and cars.

Initially I agreed, but after almost an hour of climbing in unsuitable footwear, my feet were freezing and achy. The occupants of a taxi waved happily at us as they overtook us and sprayed us with mud. I forced myself to smile back at them, resentment and grumpiness growing inside me like rising bread dough.

The walk was worth the effort though—it offered breathtaking views of the scenic Romanesque abbey which had been built on the edge of a mountain ridge. Stout and massive, it gave me the impression that the slightest gush of wind would send it rolling down the cliff. It seemed a miracle it had managed to withstand so many centuries of wind and snow.

"Look what I found on the internet," Carlo said, reading from his phone, "*Alcazar Abbey is a Romanesque construction built on an abrupt mountain range of the Pyrenees, right on the border between France and Spain. A former monastery, legend has it that the Knights Templar were its first owners. In present times, it has been turned into a museum, and thanks to the dramatic views, it has also become a tourist hotspot and a very popular destination for celebrities to get married.*" He grinned. "Are we celebrities yet?"

I took a couple of strides away from Carlo, tired of his ongoing joke. We must be less than half a mile away from the abbey, which was already visible beyond a peaceful meadow by the road. Under the shadow of the abbey's timeworn stone walls stood an abandoned graveyard with ancient tombstones in various states of decay scattered randomly over it. A sign informed us this was the Sinners' Cemetery of Alcazar: the place where locals buried those who weren't allowed to rest in sacred ground, such as unbaptized children, excommunicates, and of course, witches.

The abbey was closed, as we already suspected, save for the little café by the entrance and an uninspiring museum gift shop plagued with useless jumble such as key chains, toy swords and postcards. I considered buying one for Elizabeth but changed my mind at the last minute.

We strolled around the colossal walls, admiring the square and sturdy bell tower. A heavy iron gate prevented passersby from going further, but we got a glimpse of a large courtyard, where some workers were setting up a stage and several spotlights and loudspeakers for the coming party.

"I doubt there's much more we can do here today, apart from freezing to death," I said to Carlo, rubbing my numb ankles. "We should find a place to stay, unless we intend to sleep in the car."

Carlo approved, and we started the hike back to the village. On the way there, a piercing pain in my chest paralyzed me, forcing me to stop and hold onto a tree trunk for a second.

"Everything okay?" Carlo asked, a tinge of apprehension in his voice.

I stretched my neck left and right, trying to shrug off the sudden chill that had raced down my spine like a stream of icy water. It went away, but I still felt cold and uneasy afterwards. "Yeah, I'm fine. I don't know what got me. I think I'm just tired. So many things have been going on lately."

"*Hmm*, I can imagine," Carlo said, shrugging. "Can't wait to put my feet up for an hour or two."

We found two decently-priced rooms in a small B&B near the medieval market at the central square of Alcazar. After that, we grabbed a quick lunch at one of the stalls and took a couple of hours to relax in our respective rooms. Once it was dark outside, we strolled back to the small picnic area where our car—and Clarence—must be waiting, in order to retrieve our bags and say hi to my favorite vampire.

As we got closer to the edge of the village, following the yellow glow of the forged iron streetlamps, I was crippled by the same sinking, cold feeling I had felt earlier, only this time, it was radiating off the left side of my chest. I had to stop and take a few deep breaths, clutching my chest. Meanwhile, Carlo plodded lazily a few steps ahead, and I wasn't even surprised when I heard his angry shouts coming from under the fir trees.

The car was still there, but the trunk lid hung broken and wide open, its contents clearly visible from where I stood.

There was a blanket, a few bags, and nothing else.

Nothing.

Nobody.

There were footprints all over the clearing, plainly visible all over the trampled frosty grass and mud. My stomach turned as I followed them frantically, clutching my purse against my chest in the cold evening.

I called Clarence, my voice broken with worry, but the only thing I could hear were my own panicked steps crushing the mulch. I found the blanket I had covered him with, torn and laying near the car in a soiled bundle.

Carlo leaned against the car and lit a cigarette, watching me in silence with a mixture of worry and scorn.

"He's gone," I said, choking on my words.

"And?" He closed his eyes, inhaling the smoke with visible pleasure. "He might be a bit clingy, but he has legs, you know? I think you are overreacting… big time."

"Something must have gone wrong. He wouldn't have left without telling me."

Carlo puffed, leaving behind a gray cloud and stroking the bent lid of the trunk. "Whatever. You know what he is. You know what they do at night. Stop running around like the world is ending, will you?"

"Someone was here, Carlo, can't you see the footprints? What if Natasha followed us? What if something horrible happened to him? I have a feeling something is very wrong."

Carlo snorted. He obviously couldn't care less if something had happened to Clarence. "The only thing that worries me right now is that he broke the lock of the trunk to get out, and now I have to add one more repair to my long list of expenses. We must find a mechanic, by the way."

"You don't understand," I grunted with frustration, but all I got back was a fed-up glance. "He wasn't feeling well." Carlo kept staring, unfazed. "Fine. Stay there. I will search the woods on my own until I find out what happened to him. You can smoke until your lungs turn black, as far as I'm concerned."

I combed the woods the best I could in the darkness, helping myself with the flashlight on my phone. All the footprints ended abruptly at the edge of the asphalted road, leading nowhere. Finally, I gave up and dragged myself back to the car, where Carlo was still waiting, his features softer now.

"Lumin," he said quietly, offering me a hand. "Stop it. It's dark. And cold. And you are wearing some stupid office shoes which are going to give you hypothermia. If we don't leave soon, you are going to get sick. Let's go to the hotel, and we can come back tomorrow morning, okay?"

I growled and slapped his hand away, walking in large, stubborn strides. Yes, I should have bought a pair of winter boots in Emberbury. No, I didn't care that my feet had turned into icicles, because I had more important concerns.

Like, for example, what might have happened to my vampire lover… boyfriend… whatever. It was not like him to leave like that. I knew it. And the cold inside my chest confirmed it.

Once we reached the hotel, Carlo invited me to watch a movie in his room, but I declined with a stifled sob and locked myself in my room to worry about Clarence for the rest of the night. I could not sleep, so I flipped through pictures of my daughters on my phone and wrote a brief message to Minnie.

"We have a surprise for you!" flew in her answer as I was dozing off, scrolling the news. "You'll find out very soon!"

Chapter 18

Clarence

The taste of blood woke me up. It was dense and bitter; richer than usual. Two female voices whispered anxiously in the background, but only one was familiar. *Too familiar.* It belonged to someone I had given up for dead. Darkness had fallen, and I was still in the boot of that car; the blinding rays of the moon bathing the clearing with their silver glimmer.

"He is awake," the voice said, addressing me sweetly. The stranger, who perhaps wasn't so, brought a bleeding wrist closer to my lips. "Drink."

I took her hand with trembling hands and licked the thick, dark liquid, feeling its strength running through my veins and rekindling my dormant limbs.

"Can you move?" she asked, helping me stand up.

I stirred, and a shiver shook me violently. "I am so cold," I mumbled. "I don't feel well. But yes. I can move if I must."

"No wonder he's cold," said the other woman. Her voice was eerie as she chanted the words of a spell, and she smelled like a witch. "It's in the curse. *Gelid like silver, silver death; I curse thee now...*"

"Stop. Those are dangerous words."

The other one giggled. "I only know the beginning. You are completely safe."

A sigh came from the other side.

"He already has *the glow...*" the younger one continued, "you know what that means."

The glow. Yes, I knew about it too. *The final stages of the curse.* A faint glow first, slowly vanishing into nothing after that.

"You need to come with us, Clarence."

"I am not going anywhere. I must wait for Alba," I protested, trying to straighten my back to look at both women face to face.

"No. You must come now. You have no choice: either you come with us, or she will just find a heap of old dust by the time she's back. You can leave a message for her. She will be fine on her own, but you won't."

I knew they were right. I could feel it. I did not understand why it had happened so fast, but there was truth in their words. "How did you find me?"

The petite one licked the wound on her wrist and watched it close magically, without leaving any traces. She sat by my side in the trunk, rubbing the butterfly ring Alba had brought me all the way from Emberbury. "What do you think?"

"I see," I leaned back, too weary to sit straight. "It took half a century, but now we know those witches are no con artists."

"Yes. Scrying helped too. But the ring made it easier." She nodded. "I know you are concerned about Alba, but now you need us more than she needs you." She kissed my cheek, her caress bearing more memories than one could care to count. The other woman squinted at us, a nervous look overshadowing her features.

"So, are you alive?" I blinked, framing her face with my hands, her silky locks tickling my knuckles. "Or… am I dead?"

She laughed. "Such a tough question. We can discuss it on the way there."

"There, where?"

"Somewhere safer and more discreet."

She waited as the taller woman scribbled a brief note and placed it sloppily under the windscreen wipers, drying her damp hands on her trousers. The piece of paper flapped furiously, fighting the evening breeze.

"I had missed you," she said, hugging me, and I returned the hug, swaying under the weight of so many fond memories, come and gone but never lost. "But now is not the time for that," she added, pulling away. "Come. We must try a spell… before it's too late."

Chapter 19

Alba

Carlo was nice enough to come with me and help me comb the area where Clarence had disappeared. We spent the whole morning there, until we were both frozen, cranky and muddy beyond recognition.

After so many hours of searching, his patience ran out, and he declared he wasn't spending a minute longer searching for someone he didn't even want to find in the first place.

"The vampire can remain lost forever. I don't care," he grunted, lighting what must have been the fifteenth cigarette of the day. "Just tell me whether we're still going to that ball or not."

I sighed. "I don't know? I guess?"

Hopefully, Clarence would be back sooner or later, and it only made sense to try to get hold of the counterspell while I had a chance. The curse wasn't going to disappear on its own, and the abbey would be closed for weeks after the ball.

"Okay then," Carlo said, emptying his pockets of old receipts and letting them fall carelessly on the ground, together with a cigarette stub. "Time to go back to the hotel and get ready for the party."

A reddish glow caught my attention. Carlo's cigarette had set a bunch of dry leaves on fire, causing the flames to spread. I stomped on them repeatedly, cursing as the heat scorched the tips of my shoes.

"Look what you almost did! You could have caused a fire!"

Carlo rolled his eyes and crouched to pick up the cigarette. "Come on. You are exaggerating so much. It was just a tiny spark."

"I can't believe you're saying this, particularly after we almost burned alive in Italy last Christmas. So irresponsible of you."

"Yeah, whatever. I'll pick up my stuff. No big deal." Carlo groaned. He started to collect his litter, then paused, lifting a half-burnt piece of paper off the ground. "What's this?" he said, handing it to me. "This one is not mine."

I studied the remains of what looked like a handwritten note, trying to find a proper place to dispose of it. "No idea. People are disgusting. There's a trashcan six feet away from this spot, why can't they just use it? It's disgraceful."

"Okay, spare me the lecture, please," Carlo said, raising his hands. "That's not what I meant. The name of your bloodsucker boyfriend is written on it, if you haven't noticed."

"What?" I yelled, looking at the note with new eyes. Most of it had burned to ashes, and the only remaining words I could still read were *"Clarence is with us."*

"With us… with *whom*?" I yelled in frustration, flipping the charred piece of paper back and forth. It was one of those extremely thin and useless napkins one got in most cafés around Alcazar, and I couldn't recognize the rushed, spidery handwriting.

"You should thank me for smoking. If it wasn't for me and my nasty habits, you would have never found that note. So I think I deserve an apology and maybe a hug too," Carlo said.

"Damn. I have no idea what we should do now," I said with a grunt of desperation, fighting the urge to punch him. So many unanswered questions drifted recklessly through my mind. And the last thing I wished to do was to attend a stupid carnival ball while Clarence might be in danger.

"The only thing we know for sure is that he's not here, and there's no point in searching for him, because he's with… *someone else*," Carlo declared, and I grumbled in reluctant agreement. "*Someone else* who bothered to leave a note and knew him by name. So I suggest we stick to the original plan. He might come back. Or not. Hard to tell right now. If nothing else, we get to attend a party. Maybe get laid, with some luck."

"Okay," I said, ignoring his last statement, "You have a point. Let's go."

∗∗∗

Carlo took the wrecked rental car to a local mechanic while I showered and got ready for the party. It took me a while to figure out how to tie the atrocious princess dress I had bought at the market without revealing half of my sad-looking and extremely unflattering underwear. The pink satin skirt was wrinkled, and I did my best to steam iron it, hanging it in the bathroom as I took a long, toe-thawing shower. When I came out of my room, wearing the dress under my coat and a loose side braid, Carlo started to snigger so hard that I thought he would die on the spot from asphyxiation.

This time—lesson learned—we booked a 4x4 taxi to drive us to the abbey. The day spent combing the forest in the cold had left me exhausted once again, and I would have paid cash in exchange for a good nap; but sleeping wasn't in the cards for me, as usual, so I took out my phone and dialed Minnie's number during the car ride.

"Minnie, can you get me Iris or Katie on the phone?" I asked, watching the trees pass by in the darkness behind Carlo's tall profile.

"Sure," she answered, "wait a second."

"Mommy!" I heard Katie squealing from the other side. "Where are you?"

"Oh, I'm..." I hesitated. "I was about to go to a little party."

"A birthday party?" There was clear excitement in her voice. She was probably picturing

168

cakes and presents, and not a cold stone building full of strangers holding champagne flutes.

"Well, no… more like a costume party."

More squealing ensued. "You have a costume? Minnie got us costumes, too!"

Minnie was always so cool. Sigh.

"Actually yes, I do. I'm going as a…" I hesitated, smoothing the sloppily embroidered bodice, which in turn caused a few plastic gemstones to detach and disappear among the folds of my skirts. "A princess. It's a pink princess dress." There was a silence on the other side, so long that I thought I might have lost the connection. "Katie? Are you still there?"

"Yes, mommy." She sounded… worried? Upset?

"What's wrong?"

"I don't think old witches like you should wear pink princess dresses," she whispered with concern.

"Katie! Minnie could hear you!"

Old *witches? What the…*

"Sorry, mommy. But it's true."

"I think witches can wear whatever dresses they want," I whispered, trying to conceal my dismay.

She wavered for a second. "Well, not in the books Minnie reads us at night… they always wear black. And they are *evil.*"

"Give me Minnie back," I growled. "I have a thing or two to discuss with her."

I needed all my self-control to refrain from

scolding Minnie. She wouldn't have understood the problem anyway. I ended the conversation in a bad mood and turned to Carlo, who had been watching me with an amused expression on his face.

"So, *Rapunzel*," he said, "I have been googling the program. It seems the dance will take place in the monastery's cloister, but most rooms are open to visitors, including the library. Everything except for some service areas and the crypt. Where do you think that book of yours might be?"

"I'd like to think it's in the library, but with my luck, it's probably in the crypt," I grunted.

"I was thinking the same," he agreed as the taxi stopped at the end of a long queue of identical cabs.

"We can check the library first, and if there's nothing there, we'll have to find a way to get into the crypt," I whispered so the driver wouldn't hear me. "Do you think one of us could sneak into the gatehouse and borrow a set of keys somehow?"

Carlo smiled smugly. "If the concierge is a *she*, I see no problem at all," he said after a brief consideration.

I rolled my eyes, but I admitted to myself he was probably right. Carlo was tall and good-looking; it was just a shame he had been born with fully-working vocal cords.

"Okay," I said, opening the door and hopping out of the car. "You see to the keys and the crypt, and I will check out the rest of the rooms. The first one who finds something sends a message to the other. Deal?" Carlo gave me a mock military salute in agreement. "Good. Try to be discreet and keep your phone close."

***

An army of florists must have been at work since dawn, spreading fresh ivy leaves and white rose petals all over the cobblestone path which led to the abbey. A pageboy took our tickets and reminded us this was a masquerade party and masks were compulsory until midnight. Carlo protested; but the pageboy would not yield, and he had to oblige and put on his butterfly-bird mask. It covered his nose and forehead, and it was actually quite flattering, at least in my opinion. Once we were properly attired, the pageboy bowed and allowed us to cross the red rope barrier in front of the ancient building.

A path of candles and evergreen pine branches led us to the old monastery cloister, where we were greeted by an ample square outdoor space surrounded by arcades. Long, lavish tables awaited us under the arcades, all dressed in white bows and roses and covered in platters with tiny pieces of bread and delicious-looking toppings. At the furthest end of the courtyard, an orchestra played a lively version of Liszt's Hungarian Rhapsody as guests sauntered in and talked casually to each other, all dressed in costumes which looked definitely better than ours. Despite the strategically spread outdoor patio heaters, I wasn't thrilled to give my coat away to the cloakroom attendant, but I did it anyway to look less out of place among the rest of the bare-shouldered guests. The amount of skin on display despite the frosty night made me wonder whether the whole event was just an excuse for a covert vampire dance.

Carlo made a ladylike curtsy and took my hand. "Dance with me?" he asked, wiggling an eyebrow. "Before we get down to business?"

I hesitated. The setting was lovely and the music enthralling. Everyone seemed to be enjoying themselves, and it would have been so easy to let go, have a drink or two and forget about everything that needed to be done.

"We will raise fewer suspicions if we behave like we came here to have fun, just like everyone else," Carlo encouraged me.

"Okay," I conceded, taking his hand with two fingers. "But just one dance. We have lots of things to do."

Carlo's expert hands made my long skirt spin among the ancient arcades, and one dance led to the next, and the next. Even though I didn't want to admit it, I was enjoying myself, so I purposely forgot about my one-dance-only request.

Lost in the music, at first I didn't notice Carlo was getting bolder with each subsequent piece the orchestra played. But as his hands started to move down my back and his confidence built up, I decided it was time to get to work before I had to slap him. As soon as the waltz ended, I detached from him and headed for the tables under the gallery, which were covered in trays and champagne glasses.

"Thirsty," I said, waving at him without looking back. "And busy. I'm going to find the library. I'll text you when I'm done."

When I turned around once again, Carlo was gone, hopefully in pursuit of a gullible female janitor to steal a set of keys from.

I grabbed a glass of champagne and leaned in to look at a wall bedecked with an enormous glass blueprint of the abbey. Starting at the "*you are here*" dot, I traced with my fingertips a few possible routes to search the whole complex as quickly as possible.

I was trying to decide whether to head upstairs first or scour the ground floor instead, when the clamor of applause took me out of my elucubrations, forcing me to check whatever was happening on the dance floor.

Two masked women were twirling in the middle of the cloister with such expertise that the whole party had grown quiet in order to stare at them in awe. The tallest one was wearing a gothic sheet dress with an open back made out of dozens of straps, which mimicked a spiderweb and exposed her heavily tattooed skin. The other one was smaller and clad in a sumptuous black velvet gown, sunflower golden ringlets flowing behind her. The tallest dancer hurled the smaller one in the air and caught her like a dove in her arms, right as the song ended. Both moved with the dexterity of professional dancing contestants.

For a second, silence fell over the abbey's patio; even the orchestra had stopped playing to admire the best dancers in the party. A shy bystander started to clap her hands, and soon, everyone joined her in impressed cheers and hoots. The two expert dancers bowed at their unexpected audience, seeming surprised and pleased at the same time. They held their skirts with gracility, looked at each other, and finally joined in a passionate kiss.

Only then I noticed the thick tuft of white and green hair sprouting over the taller woman's black and gold mask, and I knew exactly where I had seen green hair like that before; this was the last place I had expected to encounter it again.

I elbowed my way through the crowd that had resumed their previous activities and weren't interested in the dancers anymore. Swallowing my shyness, I approached the two women, who weren't kissing anymore and had started to swing softly to the new piece chosen by the orchestra.

Taking a deep breath, I tapped on the shoulder of the green-haired girl, and she turned to look at me, a soft smile emerging as she lifted the mask off her eyes and allowed me to see her whole face.

"Alba," she said, releasing her partner in order to hug me, "finally."

"Alice?" I muttered, my brain cells doing somersaults as I tried to comprehend how on earth I could have accidentally run into one of the few witches who didn't hate me and in a secluded abbey atop the Pyrenees of all places. Then I turned to the petite blonde next to her, my lungs emptying of air as I recognized her delicate features under the mask.

"Francesca," I gasped, throwing myself into her arms. "I thought I would never see you again."

Chapter 20

Alba

I sniffed Francesca's hair, relishing her familiar scent of rusty blood and roses. Her body tensed when I tried to hug her, deceivingly small and birdlike in my arms. She was wearing a spiked bracelet that contrasted with her otherwise elegant attire—a gift from Alice, perhaps—and the spikes dug into my back, but I was too glad to see her to care. "Oh, Francesca…" I said, my voice trailing off and dissolving into a teary gurgle.

"It's all right," she said, grabbing my wrists and pushing me away, then studying me from head to toe, "I am fine. And I'm happy to see you too."

"How did you find me?" I stammered. "This makes no sense."

Francesca was safe. Elizabeth wasn't going to kill me. My head was spinning with relief, and I thanked the Universe for this welcome and unexpected lucky streak.

"It's a long story," Alice said, looking around nervously. "I used a pendulum to pinpoint your exact location. It wasn't that hard, thanks to that magical trinket you had..."

I shook my head, too overwhelmed to think. "But… that house in Venice… it collapsed on you… we feared you might have died in the canals… disappeared forever under the sun…" I sobbed, and Francesca caressed my hair softly, wiping off my tears with tenderness.

"It's fine. Vampires can't drown, and Alice saved me from sunrise. If it wasn't for her, I wouldn't be here now," Francesca whispered softly.

"But… how…?" Words didn't come easy. I kept touching her arms and shoulders, reluctant to believe she was real, in front of me, and not just a product of my imagination.

"Alice found me the night of the explosion, unconscious and floating in the canals. She took me to shelter and nursed me back to health," Francesca explained, threading her delicate fingers through the many straps on the back of the other woman's dress. "*Magicked* me back to health, to be precise." She winked at the stout witch beside her, and a look of fondness and complicity traveled from one woman to the other, hinting at the deep bond created between them by the time spent together in Venice.

Both women looked at each other with such longing that I considered lending them the keys of my hotel room. "I still can't believe you are here. This is all so… unexpected."

"I feel responsible for what happened in Venice," Alice said, frowning her lips. "It was my coven that caused this, so it's also my fault in a way."

"It was not your fault," Francesca assured her, standing on her toes to kiss Alice's cheek. "We are not our past."

Alice leaned against the deceivingly small vampire. "Ah, Frannie… we better discuss all this somewhere else. There are prying ears everywhere."

"Yes, I agree," Francesca said, assessing my choice of attire. The expression on her face revealed clear dissatisfaction. "So, what exactly are you dressed up as?"

"*Uh*… princess?" I ventured with a nervous grin, opening my arms so she could admire the kitschy gown in all its synthetic glory. Noticing her displeasure, I squinted with malevolence—or at least, I tried—and offered an alternative. "Witch?"

"It's hideous," she declared, shaking her locks. "I have never seen anything this bad."

"Why, thank you," I said. "Still, I didn't come here to boast about my luxurious wardrobe. I have more important things to do… *to find,* actually."

"The grimoire, I suppose," Alice murmured. "We know about it, and we have a plan."

"But perhaps…" Francesca said, coiling a slight arm around Alice's firm waist, "you might want to have a look at something else first. Something even *more important.*"

"Really? I doubt there's such a thing, but…"

I couldn't think of one single thing I desired more than finding the spell to break Clarence's curse.

Except, perhaps…

Francesca tilted her head sideways, toward the furthest end of the patio, where a dashing man in a black mask and a light silver tuxedo was leaning against a pillar, his legs crossed casually and a pale hand half-hidden in a pocket.

"He was *dying* to see you," Alice drawled with a wink, and I let out a girlish cry of happiness as I ran across the dancefloor and into the arms of the only man I wanted to dance with at that or any party, wrapping my arms around him with a squeal.

Clarence returned the embrace with his eyes closed and a relieved smile, letting out an oddly human sigh. We melted into a hungry, desperate kiss, full of questions, desire and relief.

"Where were you? What happened?" I mumbled into his soothingly familiar chest, catching my breath.

"*Shh*... not here. Later." He dragged me gently toward the center of the dimly lit courtyard and bowed formally. "May I have this dance?" he asked, leaving a butterfly kiss on the back of my hand. "Unless your dance card is full already…"

I watched him through half-closed eyes.

"Not sure. I'll see if I can make room for a truant vampire."

I let myself go in his steady arms, shaking off the stress of the last twenty-four hours. Dancing with him was like traveling back to bygone, olden times of grand balls and banquets. Times he had lived in, when I didn't even exist. As we cruised around the dance floor, drawing perfect figure eights on the centuries-old stone slabs, I imagined us standing on a boat, sailing from island to island at the sound of a whimsical waltz. Alcazar Abbey had become our very own Titanic, as we swayed with abandonment, surrounded by shallow luxury and oblivious to the many unresolved problems looming over us, about to sink us… just not yet.

I shut my eyes.

Problems could wait.

Just one more dance.

When I opened them again, Clarence was staring fondly into mine, a faint reddish glow shining behind his black mask.

"I hope you found the note Alice left for you," he said, kissing my hair in passing as he made me twirl once again.

"Carlo burned it," I answered. His eyes flared with hardly-contained anger, so I added hastily. "By accident." I was starting to feel dizzy, what with the plentiful whirling, the champagne, and all those missing people showing up all of a sudden.

Clarence rolled his eyes, and I was almost sure he swore under his breath, the name of a certain corrupt policeman standing out among the rest of garbled words. "I must confess, I watched you dance with him for a while, and his behavior was starting to… irritate me."

We passed close to Alice and Francesca, who were so enraptured with each other that neither of them bothered to glance at us. They made a sweet, though contrasting, couple.

"Really? Well next time, instead of vanishing without a trace, then stalking me from a dark corner, why not come and scare the competition off with those claws of yours?"

Clarence stared down at his nails, now blunt and neat while he held my hand in a waltzing pose. His jaw tensed, making me regret my silly remark. I was aware that Carlo and his claws were already well-acquainted, and neither of them was very proud of that moment.

"Who am I to tell you what you can and can't do?" he said sullenly. "He kissed you once in front of my very eyes, and it's evident he wouldn't mind doing it again."

"You know I'm not interested," I assured him, adjusting my steps to the brisk rhythm of the music. "I only care about you. I barely slept worrying about you."

"I am so sorry," he said. "An urgent matter came up, but hopefully the problem is dealt with… for a while, if nothing else."

I tripped over his feet, but he lifted me off the floor and kept moving, his back straight and slightly bent backwards with impeccable dancing etiquette. I wondered about the many dancing cards his name must have been penciled on during his unusually long existence, and my lungs constricted for a second. How many gorgeous ladies had he stolen a kiss from? How many had ended up in his bed after two centuries of extravagant parties?

But no. I wasn't going there. *Not tonight.*

"What kind of urgent matter?" I asked as the music trailed off, and I caught my breath, waiting for the next one to start. He glanced away, and I frowned. "Seems like nobody wants to tell me anything today."

He smirked mischievously and stroked the small of my back, staring at the ridiculous plastic gems on my frock. "I shall explain everything at the right time, but only if you first confess the name of the poor child you stole that costume from."

I winced. "Not funny, Clarence. Excuse me if I didn't bring a ballgown to our impromptu mountain trip. Also, I was wondering the same about yours. A silver tux? Really? So *not* your style."

"It was *not* easy to find a last-minute donator as tall and alluring as yours truly, as you can imagine." He smirked. "However, it's significantly better than yours… but worry not, Isolde. You would look stunning even in a darned burlap sack. Not that this is far from it…" His fangs flashed for an instant, and he whispered into my ear, "And even better without it. But it's safer for you this way."

I sought Alice and Francesca across the room to hide my blushing. "We need to talk."

"Yes. But outside. There are… *others*," he said, silently mouthing the word "*witches*".

"Oh, I see." I nodded, reluctantly disentangling myself from his embrace as I studied the rest of the attendants with new eyes. "Okay.

You know I'd love to spend the rest of the night dancing with you, but we are here to fulfill a mission."

"I know," he said, his voice suddenly raspy. "Just one more dance, and I'll set you free," he pleaded, nuzzling my cheek and tugging gently at my arm as the first notes filled the air once again. "This is the *Vienna Blood* waltz. One of my favorites."

"It had to be," I concurred, stepping on my own toes as I struggled to follow his proficient rise and fall.

"Once, many moons ago, I danced to it in Vienna," he explained, a dreamy haze marring his maroon irises. "It would have been the perfect place to take you to see your first opera, as I promised I would..." he slowed down the pace, a sudden gloom darkening his well-chiseled features under the mask. "But I might be compelled to break my promise, after all..."

"What do you mean?"

My question lingered in the air for a couple of seconds, until he shook his head, as if to dispel a bad omen, and swiveled to face the orchestra.

"Never mind," he whispered, holding me tighter. "Let's dance now. While we still can."

Chapter 21

Clarence

Vienna, Austria, Carnival 1957

Francesca giggled as we ran past the large lobby mirror of the lusciously Baroque opera house, unnoticed by the rest of guests at the most exclusive *Faschingsball* in the city. Luckily for us, they were all too busy complimenting each other on their attire and doing the typical small talk common among wealthy socialites, preventing them from noticing us: the beautiful, young and flawless couple who blended impeccably with their surroundings—except for the fact that they had no reflections.

"Francesca! I thought you had checked for mirrors this morning, when you flew by," I scolded her as we reached the ballroom, which was as ornate as the rest of the rooms but blissfully mirrorless.

"I was wrong," she admitted with a grin, planting a brief kiss on my neck, "which is delightfully unusual."

I returned her kiss with nervousness, still concerned we might have been noticed by someone. Nobody was looking at us, and I took a deep breath before answering. "Do *not* do this to me ever again. What we just did was reckless."

"So… what if I do it again?" she asked, a daring glint in her azure eyes. "What will you do?"

Holding her gaze, I ran the tips of my fingers over her spine, starting at the base of her neck and feeling each backbone under her spotless white dress until she shuddered, just as I wanted, when I reached the small of her back. "You know *what*," I said quietly, and she regaled me with a pretend scandalized glance.

We retreated to a corner, admiring the majestic crystal chandeliers and gilded decorations. The loges over us were starting to fill with high society guests, and I studied their occupants, trying to catch a glimpse of the very familiar profile of the man we were hunting that evening.

"Perhaps we should part ways here," I suggested. "You search the left wing, and I will have a look at the right one." When she didn't answer, I turned around and looked at her. Her knuckles had turned white and were crumpling her skirt, and a red rim had taken over the perfect whites of her eyes. "Francesca." I pressed her tiny figure against my chest, taken aback by her sudden—and rare—change of humor. "What's the matter?"

She shook her head and composed herself

but remained cradled in my arms for a minute longer than she would have in normal circumstances. "I thought I had seen Ludovic," she whispered, rearranging her dress around her shoulders. She might have sobbed, but if she did, she hid it well and fast. "But it wasn't him. Just the same hair… the same height…"

I nodded, knowing how family, and moreover Ludovic, were Francesca's only weakness. She was far from weak. But her heart broke a little each time she remembered her missing brother and daughter. Both lost. Both out of reach. A pain she concealed flawlessly from the world, save for the few select ones she opened up to on occasion. Like me, now and then.

"He would not come here," I said, stroking her cheek. "Particularly not today, when Vlad might be nearby. Too dangerous."

"Vlad doesn't want Ludovic," she pointed out, straightening herself. No traces of her passing episode of grief were left by then. "He wants *you.*"

"And thus, here I am tonight," I said.

Francesca tucked a stray lock of hair behind her ear, and the ring on her middle finger shone under the bright chandeliers, making me smile. "I'm glad you decided to wear my present, despite your initial qualms."

"Solely because it matches my tiara," she replied with a squint. "I don't need your protection, Clarence, nor anyone else's."

"I almost had to sell my soul to a witch so she would charm that ring for me," I said, and she laughed.

"I still don't know how you got a witch to charm *anything* for you."

"I can be charming as well, if needed," I simpered. "But perhaps my pilfering talents helped a little too… you know I'm an honest man, but I'd do anything for the sake of a lovely Italian lady of my acquaintance."

She snuggled against my chest once again. Even though she denied it, there was contained fear in her demeanor. "Honest…? I'm not sure… you were always so adept at petty theft…"

"Anything for you, my dear Francesca."

The débutants made their appearance in the ballroom, ready for the opening dance, and Francesca brought a finger to her lips as she studied the pristine-looking couples, paying special attention to the lovely young ladies draped in floor-length dove-white gowns.

"Which one do you think he will settle on this year?" she asked in a thin whisper.

Scanning the dancers, my eyes fell on a pale, blue-eyed angel who reminded me of someone I had known a long time ago. "Who is that?" I asked, certain Francesca must have memorized the list of guests before our arrival.

"Klara Steiner. A jeweller's daughter."

I nodded, considering the rest of the candidates. Many were blonde with blue eyes, but Klara, unlike the others, had a certain frailness and inhibition to her. That was the trait Vlad relished the most: I knew him well enough to know his predilection for fragile creatures, and I had known him for longer than anyone still living. Vlad would always abduct the one who carried a stronger resemblance to his long-lost *love*. Not that he ever understood the meaning of that word, but he seemed to be fond of his lovely, sweet pets, and kept them alive while they were docile and scared, just the way he fancied them the most. Once they turned sour and broken, it was time for a new toy, and what better place to enjoy window-shopping than a flashy Vienna ball?

"Let us split up," I suggested, and Francesca nodded in agreement. "I'll keep an eye on Klara, and you watch the others… and my back. As soon as she leaves the ballroom, one of us must follow. We should never leave her unattended."

"That we should not," she agreed, straightening my tie.

"It will probably be easier if I do it. Less conspicuous. With some luck, we'll get hold of him tonight… it's about time we did."

"Are you going to kiss her?" Francesca asked in a mocking tone, though there might have been a darker tinge to her voice under the surface.

"Only if necessary," I teased her. She shrugged. *Good. She did not mind.* Better this way, because there was always a chance.

"If you need assistance, call me," she said, eyeing the frail blonde dancer with thirst and… wariness?

"Please be careful," I said, kissing Francesca's rose-scented hair one more time before leaving her side, "and I beg you, don't take off the ring. The witch said it would help me find you if you ever got lost. I would do anything to keep you safe. You know that."

"I can keep myself safe, thank you, and I don't believe in amulets."

"Neither do I," I said, struggling not to kiss her once again. "But sometimes things do work, whether we believe in them or not."

Chapter 22

Alba

The music died down, and the orchestra left the stage for a break, turning on soft, recorded ambient music to entertain the attendees in their absence. Dancers flocked to the food tables, while Clarence and I headed to a secluded corner where Alice and Francesca were drinking champagne and whispering into each other's ears.

"Who was that fine-looking gentleman dancing with you earlier?" Francesca asked, grinning sympathetically in Clarence's direction over the rim of her empty glass. "You seemed… quite close."

"Oh, that was just Carlo. Didn't you meet in Italy?" I said with a dismissive wave, ignoring Clarence's soft growl behind me. "Which reminds me… I should check what he's been up to."

I opened my purse, just to learn the signal at the abbey was virtually nonexistent, at least in the courtyard. Maybe Carlo had sent a text, but I had no way to check. There was a message from

Minnie, received an hour earlier or so. It showed a photo of Iris and Katie wearing fairytale gowns, not unlike mine—just more age-appropriate—and below a brief caption:

> *"Surprise, Mommy! Daddy and Auntie Minnie are taking us somewhere special for Mid-Winter Break. Can you guess where? We are on our way to the airport!"*

Mid-Winter Break? When was that? And why hadn't they mentioned a vacation during our phone call? Was that the *surprise* Minnie had mentioned as I was falling asleep last night? A plane ride seemed pretty much mention-worthy, and not something to *surprise me* with. Also, *Auntie* Minnie? What the…? Okay, at least she wasn't *Stepmommy* Minnie, so that was a good thing… wasn't it?

"So, what's going on with Carlo?" Alice asked, glancing at me with impatience and interrupting my endless worry loop. Minnie's unexpected text had thrown me off completely.

"He's trying to get into the crypt," I explained, shaking off the many questions I had for Minnie, which, sadly, would have to wait until I got the signal back. "We think the grimoire might be there. I should go downstairs and try to find him, by the way. My phone is not working well here, and he might have called me."

Alice started to laugh hysterically, tears and

all. "There's no way he'll break into the crypt on his own," she snorted, wiping her eyes. "It's guarded by magic, night and day. Nobody but the Daughters of Isis can enter."

"What do you know about the Daughters of Isis?" I asked as I turned my phone in all possible directions, in the hopes of catching the faintest signal.

"Oh, they're just some old, eclectic Isis-worshipping coven who appropriated the Alcazar Grimoire after the French Revolution," Alice explained, rolling her eyes. "It's the most sought-after witchcraft treaty of the Renaissance, and they are so full of themselves for keeping it safe. *Keeping it safe,* yes… but only after *stealing it*, I may add. Always boasting about their importance in the *Warty Toad Newsletter.* Just because some drunk monk happened to drop a copy on the lap of a slutty sister two-hundred years ago, they have been bragging about their superiority for the last couple of centuries." She huffed. "It's not like they wrote the spells themselves, those bit…"

"Alice!" Francesca chided her with her steeliest governess glance.

"Yes, okay. Whatever," Alice mumbled, frowning. "We aren't on the best terms, to be honest. How could we be, when they have always been such competitive, thieving b…" She squinted at Francesca, huffed, and closed her mouth again. "Anyway. Our High Priestess, Valentina, and theirs pretty much hate each other and have some passive aggressive shit going on non-stop. But the only way to get into that crypt is to get an invitation from The Daughters of Isis, and only witches can get one. Carlo has no chance in hell of getting in there on his own. Like… ever."

"But what about me?" I said. "They don't know me. I'm a witch, and I don't belong to your coven, so they might be willing to talk to me."

"You?" Alice cackled again. "I seriously doubt it. A real witch would have to vouch for you first."

"What do you mean, a *real witch*?" I blinked, offended. "Everyone has been going on about me being a witch for months, and now suddenly I'm not *witch enough*?"

"Oh, well, yes, I suppose you are…" Alice explained. "But I meant a *recognized* witch. The Daughters of Isis have the oldest roots, and they also happen to be the most secretive of all. They are a powerful, secretive coven, which guards one of the most dangerous magical treatises on Earth. You, on the other hand…"

I, on the other hand, was just a chaotic stray who sneezed and caused a traffic accident but couldn't cast a simple spell even if my life depended on it.

"Okay," I said, raising my hands in surrender, "cut it short. I suck. I get it."

Alice lifted her hands in apology. "No, no, don't get me wrong… I just mean you can't come uninvited. But I might be able to help."

In the meantime, Clarence had walked away and was analyzing the label of a tall bottle of Chardonnay with the devotion of an experienced sommelier. For someone who refused to try a single drop of wine, he seemed very much immersed in his reading. A string of golden lampions was shining above him, and it was almost as if the glow was coming from him, instead of the candles inside the lanterns.

"Clarence," I said, shaking his arm with excitement. "Why are you here alone? Would you come discuss the plan with us? If we manage to get into the crypt tonight, you could be rid of the curse very soon!"

He stared at me, something akin to sadness in his eyes. "Ah, isn't that brilliant?" he said without much enthusiasm.

I blinked, unable to understand his sudden change of heart. "What's wrong? Aren't you excited things are working out?"

"Oh, yes, of course I am…" he trailed off. "But maybe we should leave. Why take such risks, my dear…? I wouldn't want you to endanger yourself just for my sake."

I exhaled with frustration. "You are behaving very weirdly, Clarence. Why would you say something like that, when we have made it this far?" He gazed down, concentrating once again on the wine label. "Also, is it me, or do you have like a… halo?" I added, waving my hand through the faint aura around him.

"A halo?" He let out a joyless chuckle. "Of course not. I'm not a shooting star. Or a saint."

"That you are not," I agreed with a naughty wink, but he didn't even smile back.

Upset by his taciturn mood, I turned around to leave, and the change of position brought my phone back to life. The device started to beep with a dozen messages from Carlo. I called him back, wondering what kind of trouble he had run into.

"Lumin," he gurgled on the other side, sounding like his head was underwater. "I have a bit of a situation here downstairs."

"I'll be right there," I said, ending the call and rushing to check out the blueprint of the abbey. I took a quick photo to keep just in case and located the closest staircase.

"Carlo is in the basement," I told the others, who had trailed after me without a single question. "And yes, he's in trouble."

Alice exhaled with amusement. "Of course he is."

"Follow me," I said, ushering everyone away from the courtyard and toward the lower floor, "let's go find him before he does something stupid. Something… else."

We hurried downstairs, Alice and Francesca skipping beside me, the three of us gathering our ridiculous skirts like medieval princesses. Clarence walked a few steps behind, though his deep disinterest in Carlo's fate was more than evident on his face.

As I was walking down the stairs, I lost a shoe in the most Cinderella way. Just less elegant, and with shoes which, by then, resembled stable clogs more than crystal slippers.

"Go on, I'll catch you!" I told the others,

sitting on the steps to put my shoe back on while they disappeared from my sight. I flinched with pain and rubbed my poor feet, both covered in sores after too much hiking in improper footwear.

"Madam, please." A spectral whisper filled the air. I hesitated before raising my head, chiefly because I had heard that voice before, and I knew exactly what unpleasant sight awaited me.

"Laura, wasn't it…" I said, gulping slowly and still reluctant to look at the source of the voice.

"Yes, madam. Laura. We have been following you for a long time, but tonight the Angel of Death is looming over you quite low. I can see him clearly, but I can help, I promise. Just send me to where my husband and parents are waiting, and I'll do anything you need. Anything. Please, Madam."

I swallowed for courage and raised my head. Just as expected, the headless ghost from the forest and her daughter were hovering in the middle of the staircase, both see-through and luminescent.

"I'm…" I glanced away, too stressed to hold a severed head's gaze. I didn't even know whether I was supposed to talk to the head or the body. "I'm not able to do that. I'm sorry."

"There is a spell in that book you are searching for. It can send us to the other side. Please, Madam, consider my request. I shall pay you back. I will shoo the Dark Angel away in exchange or do anything you need. I swear by my daughter's life."

The daughter seemed as dead as the mother;

I wasn't sure that was a trustworthy thing to swear by.

"Okay," I nodded, exhausted. "I'll see what I can do once I find the grimoire. But I can't promise you anything."

The little ghost girl flew down, still holding her mother's head, and dropped a gooey kiss on my forehead. "Thank you, madam. I love you for trying."

And then, they vanished.

I took a few deep breaths and waited for the slimy feeling on my forehead to pass. Those Angel of Death threats reminded me of the stories about shady psychics trying to fish for clueless clients. But the child-ghost's kiss had seemed sincere.

Damn. Dealing with the undead was always so puzzling.

I rubbed my forehead and started to walk, following the footsteps of Alice and the vampires.

The stairs ended at the beginning of a dark and narrow corridor, with many closed doors on both sides. According to the visitor maps of the abbey, the corridor must be U-shaped, but said maps stopped at one end of the U, as if the hallway led nowhere, which was odd.

I turned the first corner and found the other three standing in the darkness and waiting for me.

"Where were you?" Alice asked.

"Sorry. I keep seeing strange things," I excused myself.

"At least you can *see* something," Alice complained. "It's too dark for me here, and I didn't bring a flashlight. I almost broke my head against those low beams at the end of the stairs."

"We can use my phone," I offered. "Or maybe Clarence and Francesca can go and check what's at the other end. They can see in the dark, unlike us."

Actually, Clarence himself was still glowing a little, just like in the courtyard. Only now there were no lamps and no candles to blame.

"No. That could be dangerous," Alice said. "We don't know who or what is waiting for us there, and how they might react to our presence. Witches are never too friendly to vampires found wandering around their property. It's best if I go first. We witches get each other. Well… kind of."

Alice took the lead, and the vampires and I tiptoed after her till the next bend of the passage. After a few seconds, the green-haired witch dissolved into the darkness before us.

A burst of laughter emerged from the other side, and I clung to the sleeve of Clarence's tux. He shrugged and took my hand.

"Come here!" Alice called between chuckles. "You have to see this!"

As we turned the last bend of the hallway, we were presented with an image of Carlo hanging by his belt from the lintel of a robust and antique coffered door. His underwear—and the surprisingly hairy crack of his butt—were half exposed, and his cheeks were entirely red, probably because of the prolonged upside-down position and the exposure to an unexpected audience.

"I don't see what's so funny," he grunted.

Two suits of armor flanked the door, and upon closer inspection, I observed that Carlo was hanging from two long iron halberds held by said—empty—armor while a bunch of keys lay on the floor, together with the contents of his pockets—namely money, chewing gum and an embarrassingly long strip of strawberry flavored condoms. Somehow, he had managed to keep his phone in his hand, and he was holding onto it like a lifeline.

"Strawberry? Really?" Alice was practically rolling on the floor with laughter, and I nudged her softly with the tip of my shoe so she would chill out before someone else appeared.

"Haunted armored guards," Francesca said matter-of-factly, like it was the most normal thing in the world. "A very old trick. Even I would have recognized them."

"That's no trick," Alice corrected her, her tone turning stern, "The Knights Templar were the founders of this abbey and the original lords of these lands. After they were slaughtered, their ghosts remained here to guard their possessions and make sure only worthy people enjoyed them. The Daughters of Isis were entrusted with custody of this abbey barely a few decades ago, but they are not its true owners." She rolled her eyes. "Despite their entitled attitude."

"Thanks for the history lesson," Carlo groaned. "Now can anyone help me down?"

"May I ask how exactly you got yourself up

there, Carlo?" I said, kneeling to retrieve the bunch of keys off the floor, but Clarence grasped the back of my dress to stop me.

"Don't," he said, pressing me against his chest with protectiveness. "Do not touch anything. It might be hexed."

"I must agree with the bloodsucker here," Carlo said. "Better not touch the keys. None of them fit anyway, and look what happened when I tried them."

"That's why they call you a stray witch," Alice pointed out, tsking. "Everybody knows you don't just barge into a haunted crypt. That is, everyone except you… and Carlo." She waved at the poor man, who had propped his legs against the door in a vain attempt to keep his dignity. "*Ciao bello!* Do you remember me from Como?" she asked casually, then turned back toward us. "There are certain kinds of locks one can't just pick without a minimal knowledge of witchcraft."

"Yes, yes, awesome," Carlo groaned. "Are we going to discuss history and metaphysics for the rest of the evening, or are you helping me down? I'm worried all my blood will go to my head, and I'll die." He twisted his neck in a weird angle so he could look at Clarence. "By the way, it's nice to see you back from the dead again, Auberon," he scoffed.

"How very gracious of you to say that," Clarence offered a brief but polite bow, and oddly enough, he tripped on one of the irregular flagstones which paved the floor. A fleeting flinch of pain crossed his face, and I made a mental note to ask him about his health as soon as we had a moment of privacy. He was starting to worry me.

Meanwhile, Alice was studying Carlo's situation and scratching her white and green hair like a child with head lice. "I could try to break the spell, but I'm not sure it would work," she muttered. "I'm not good at this, and I'm worried the knights could turn against us. I think we should get help," she declared, and after a brief deliberation, started to walk back to where we had come from.

"Hello?" Carlo yelled, sounding desperate. "Don't leave me here! Who are you going to call? Hopefully not the boys in blue?" He pointed at the incriminating bunch of keys, which still lay on the floor because nobody dared to touch them. "I don't want to get into trouble."

"Not the police, silly," Alice laughed. "The witches, of course."

Chapter 23

Alba

"I suggest Clarence and Francesca go back upstairs while we find the Daughters of Isis," Alice said. "I think I know where they might be, but they aren't going to be thrilled to find two vampires roaming so close to their secret quarters. So, you two go back to the ball and make an effort to blend in. Try to dance the worst you can, please—no lifts or tricks. We don't want you to attract more attention than necessary. Do you think you could do that?"

The vampires nodded, accepting Alice's orders with deceptive docility; we were deep in witch territory after all. Clarence clasped Francesca's delicate arm, and they headed back to the patio upstairs, whispering to each other with the complicity of those who have known each other for the best part of their existence.

Watching them stroll away together, I couldn't help but shudder. They made a movie-perfect couple, both so graceful and effortlessly elegant. Not only that, even though both had assured me they weren't romantically interested in each other, their shared memories from days past were always brimming close to the surface. It wasn't hard to sense the sea of unspoken recollections from a time when they had been each other's support during the long, dull nights spent enclosed in a catacomb with scarce entertainment and very few of their kind.

"You come with me," Alice said, beckoning to me as the vampires disappeared into the narrow corridor. "As for you…" She turned to Carlo, who grunted and showed us the whites of his eyes in exasperation. He was still hanging upside-down from the halberds, none of us brave enough to touch him for fear of waking up the enchanted armor. "We'll be back to rescue you soon—or at least, I hope so. Try to enjoy the benefits of inverted *asanas* in the meantime!"

"Inverted what?" he growled.

"I think she means yoga poses," I clarified. "Just relax and try not to panic. I think some extra irrigation won't damage your brain cells. The whole four of them." He growled even louder this time, a menacing quality in his voice. "Just breathe, okay? It will make the wait shorter."

Alice and I returned to the upper floor. When we reached the monastery's cloister, I tried to spot Clarence and Francesca among the crowd of dancing couples, but they must have followed Alice's advice to lie low because I didn't see either of them. As we passed the decorated banquet tables, I snatched a canapé covered in Camembert cheese and popped it into my mouth, wincing at the pungent smell and taste. I had to hurry up to catch Alice, who seemed to know the place slightly too well for a first-time visitor. After a few twists and turns, she stopped in front of a small, green door in a deserted wing of the abbey, where there was no food, no music and no decorations, and therefore no guests nosing around either.

Alice knocked on the door three times, paused, then repeated the same process twice.

"Remember," she murmured, throwing me a meaningful glance, "always three times three."

Soon, a voice rumbled a greeting from the other side.

"*Quo vadis, Soror?*" the voice said, in what I guessed might be Latin.

"*Strega Alice, ego tibi,*" Alice answered without flinching.

The door unlocked ceremoniously with a haunting screech, and a familiar-looking lady peeked out of the small crack, her eyes narrow with distrust. She was the same from the crystal stall, the one who had sold me the hideous Rapunzel costume I was currently wearing.

Alice took off her mask and gestured for me to do the same. The woman studied our faces and waved her hand around us. A blistering draft swirled with dusty orange light, whistling in my ears and threatening to get inside my head through my eyes and nose. I covered my face, trying to keep out the psychically stripping energy. Thankfully, after a few seconds, the draft abated, and the woman nodded, opening the door.

"Sisters," she hailed us with a bow, but there was suspicion in her voice, "you arrive at a very delicate moment for this coven. But you are welcome, nonetheless. Do you come in peace?"

"In peace we come," Alice said, elbowing me lightly and throwing me an expectant glance.

"Yes, of course," I confirmed, but both women stared at me with cocked eyebrows. *That mustn't be the right password.* "I… come in peace?" I said tentatively. They remained still. *Expectant.* "In peace we come?" I uttered in desperation.

It was a relief when the woman guarding the door finally nodded and said, "Very well. Enter, sisters."

She moved aside and allowed us to pass, and we entered a cozy room with stone floors, hidden under blood-red rugs and an ancient hearth with a crackling fire in a corner and a cauldron bubbling over it. Eleven women, young and old, were standing around the cauldron, all dressed in lavish witch costumes which made me want to crawl into a hole and wait for my horrid gown to turn into compost, which would have taken a while, as it was probably made of 100% polyester. On a round table rested a huge crystal ball, nested in a clawed bronze pedestal among a sea of candles and papers. There was also a golden plate, covered with precious gems arranged in a pentacle shape.

If the Witches of the Lake during my last misadventure in Italy had confused me with their excessive mellow attitude towards magic, these ones had mastered the theatrical aspect of the craft; the setting, as much as their attire, was worthy of a Halloween movie.

"Salve, Sisters," Alice said, curtsying and pulling at my skirt so I would emulate her. I did my best, though grudgingly. After a traumatic couple of weeks spent as a captive/apprentice in another coven, meeting other witches wasn't one of my favorite activities.

"I am Sister Alice from the Witches of the Lake," Alice introduced herself, "and this is my companion, Stray Alba."

Stray Alba? My mouth slammed shut with a clatter of teeth. The other witches threw me concealed glances which were a mixture of curiosity, pity and disdain, making me feel like a dog just rescued from a shelter.

"My birth name is Gloria, but among my sisters, I am known as Isadora," said the woman who had received us. She had bushy bangs and thick-rimmed glasses, similar to Alice's. "I am the High Priestess of The Daughters of Isis." She pointed at a space by the fireplace, and we found a free spot to stand near the cauldron. "What brings you here, sisters?" Isadora asked, pushing the glasses up her nose. "We rarely get any foreign visitors. Especially not unannounced. Unless they come looking for…"

Alice nodded. "I know what you are thinking," she said as I snooped over the rim of the cauldron. The concoction smelled sweet and heady, like a blend of strong spirits and honey. "And you are probably right. We need your assistance."

Isadora's eyes turned into thin, tight lines. "You are here because of the grimoire, I suppose." We didn't even have to answer before she raised her arms and continued, "How courageous of you, that you would dare ask at all."

Alice winced but composed herself quickly. The other witches, on the other hand, stirred on their feet. One of them huffed and left the room, slamming the door behind her. Isadora lifted her palm, allowing Alice to speak.

"Peace, sisters," my friend said in a confident tone. "We need to have a look at the grimoire, that's right. You are doing a mighty job safeguarding it, but it belongs to all witches, and we believe we have the right to consult it too."

"Our task is to protect it from harm, prying eyes, and those who could use it for selfish ends. What do you expect to find in it, my dear sisters?"

"We are in need of a powerful healing spell."

"I know of no healing spells in this grimoire," Isadora said sternly. "Unless you mean those to raise the departed."

"A counterspell," Alice clarified, "to reverse a curse, cast unfairly on one of our allies."

"I wonder what kind of allies you keep, Sister Alice, who could benefit from a spell originally designed to revive the undead. That's the only one which would match your description."

"I'm not allowed to disclose their identity,

but I assure you they are trustworthy and walk the Goddess's path faithfully."

I tried not to raise my eyebrows too much. Clarence had surely traveled countless paths in his many decades of unlife, but I doubted that included worshipping goddesses. Still, I kept my mouth shut and hoped Alice knew what she was doing because I definitely didn't.

"Our mission concerns all witches," Alice said. "Vampire hunters have turned against our kind. They used our coven in Italy as a stepping stone after associating with dangerous outsiders. We don't know much about these strangers or who they are working for, but they are involved with science, and we already know how derisive scientists have always been of our sacred arts."

"They told my coven in Como that they were targeting vampires, and they sought our magical help to capture them. But it wasn't just vampires they were interested in... Alba here was taken hostage, together with some of her loyal allies, including another witch, and we all know that such a grave offense can't go unpunished. Stray or not, Alba is one of us. She deserves revenge, and her allies deserve our assistance."

I stared at Alice in awe, surprised at her public speaking skills. All the witches had stopped whatever they were doing before our arrival and were listening to her story, enthralled, with only the crackling of the fire under the cauldron breaking the stillness. Alice assessed their reaction in silence.

"Why would a decent witch coven like yours

aid people who associate with *scientists*?" Isadora asked, spouting the word *scientists* like it was a terrible insult. Funnily enough, it reminded me of Elizabeth. In the end, these ladies had more in common with their archenemies than they thought. "That's unusual and unsafe. It goes against all the wisdom passed down from our ancestors."

"What do you think?" Alice sighed, leaning against the wall with her eyes lost in the contents of the bubbling cauldron. "Same as always."

"Money," Isadora growled. "I always knew your priestess Valentina was easy to corrupt, and this just proves it. I'm glad the grimoire didn't end up in her hands, or she would have already auctioned it to the highest bidder."

"Perhaps," Alice said. Her tone was polite, but her lower lip was trembling. "But remember, we need to eat, just like you. Not everybody has the luxury of a whole abbey at their disposal. We agreed to help them hunt vampires, so it seemed advantageous for all of us at the time, regardless of their background. Do you inquire into the origins of the funds from your donors?"

"I see." Isadora ignored the last question and started to pace around the cauldron room. The other witches remained still like black velvet statues. "But still, what your High Priestess did was inexcusable."

"I just know that we cannot support anyone who tries to damage our kind," Alice insisted. "They betrayed us and cast a curse on one of our allies. We need to reverse it or face a hefty energetic debt. The only thing I'm asking of you is to give us access to the grimoire for one night, so we can deal with this problem on our own. You don't have to do anything. In fact, the less you know, the safer it'll be for all of us."

"I sense half-truths in your story, sister," Isadora said. "You can't hide that from me."

"That's right," I interrupted them, and Alice threw me a murderous glance, "but it's not Alice. It's me. I have personal reasons to do this, aside from the higher good of all witches."

"Now, now. I knew there was something more." Isadora leaned in our direction with heightened interest, her cleavage overflowing her low-cut dress. "And those reasons are…?"

"Private," Alice answered, holding her gaze with bravery and grabbing my arm to stop me from saying anything else.

"*Private* is not good enough," Isadora said. "Tell us the whole truth or walk away."

"I nearly died at the hands of hunters," I explained, "and not just me. There were members of my… family. Some died; some disappeared; another one is slowly dying from a lethal curse."

I didn't mention it had been Alice's High Priestess, Valentina, who had cast said curse, nor the fact that the victim had been a vampire. Hopefully, Isadora wouldn't ask that.

Isadora nodded. "That makes sense." She clapped her hands, motioning us to stand up and follow her to the door. "My sisters and I need to discuss this in council. Wait outside."

Alice bowed, appeased by the other witch's answer. "Thank you, sister. We really appreciate your consideration."

Chapter 24

Alba

After a tense wait, the green door of the coven reopened, and Isadora ushered us back into the cauldron room, where several pairs of eyes surveyed us—actually, *me*—with clear animosity.

"We reached an agreement," she said, "and we decided we can trust you." She pointed at Alice, then turned toward me and frowned. "But you, on the other hand, don't seem trustworthy."

I gasped. "What makes you think that?" I was affronted, but I tried to sound respectful for the sake of our quest. "I'm just here to help someone I care about. There's nothing shady about that."

"You're a stray…" Isadora twisted her lip with disgust. "You strays are bad weeds with soiled roots, growing where you shouldn't; always causing more harm than good… unpredictable, without a proper code of ethics!" She clicked her tongue. "A dangerous sort. Deceitful too. And no proper manners."

Thanks for the kind words, I thought, biting my tongue to the point of bleeding.

"But Alba is different. She was trained by our High Priestess, Valentina," Alice intervened, saving me from saying something completely inappropriate, which would have only proved Isadora's affirmations. I hadn't been exactly *trained* by Valentina, unless by *trained* she meant kidnapped and forced to meditate, but it was true that I had learned a couple of useful things during my forceful stay with the Witches of the Lake in Como.

"*Hm.*" Isadora's eyes traveled from Alice to me several times. "The only solution would be to test her," Isadora concluded, shaking her head. "Let's go to the crypt. The grimoire shall decide."

***

As we followed the stone corridor which led to the crypt, Alice jolted and grabbed Isadora's forearm, forcing her to stop.

"There's one little thing I forgot to tell you!" she exclaimed. "Please, don't be cross, but we came with a friend, and somehow he… ended up dangling from a halberd… by the crypt… and we have to get him down. I'm really sorry. He was curious, nothing else…"

Isadora stared at us with dismay—seemingly, stealing a grimoire wasn't the best way to win a witch's heart—when an attractive, red-haired witch in the back huffed, her face crimson and her fists balled with rage.

"No freaking way!" she yelled. "Are you talking about a handsome, blond guy who never shuts up?"

"That would be him," I agreed.

"The bastard," she growled, "I danced with him, and he stole my purse. Right after kissing me! If I catch him, I..."

"Well..." Alice interrupted her, a faint grin on her lips, "he's dangling upside down from his undies, so wait a minute, and you will be able to tell him whatever you want... in person."

The red-haired witch ran down the stairs with a furious huff. When we reached the doors of the vault, we found her murmuring an incantation in front of a terrified Carlo. With a wave of her hand, she motioned for the invisible knights to let go of him, making the halberds turn like the hands of a clock. Carlo crashed to the floor with a loud thump and a groan, and the witch slapped him, not before retrieving a small pink purse which lay somewhere near the door of the crypt. Carlo glowered at me—after all, he had ended up there while trying to help me—but he was kind enough to remain silent about the particulars of his magical misadventure.

"I'm sorry," I mouthed with a tight grin, then added in a normal tone, "Are you okay?"

Carlo pointed at the affronted red-haired witch. "She said she was going to turn me into a cockroach."

The other women cackled in the most witchy way, pointed hats and all, and one said, "So you really believe we can do things like that?"

Carlo shrugged, and none of them clarified whether turning trespassers into cockroaches was an actual possibility or not.

"I will go in alone with the newcomers," Isadora said. "The rest of you wait outside and guard the doors."

The witches moved aside, and Carlo waved at us, sullen. "I'll be upstairs grabbing a drink or two. See you later."

Once he disappeared, Isadora knelt and saluted the invisible knights in Spanish. "*Salve, fieles Caballeros de la Abadía,*" she said, and Alice threw me a furtive glance of complicity.

The halberds, which had been crossed over the doors, pivoted to let us in with a rusty screech. Isadora reached for the pendant around her neck, the one that resembled Jean-Pierre's drawing, and stuck it into the large iron keyhole.

Okay. So that was why none of the keys Carlo had found fit the lock.

"Come here," Isadora beckoned, pushing the coffered door open.

We ducked our heads to cross the low doorway and entered a vaulted space. Isadora turned on the lights, which were dim and yellowish and barely offered enough brightness to see properly, and we were presented with a large, rectangular room, with a dirt floor and walls built out of rough-cut stone. The floor was damp and stained, and the smell of blood and smoke lingered in the air. Despite its large size, the low vaulted ceiling made the room claustrophobic.

The crypt was mostly empty, save for an ebony podium in the middle of the space, resembling a preacher's pulpit.

I had expected to find the famous Alcazar grimoire in a magnificent library, similar to the one in The Cloister. Instead, the witches seemed to be keeping the powerful magical treaty in a humble medieval vault that stank of stale, decades-old air.

"This is our sacred place," Isadora said with solemnity, and Alice bowed. I mimicked her, even though I couldn't help thinking that I had seen prettier garages.

Isadora sauntered to the center of the room, her hands raised in prayer in front of the pulpit. "I brought you here to test your suitability," she explained, opening the book that lay on the podium. It was a large, antique manuscript with leather covers, darkened by the passage of time.

Alice's eyes widened. "*The Alcazar Grimoire,*" she gasped. "Can I have a look?"

"Of course not," Isadora puffed and turned the aged pages with extreme care. She read a passage to herself, her lips moving in silence, then closed the book again. "At least not yet. Place your hand here," she ordered, pointing at the leather cover. "You will go first."

Alice obeyed. Soon, a faint pink glow started to radiate from her hand, or perhaps from the book. Isadora nodded in approval.

"Good. You are accepted by the ancestors and the spirits guarding the grimoire."

"Thank you, sister," Alice said, stepping back with a curtsy.

"Your turn," Isadora said.

My hand was shaking when I placed it on the grimoire, but the grumpy old book ignored me.

No glow, nothing whatsoever.

Please, do the glow thing already, I screamed inside my head.

"Can you please keep your hand still?" Isadora requested, and her features tightened with irritation.

"I'm trying," I muttered. My heart was pounding. I needed to calm down.

I took three deep, slow breaths, then imagined a beam of light radiating from my heart—one of the few useful things I had learned from The Witches of the Lake. The shaking improved, and I concentrated harder.

"That's better," Alice whispered. "Keep going. Think about something nice. You can do this."

Something nice…

Katie and Iris chasing butterflies.

Clarence and I, dangling our feet over the roof of Saint Mary Magdalene church.

Kissing him in Italy, among the ruins of a fire-ravished inn, while hovering above the ground as an astral projection…

I was so lost in my sea of spinning memories that, at first, I didn't notice the faint purple glow originating under the palm of my hand.

It started as a soft lavender light, not unlike

Alice's. But slowly, the sweet lilac turned into a deep shade of plum; just to flow into a dark shade of crimson. Alice and Isadora's eyes were fixed on my hand, indecipherable expressions on their faces.

The glow turned into a ruby-red six-feet sphere, enveloping me, together with the book and the podium where it stood, up to the sooty ceiling. The large light orb started to turn into smoke, losing its initial shine and making it hard to breathe in the enclosed, windowless space. I kept my hand on the book, fearful that Isadora would declare me unsuitable. I had to finish what I had started.

I threw a sidelong glance toward the other two women, just to realize they had withdrawn to the furthest end of the crypt, their backs pressed against the wall in dismay.

Perhaps I should stop after all?

I tried to detach my hand from the grimoire, but it had gotten stuck to it with an invisible magnetic force.

The vermilion mist took over the whole crypt, and it started to gather on the ceiling and shrink, forming a thick, sticky red layer above our heads, which condensed into tiny wine-red droplets.

And then… it started raining.

Raining *blood*.

Not unlike the day I had blown up Carlo's wine cellar, but this time, it was *real* blood. It smelled like blood. It tasted like blood as it sprinkled my lips and face. Because it *was* blood.

Isadora covered her mouth, and Alice

gasped with horror.

"A blood oath," Isadora shouted, revulsion clear in her voice. "Did you seal a blood contract with the Creatures of Darkness?"

My hand finally separated from the book, and I removed it swiftly, hoping that would stop the warm, iron-tasting rainfall.

"Maybe?" I uttered, shuddering at the gush of memories of the fatidic day when Elizabeth had sliced my wrist and drunk my blood to seal our lifelong agreement. I would never forgive the vampire queen for that, particularly because she hadn't even bothered to warn me beforehand. But never in my life could I have imagined that said blood oath would have further consequences along the road.

Just as the blood rain receded, the healed scar on my wrist, proof of that old blood oath, started to burn and throb.

"What if I did?" I asked, pressing my forearm against the back of my skirt. The rain had stopped completely, and the dirt floor soaked up all the blood with thirsty slurps.

"Get. Out," Isadora barked.

I stood frozen, glancing left and right, unsure what to do next. Isadora grabbed my sleeve, still damp with fresh blood, and pushed me out of the crypt with a furious yank. Alice ran after me, and both of us climbed the stairs as fast as we could, the echoes of screaming witches following us.

"How dare you bring this cursed woman

into our sanctuary?" Isadora spat, chasing Alice with a fist in the air, "How dare you reveal our secrets to a traitor? She sold her soul to the Creatures of Darkness; she's tainted forever! None of you is ever welcome in this house again. Go away and never return; otherwise I'll pluck out your eyes with my own hands so you never find the way back again!"

When we reached the courtyard, her voice was still resounding in my head. My wrist was bleeding, so I tore a small strip of tulle off my tacky dress and bandaged the wound the best I could. Outside, people were still dancing, drinking and laughing, unaware of the blood rain and turmoil that had just taken place a few feet below.

"Shit," Alice said, holding onto a buffet table and wiping the blood off her face with a napkin, "that didn't go well at all. What now?"

Chapter 25

Clarence

Francesca threw me an intent glance and tossed a wavy lock of hair behind her shoulder. The golden glow of the party lanterns in the distance made her skin glimmer with a soft golden shine, giving her the appearance of a fallen angel.

After Alba and Alice had gone in search of the witches, Francesca and I had left the abbey, the ball too loud and full of human scents for two hungry vampires to loiter. The curse was creeping back faster this time. Alice's sorcery had helped for a few hours, but the cold in my veins was returning with a vengeance, and the crippling nausea was making it hard to concentrate on anything but sheer survival.

"So, what are you going to tell her?" Francesca asked.

"I don't understand your question," I said as the music fizzed off behind us, the voices and notes turning into a humming medley in the crispy night air. "The truth, what else?"

Francesca dropped her eyelids in that slow, characteristic fashion of hers, and sniffed the air around us. We were alone. "Aren't you concerned about her reaction?"

"She talked to Jean-Pierre. She knows what this curse can do."

"But she is not aware of its advanced state."

"That, she is not," I agreed, exhaling loudly and trudging toward the nearby trees. Perhaps the wilderness would present us with a lost, wandering stranger to quench our thirst. Not that it would help against the freezing, paralyzing cold.

"The glow is returning… how long do you estimate?" Francesca asked. Even though her voice was steady, sorrow was apparent in her eyes.

"I don't know. I wasn't expecting this. Perhaps a few weeks. Days?" I stumbled and had to stop in the middle of the rough path. I took in her small, serene figure. Her impassive stance hid an ocean of sadness, a sadness others might not see but clear as day to me. She was sadder than she had been in decades. "You heard what Alice said, and I think she was right."

I would already be dead for good if they had not found me. Francesca's blood and a healing spell from Alice had achieved a semblance of normalcy, enough to weather the soirée with grace. But just a few hours later, I could feel its merciless, unflinching attack once again. A simple healing incantation was barely enough to cure a minor human ailment, let alone reverse a curse meant to kill the immortal.

"Perhaps Alba has good intentions, but Alice is much more experienced," Francesca said quietly, embracing me and resting her head on my chest. "And even she couldn't do much."

"But Alba has done remarkable things when faced with adversity. I trust her."

"You are placing all your faith in a woman who can barely light a match with her unsteady magic," Francesca pointed out, "and you expect her to reverse a spell older than this abbey standing behind us?"

"At my age, I have learned not to have any expectations beyond the present day, and I will not resist fate because it is utterly pointless. I don't expect anything from anyone anymore."

"She's not ready, and you know it. Healing magic comes at a price. A price she might not be able to afford."

I closed my eyes and let out a ragged breath. That possibility had occurred to me during the ball too, when finding the grimoire had become an actual prospect and not just an irrational dream.

"So, I will repeat my question," Francesca whispered softly. "What are you going to tell her?"

Tears pooled in my eyes, but I blinked them away. "I understand where you are coming from, and I don't know. Yet."

She released me and took my hand in both of hers. They were slight, but hard as iron. She fidgeted with the ring I was wearing, reminding me that it was still there. I took it off and handed it to her.

"It is yours," I said.

"No," she replied, placing it on the palm of my hand and closing my fist around it, "keep it. You need it more than I do now."

I tried to refuse, but the cold had started to crawl down my limbs again, taking away the feeble determination I might have still had.

"Very well." I slid it back on my little finger. "I shall keep it then."

"Find it a new owner," she suggested. "There are many things you can do with a ring like that. I hope you choose the right one."

I raised my eyes, holding her daring gaze.

"I will weigh up my options, thank you."

She gave me a weak smile, dragging me toward her. "Come here now, before everyone shows up and starts asking uncomfortable questions," she whispered, sliding her dress down her shoulders. The luscious sight brought up memories from other balls and other nights, many years ago, and my breath caught in my chest. "Let me help you... the only way I can."

Chapter 26

Alba

After leaving the crypt, Alice and I scanned the dance floor for signs of Carlo, Clarence and Francesca. None of them were there, but my phone was working again, so I dialed Carlo's number. He told us he was waiting outside by the line of taxis on his own, but he knew nothing about the vampires' whereabouts.

The blood oath scar had turned into a bleeding, open wound, and it was throbbing painfully by the time we reached the main gates of the abbey, the tulle bandaging soaked and useless. The pageboy by the door bowed, and I rushed past him with a tight smile, hoping he wouldn't notice the dark red stain on the back of my skirt.

Once we were outside and away from the chatting, drinking and smoking crowd, Alice halted on the frosty grass and lay a hand over my shoulders with sympathy.

"I'm sorry things turned out like this," she said. "I know how important this is to you."

"Thank you," I answered quietly, and I kicked a large stone, realizing too late how deeply rooted it was into the frozen ground. "We can't just give up now. We've come so far..."

"But you should know..." Alice hesitated, walking away from the abbey and toward the area where cabs were waiting, "perhaps it's for the best you didn't get that spell. Yes, you can cast the *Fulminatio*, but in magic, we work with opposites. *Yin and yang. Black and white. Darkness and light.* You always need to learn to control both because you can't have one without the other, without disturbing the overall energy balance of the universe. There's no good or bad by themselves, just dangerous imbalances."

She pointed at the taxis, and we started to walk toward them as she continued.

"Sometimes, one of the extremes is easier. But a proficient witch must master both before trying highly complex spells. Persuasion and dissuasion, chaos and order, healing and destruction..."

"I'm definitely good at destruction," I commented.

"Of course you are." She smiled apologetically. "Because that's the easiest magic of all. Destroying things? No big deal. Some don't even need magic for that, just brute force. But building, conjuring things that weren't there before? *Healing?* Ah, that's much, much harder.

That's where the difference between a good witch and a beginner lies."

I grunted. "So, if I understand correctly, you think even if we get the grimoire, I won't be able to reverse the curse."

We strolled toward the parking area, trying to spot Carlo among the visitors waiting for a ride back to the village.

"I don't know what to tell you." Alice exhaled. "I just think you might cause an energy imbalance, and the power needed for the spell would have to be sourced from somewhere. If you don't know how to channel it from the outside, you might end up draining your own."

I sighed, nodding in silence.

"Look, there's Carlo," Alice pointed at a tall, suited figure holding a cigarette under a forged iron streetlight. "Maybe the other two flew back to the hotel. It's getting late, I'm tired, and you look cold in that ridiculous gown, so I suggest we leave before you freeze. Clarence and Francesca are old enough to find their way back."

I didn't like the idea of leaving the abbey without the two vampires, but Alice was right; the cold mountain breeze was seeping into my bones through the sheer fabric of the dress, and the sleepless nights were starting to take their toll.

"Okay, but I need a bathroom first," I said, remembering the long ride ahead. "Go with Carlo, and I'll meet you by the taxis in a minute."

I searched for the restrooms, but the queue in front of them was so long that I gave up and decided to venture into the bushes instead. I left the abbey behind, breathing the mountain air and relishing the growing calm and silence.

Blissful peace.

I was scanning the forested area for a discreet spot among the vegetation, when I noticed a metallic object peeking out of the muddy dirt. I picked it up: it was a spiked bracelet with a broken clasp, just like the one Francesca had been wearing at the party. It was hard to mistake because it had contrasted so starkly with her usual style.

The ground was damp and covered in sprinkles of dusty frost, and a trail of footprints was clearly visible in the mud. I tracked them down a steep slope which followed one of the side walls of the abbey, until the terrain started to turn steeper and became covered in slippery rocks and gravel; not particularly daunting for a vampire, but too dangerous for me to continue. I sighed and decided to give up.

As I was making my way back toward the taxis, a soft rustle of crushed leaves broke the silence, forcing me to stop and listen.

Two graceful silhouettes juxtaposed against the black, starlight sky: a tall man and a petite woman, blending into such a smoldering embrace that it could have melted all the snow in the Pyrenees. Clarence and Francesca.

I stumbled at the sight, bending to avoid being seen but falling on my knees. I remained crouched behind the shrubbery, struggling to get a better view, though not sure I wanted to see what was about to happen… or not.

Francesca sniffed the air, but thankfully for me, the wind was blowing in the opposite direction from them. She shook her head and turned to Clarence, who had knelt in front of her, holding her hand with reverence. She stood, petite but majestic, and her black, heavy skirt billowed in the breeze like the sails of a ghost ship, never tangling in the surrounding brambles, as if guided by an enchantment. She lowered the straps of her dress, revealing the perfect curves of her eternally young bust. Her head fell backwards, sandy ringlets cascading past her waist and shining white in the moonlight.

For a heartbeat, Clarence seemed to hesitate. But she tugged at his arm, waking him up from his reverie, and he started to kiss her wrist, all the way up to her shoulder, just like he had done with me so many times before. My stomach turned to knots, but I remained where I was, mesmerized by their sensual ballet. Watching them was the worst torture I had ever endured, but there was an eerie beauty to it—their motions so smooth they were clearly out of this world.

With a rough grunt, Clarence sank his fangs into Francesca's marble-white skin. She winced and contorted for a second, while he alternately kissed her neck and drank from it. There was a deeply erotic, wild and visceral air to their interaction which kept me glued to the spot: a tormented voyeur, dying inside but unable to look away. A thin trickle of blood left a dark trail down

Francesca's arm, and Clarence licked it off with his eyes closed, then kept biting, until Francesca's knees wobbled, and she pushed him away, turning her back to him to lean against a frosty fir tree.

Clarence stood up and hugged her with infinite tenderness, encompassing both her impossibly thin waist and the tree trunk with just one arm as she kissed his cheek.

Francesca wiped the blood off the corner of his lips with one finger, and they stood in silence, gazing into each other's eyes, their familiarity screaming to the wind that this wasn't the first time, nor the hundredth one, they had shared such a moment of closeness.

The spiked bracelet fell out of my hands, and its clinking sound against the frozen pine needles echoed my heart as it shattered into shards like a frail porcelain vase.

What the hell did I just watch, was my first coherent thought.

Stifling a gasp, I made an effort not to throw up all over the hawthorn and turned back to head up the slope I had come from. My dress got tangled in the spines, and I heard the cheap pink fabric tear as I tried to escape the sharp barbs.

"Alba, hold on!" I heard Clarence call from the shrubbery. They had heard me, but I was too shaken to stop or answer.

I ran until I reached the row of taxis, where Alice and Carlo were getting impatient and considering leaving without me.

"What took you so long, Lumin?" Carlo

snapped, "How much champagne did you soak up to spend thirty minutes peeing?" Assessing the state of my dress, he stopped abruptly and reached out to study the remainders of my skirt and throw a tentative look at my torn stockings, an unexpected glimpse of empathy growing in his astonished eyes. "Are you okay? What happened?"

"It's nothing," I lied. "I got lost and fell. Just a few scratches, that's it. Let's go."

He shrugged, satisfied with the answer, and he clambered into the first taxi of the row, while Alice helped herself and sat at the back of the vehicle.

"Did you find the others?" she asked before hopping in. "It's okay if we don't wait for them, isn't it?"

"Eh, yeah, no clue where they might be. I'm sure they'll find their way back," I said.

A shadow wheezed by, opening the taxi door for me.

"Hey," I mumbled, "Clarence."

"Ah, look," Alice said, "there they are. Hurry up, you two, we were about to leave." She stretched her neck to wave at Francesca, who nodded sultrily and gazed away as soon as I turned around, scanning the ground as if searching for something—not sure if it was for her lost bracelet, or for her honesty. Was she too mortified to face me?

I let out a ragged exhale to calm down my nerves. Questions were burning my throat, but I didn't feel like asking Clarence in front of everyone.

Thorny conversations would have to wait. He tried to offer his hand and help me, but I just grabbed the door handle and pulled myself up into the monstrous 4x4 the best I could.

"It's fine, thanks," I said, closing the door. I couldn't help but notice the red tinge on his lips—Francesca's blood—and I had to avert my eyes. "I think you should hail another taxi," I added pointing at the long row of cars waiting behind ours. "Not enough space in this one for all of us."

Clarence tapped on the window, asking me to roll it down, but I stared at him blankly, unwilling to make a scene. If he kept insisting, I might start crying in front of everyone. The driver turned on the engine and asked Carlo for an address. Clarence finally understood I didn't want to tackle the subject in public and pulled the door open just a tiny bit; just enough for me to hear him over the roar of the engine. "Francesca's hotel is by the Romanesque chapel. Join me there; we should talk. Here is the address." He slipped me a note, and I tucked it into my purse without reading it.

He tried to kiss me, but I retreated into the seat. With a sigh of resignation, Clarence caressed my hair before leaving, and his eyes widened with surprise as he retrieved a small, moving item from the tip of my braid.

"Look what you had in your hair. A caterpillar, isn't that strange?"

I stared at the creature in disgust before he quietly released it onto the ground.

"Please, come to Francesca's hotel,"

Clarence repeated, his eyes dusky and bitter, faint red sparkles glistening in his troubled irises. "Please do. I can explain."

Chapter 27

Alba

The sturdy Land Rover taxi breezed down the bumpy road, and I tuned out Carlo and Alice's voices, evading the present in order to avoid revisiting the scene from the forest in my mind. In the meantime, I devised several absurd ways to go back to the crypt and get hold of the grimoire, none of them very reasonable. The only spell I knew was meant to blow things up in the air, and the last time I had tried it in a basement, a whole house had collapsed on my head. Attempting the *Fulminatio* in the crypt of a historical monument didn't seem like a very good option.

"Don't you agree, Alba?" Alice asked. She was sitting next to me in the car, but her voice sounded muffled and far, far away.

I turned to her, forcing myself to remember whatever she had said last. Despite my efforts, I had absolutely no idea.

"Yeah, sure," I answered, to be safe.

"You weren't listening, were you?" Alice

rubbed my back with empathy. "I know you are nervous because of the grimoire, but try not to worry, okay? We will find a solution, I'm sure."

I shook my head. "You are right. I wasn't paying attention. But yes, I do worry. I can't help it. And I don't know how you can be so sure things are going to be okay."

"What happened up there with those witches, by the way?" Carlo asked, propping himself between the two front seats in order to look at us. Noticing my look of horror, he glanced discreetly toward the chauffeur. "Don't worry. He doesn't understand a thing. Could barely make out the word 'hotel'. So, did you manage to…" he paused, "to pull Excalibur from the stone? Have you been knighted… by the Knights of the Round Table?"

Alice and I grunted in unison.

"*Uh-oh.* They didn't like you, did they?" We grunted some more, and Carlo nodded. "Yeah, they gave me such bad vibes. And that trick with the armor… creepy."

"I enjoyed that part," I pointed out, a smile escaping my lips for the first time since I had left the dance floor. "One of the highlights of the night, truth be told."

Carlo arched an eyebrow. "I preferred the part where I kissed that French concierge girl. Although I did it purely out of duty, and she tasted a bit like… roach spray. Not my favorite flavor."

"No, your favorite flavor is obviously *strawberry*," Alice snorted.

"Shut up, kiwi-head."

"Chill, you two," I chided them, because Alice had bared her teeth, and I knew for a fact that angering a witch could never end well. "Where are we going first?"

"We'll drop Carlo at your hotel, and then you can come with me, if you want," she suggested as our lodgings appeared in the distance.

"Awesome, thanks. I'll go get a few things from my room, if you can wait for a minute."

The driver stopped by our B&B, and Carlo and I entered the deserted reception, shaking the frost off our shoes.

After his customary, not-entirely-mock offer to share my bed, Carlo disappeared to his room, and I remained in the hallway, taking deep breaths to process the latest events as much as I could before returning to Alice.

How was I going to get hold of that grimoire against the witches' will?

What exactly were Clarence and Francesca doing, hidden behind those bushes?

I leaned against the door of my room, fumbling in my purse for the magnetic card to open it. The door gave way under my weight, and I had to hold onto the doorframe to avoid falling on my rear. Which in turn added a new question to my growing list: *Why was the door of my room unlocked?*

"Carlo?" I called in a whisper, rapping on the neighboring door.

It didn't take him long to come out, dressed only in his boxers—I didn't even flinch at the sight,

236

as I had become well-acquainted with them while he was hanging from a halberd in the abbey.

"Yes?" he asked in his sexiest voice, and I covered my eyes to avoid looking at his underwear.

"Look, Lombardi, I really hate to ask, but would you come inside with me for a minute?"

He raised an eyebrow in a clear come-on gesture, and I took a deep sigh in desperation. "No, that's not what I meant. I suspect someone broke into my room, and I'm not sure I want to go in there alone."

"Oh, okay." He sounded disappointed but recovered quickly. Raising his palm, he motioned for me to wait where I was and came back after a minute, this time wearing pants. There was also something metallic and heavy bulging in his back pocket.

"Is that a gun?" I asked, not sure I wanted to start a shooting in a remote mountain hotel.

"Yep. Can be useful to assist damsels in distress, don't you think?" he declared proudly. "If I do a good job, maybe you'll change your mind about our sleeping arrangements. Where is that boyfriend when you need him, huh?"

Punching him seemed tempting, but stepping into that room on my own was slightly less so, so I merely rolled my eyes and let him go first.

Carlo kicked the door banzai style, then entered the room sideways, holding his gun just like in action movies. I used him as a shield and remained behind him, all the while watching his solo martial arts show.

Without thinking, I turned on the lights. Carlo glanced at me in anger, muttering something about only idiots turning on the lights when trespassers might still be around. *Oops. Too late to turn them off again.*

The place was completely trashed, my laptop was gone, and the few clothes I had brought with me were lying all over the place.

"There's nobody here anymore," Carlo said, putting the gun back into his pocket. "It's okay. You can come in."

"Well, I'm not staying here longer than ten seconds, just in case." I picked up my things as quickly as possible and threw them into the bag. Carlo eyed me with interest, perhaps hopeful I might accept his invitation after all. "Wait there," I said, "you are escorting me back to the taxi."

***

I got into the taxi with Alice, leaving a grumpy Carlo behind. Not that he was afraid to stay in his room alone, but he seemed offended he wasn't allowed to join in *the fun,* as he put it. It took us less than ten minutes to cross the deserted mountain village and reach the rough stone building where she and the vampires were staying, and once we got there, we found the main door locked and the reception closed.

"Well, I wasn't expecting this," she said, puzzled, checking her keys to see whether any of them fit the lock. "I wonder how they got in?"

I glanced at the open window on the second floor, assessing whether a vampire might be able to leap to such height. It didn't seem too far-fetched. Not only that; it was strange they hadn't heard us coming, given their fine sense of hearing.

"Clarence," I whispered, looking up toward the wooden shutters which swung in the chilly breeze, hitting the brown façade with low, intermittent thumps.

To my surprise, Clarence wasn't the one to show up at the window, but rather a very distressed-looking—and even more naked than earlier—Francesca.

"Can anyone come down to open the door? It's cold outside," I asked, trying to ignore the silver threads embedded in the straps of her see-through lingerie as they glistened shamelessly in the moonlight.

"Wait," she said and disappeared inside.

It took her a long while to return, but she finally did and dropped a key at our feet without further pleasantries, vanishing again without a word.

"What's wrong with her?" I muttered, retrieving the key from the paved ground. "Could have said hello at least."

Alice shrugged, and we went inside, climbing the stairs of the hotel as we rubbed our hands to return the blood flow to our numb fingertips.

Alice disappeared into her room after

pointing at Clarence's door, which was marked with an ominous number 13. I knocked, still wondering who might have stolen my laptop and why, and mulling over Francesca's silhouette, standing by the window with scarcely any clothing on and an expression that revealed she wasn't happy to see me.

There were noises coming from the inside of the room, but Clarence didn't come to open the door. I knocked harder. What was taking him so long? He was expecting me, wasn't he? He had invited me, after all.

"Clarence, are you there?" I whispered.

A loud thump ensued, followed by the sound of a glass object crashing to the floor. *Someone* was there for sure.

I called his name several times more, but there was no answer. Finally, I gave up and went to check on Alice, who burst out of her room with a puzzled expression.

"Francesca is not here," she announced.

Our eyes met and simultaneously fell on room number thirteen—I imagined Alice's mind was swirling with similar ominous thoughts to mine.

"Have you tried knocking?" she asked.

"He won't open the door," I whined.

"So strange." She tested the doorknob and frowned, trying to peek through the keyhole. "*Frannie, amore*, are you there?"

Again, no answer.

"Frannie! Open the door!" shouted Alice, her patience waning.

"No!" came Francesca's voice from inside.

"Why not?" I asked, perplexed.

What the hell were those two doing in that room?

"Stay outside!" Francesca replied, sounding breathless. "Or go to the other room!"

"We aren't going anywhere!" I said, grabbing a chair from the hallway and trying to charge against the door with it. "What are you hiding?"

Alice motioned for me to wait with the chair and started to move her hands above the lock in a soft, circular motion, in what seemed like the beginning of a spell. A lockpicking spell, perhaps.

"I can't explain now," Francesca roared back. "Please, don't insist."

"What do you think they are doing?" Alice whispered, still working on the lock.

I shrugged, although I had a few theories.

"Those two have a history, don't they?" Alice blurted, a glint of jealousy in her eyes.

"Yes…"

Before I could finish the sentence, Alice muttered a few foreign words, and the door unlocked with a soft click. She strode into the room in a rage, disappearing beyond the hallway. I couldn't see the bedroom area from the entrance, and I wasn't even sure I wanted to.

A catlike hiss shook the air, and it sounded a lot like Francesca. I heard Alice gasp, and she barreled out of the bedroom. She pushed me out, knocking the air from my lungs with all of her weight.

"Let's get out of here," she growled, holding me against my will. "Francesca was right."

I squirmed to get away from her. "What the hell is going on? Why would I go away?"

Alice relaxed her grip on me, and only then I realized she had tiny droplets of fresh blood sprinkled all over her face.

"Because... Alba..." she hesitated, "I'm not sure you're ready to see what's in there."

Chapter 28

Alba

Blood.
Blood everywhere.

Blood soaking the pillows and the mattress; blood staining the elegant beige carpet. Bloody handprints on the bed head and even on the old, still open book on the nightstand. There was blood even on my hands, my fingers sticky and smeared with crimson after flipping the light switch to make sense of my surroundings.

Francesca's hands and face were tarnished with scarlet stains, some dry, some fresh. She was kneeling on the once white bedspread, her fangs sharp and soiled, her knees apart, straddling Clarence's body over the sheets and a desperate expression washing over her eternally young features. Her black gown was torn and stained, just like Clarence's shirt.

"What...?" I couldn't speak. I leaned against the wall behind me to avoid collapsing on the carpet.

"I told you not to come in," Francesca croaked, wiping the blood off the corners of her lips. "You didn't listen." She panted and closed her eyes, which glimmered with a weak azure glow, and slithered to the edge of the bed. "I wanted to spare you this… this mess."

Clarence was unconscious, his hands peacefully woven over his chest. His cheeks were dark and sunken, stained with red; his nose seemed shockingly sharp and angular all of a sudden. And that eerie glow… like an aura glowing around him, now obvious and bright.

"You had no right to hide this from me," I growled, slowly approaching both vampires and caressing Clarence's stiff arm. "I'm not a child. Just tell me what the hell is going on."

Clarence's hand was heavy and rigid like a statue's, and I winced when his fingers refused to intertwine with mine as they usually did.

"Francesca!" I roared, directing all my anger and fear toward her. "Say something! What have you done? Why is there blood everywhere?"

When I turned around, there were hefty, round tears rolling down Francesca's face. Francesca, who was always calm and collected.

"I was trying to…" she trailed off, retracting her fangs with a pained wince. There were dark circles under her eyes and fine wrinkles around her mouth, and none had been there before.

Silence fell over the room.

"Trying to *what*?" I swallowed. The more I observed the gruesome scene, the less sense anything made. It almost seemed as if they had been trying to kill each other.

Alice approached me cautiously and lay a hand on my shoulder. "She was trying to help him, Alba."

I swayed back. "Excuse me if I don't see how this… bloodbath could help anyone."

"The curse was spreading so fast…" Francesca murmured, her eyes low but still glowing through her long eyelashes. "Alice tried a regular healing spell, but it didn't help. So she suggested we try vampire blood. Clarence agreed at first but later changed his mind. He was worried… worried about me. He refused to feed anymore, to avoid harming me." Francesca sighed and rolled her eyes. "So, I had to be a bit more persuasive." Licking a drop of blood off her knuckle, she left it clear what kind of persuasion techniques she might have been using. "I had no choice."

"We were dancing together two hours ago," I snapped. "How can he be unconscious now? He seemed perfectly okay at the abbey. Why the hell didn't I notice any of this, and why didn't anyone bother to tell me?"

"Well, I don't have an answer for that," Alice whispered. "Nobody knows why the curse works faster on some and slower on others, although some say that the harder the heart, the longer it takes for the silver cast to consume it. But honestly, I can't believe you didn't notice his health was deteriorating. Even a stray should be able to pick up on such things."

I blinked.

I remembered all the times I had voiced hunches about Clarence's health dwindling. He had always denied it, so I had dismissed my own intuition and believed him. The main reason being that I *wanted* to believe him.

"But he said he was fine!" I protested.

"Never trust an English vampire when he tells you he is *fine,*" Francesca observed, slumping on the bed next to Clarence.

I crept to his other side and leaned over him, brushing raven black waves of hair away from his forehead. I could feel his breath on my skin; it was cold and sporadic but still there.

"He's just asleep. Must have fallen into slumber," I declared.

"No." Alice sighed and took Clarence's hand from mine. She turned it over to show me the thin veins in his wrist, clearly visible through his almost transparent skin. "This is no ordinary slumber. See this?"

I shook my head, about to say no, but then I saw what she meant: the same thing I had observed a hundred times and deliberately overlooked. His veins were shiny grey and traced a map of silver rivers all over his body, and they were the source of the halo of light surrounding him.

"This is the Silver Cast, spreading from the heart and throughout all his veins. It moves only forward, and there's no way to stop it without the counterspell. If we don't get hold of the grimoire soon, I doubt he'll wake up ever again."

"No," I gasped. "I don't believe you."

"Alba," Francesca's voice was softer, and she had recovered her characteristic restraint. "I've seen this before. It's merciless. I know it's hard for you to accept this, and it isn't any easier for me, but the time to say our good-byes might be imminent."

"He's not dead yet," I said, crossing my arms.

Alice watched me with sympathy. No. Not sympathy. Pity.

"Alice," I said, "please. Don't look at me like that. Tell me we can fix this."

She tilted her head, her eyes immense and sad, but she didn't answer. Instead, both of them stared at me in silence, with dejected half-smiles which felt like an invisible blow to my stomach.

"Okay then," I said, using all the courage I could muster to get up on my feet, "Then don't say anything, but I'm going to get that grimoire, and I'm going to do it right now or die trying."

Chapter 29

Clarence

London, 1835

Harold Jamieson was my self-appointed best friend and fellow opium enthusiast, and he happened to be the first human I was tempted to turn into a vampire. We were as thick as thieves for many, many years. He was a failure at art as much as I was one at medicine, but we both excelled at ruining our lives and enjoyed doing so together. My sudden disappearance after I became Anne's shadow must have been an unbearable shock for him, accustomed as he was to sharing most of his shenanigans with me.

Following Anne's instructions, I strove to leave my old life behind and start a new one with her as my master. But Harold was not one to give up easily; he combed all of London searching for me. I laughed grimly when I heard he had been asking for me at the morgue—among the dead, and not the living medical professionals of which I used to be a member. This was ironic and also remarkably accurate, a sign he knew me well, the old devil.

When Anne disappeared forever in the parliament fire, together with her lover of the day, I dismissed all her lessons and let go, becoming an even worse version of myself than the one she had turned me into.

The only good thing I ever did during those months was to regularly visit my mother, who was dying of consumption. There must have been a minute part of my brain which still remembered being human, and it desperately drew me to her. My thirst was hard to withhold in the presence of mortals, but Rose Auberon had an almost magical gift: just one of her fond, sympathetic gazes, or a calm word from her sufficed to remind me that somewhere in my heart, I was still her child. This helped me forego my need to be a predator around warm-blooded mortals, at least for the brief moments we spent together. Around her, I was still a creature able to suffer, grieve, and feel human feelings again. Still a monster, yes, but a monster able to remember how to love another, forgiven for my sins during those fleeting hours when the whole house was sleeping, with only the flickering flame of a candle between us.

Whenever I was there, she pretended not to know what I was, and I pretended to be the person I used to be before Father broke us. It was our tacit agreement, and we kept it religiously, no questions asked.

Those soul-baring evenings with Rose were the very reason I held onto a minute fraction of my humanity, unlike many others of my kind. And so, I cherished them and dreaded my mother's imminent death, knowing that each time I visited, it might be the last one. And after that, many things could happen, none of them good.

One night, as I was leaving my parents' home cloaked by fog and darkness, Harold Jamieson came running from the other side of the street and stared at me with disbelief.

"Christ, Auberon!" he gasped, repositioning the round, brass spectacles over his nose. "Where have you been all this time? You look… different. Have you been sick?"

"Harold," I said, swallowing and trying to dispel my growing thirst as I stepped back. I had spent two hours with Mother, and despite her efforts to keep me sane, it was hard to think clearly around humans when darkness fell. "Excuse me, but I really need to go."

Harold scoffed and placed a hand on my shoulder, scrutinizing me with suspicion. "What's the rush? What is so urgent that you can't greet an old friend after a months-long disappearance?"

"Harold, please," I repeated, closing my eyes and striving to divert my attention to something else; anything that could distract me from the sweet scent of his blood and the sound of his heart pumping it into his arteries. "I'll call on you tomorrow," I lied, but it sounded like a lie, and he knew me too well. "I cannot talk now."

I started to walk away from him, turning into a dark alley. I avoided looking back, but I could hear him following me. I could have run and got away from him, but curiosity was stronger than caution. As much as I knew it wasn't wise to talk to Jamieson, the thirst for information was as strong as the one for blood. I, too, had missed him.

"Fine," I huffed, stopping in my tracks. "What do you want?"

"I want to know why you disappeared. I want to know why suddenly I am not worthy of a proper hello or five minutes of polite conversation. Did I offend you in any way? Are you embarrassed to be seen with me now?"

"No." I paused. "I have changed. That's all."

"I can see that." He sounded disappointed.

"Will that be all?" I asked. His heartbeat was so loud, it was deafening. If I didn't slip away quickly, I would lose control, and my fangs would be on his throat before he could even take his leave.

"I suppose," he said, shaking his head, offended. "All right, Clarence. I think you have made yourself clear. Thank you."

He turned around.

Too late.

Harold screamed and implored when I ambushed him in the alley. I could not think. All I could hear was his heartbeat: too loud, too enticing, too sweet. I had tried to warn him that I wasn't his old friend anymore, but he hadn't listened. The side street was dark, and my self-control was nonexistent. The beast took control, and when I finally recovered my lucidity, he was unconscious and on the brink of death.

"Auberon. Please," he panted, "I don't want to die."

I squeezed my eyelids together, pain and guilt gripping my chest as awareness crept back.

"Help me," Harold pleaded. "I know you can."

"Please forgive me, Harold," I said, kneeling by his side. "I could never do to you what was done to me. I can't curse you with this existence."

His eyes fluttered one last time, shining with a flash of sympathy before they fell open, and life abandoned his body.

"Farewell, my friend," I whispered, closing his eyes. I said a prayer for his soul, not that any of us ever cared about the hereafter. After that, I left my only and last mortal friend to the mercy of the ravenous, implacable London rats and trudged all the way back to Anne's empty house, while muttering to myself, and perhaps to the ghosts of those my bloodthirst had killed, "I am so, so sorry."

Chapter 30

Alba

"Going back to the abbey right now is a horrible idea," Alice said, pulling at my arm and forcing me to sit back on the bed. "We are both too tired to cast even the easiest spell. It would be pointless to face those witches while we are drained. Heck, no, it would be *suicidal*."

I growled in frustration, knowing Alice was right. The events of the day had left me exhausted, mentally as well as physically.

"Sleep now," Francesca commanded, leaning over me and caressing my hair. "I'm famished too. I need to go out for half an hour. But I'll be back very soon to watch over your sleep."

She jumped out the window with a rustle of skirts, leaving behind her characteristic scent of blood and roses.

"I'll go to my room, if you don't mind," Alice said, eyeing the tiny crimson smudges on the cream bedspread—and the unconscious vampire—with reluctance. "Would you like to come with me? It's cleaner, and we have a couch too."

I shook my head. "No, I'll be okay here. I'd rather be close to him."

Alice nodded. "Yes, of course." She was about to leave when she paused, her hand over the light switch. "Should I turn off the lights? Or would you feel better if it's not so dark?"

"It's okay. I don't mind the darkness."

Alice left, and I remained alone with Clarence. He wasn't breathing, and his skin had that distracting silver glow. It was faint around his fingertips, becoming almost blinding over his chest, even through the fabric of his half-torn shirt.

As usual, I was tired but not sleepy, so I turned on the little bedside lamp and took the thick tome forgotten on the nightstand. *War and Peace.* Yes, it sounded like the perfect antidote to pernicious insomnia. I checked the page where Clarence must have stopped reading before leaving for the ball, a passage underlined with a sharp pencil as he often did:

> *Chapter XI*
> *"I have been in love a thousand times*
> *and shall fall in love again, though for*
> *no one have I such a feeling of*
> *friendship, confidence, and love as I have*
> *for you…"*

Ah. Clarence.

I kept flipping the pages, just to find yet another highlighted paragraph:

> *Chapter XXXII*
> *"...when loving with human love, one may pass from love to hatred, but divine love cannot change. No, neither-death nor anything else can destroy it. It is the very essence of the soul. Yet how many people have I hated in my life? And of them all, I loved and hated none as I did her..."*

"Damn."

Wasn't this supposed to be a book about wars?

I slammed the book closed and slipped it into my purse, turning off the lights once again. No. I wasn't in the mood for that kind of torture. I'd just lie there until sunrise, allowing my worries to devour my soul as they should.

But in the darkness of the room, Clarence's body kept glowing, and its eerie luminosity was but a mute testimony of the curse which would soon bring about his demise. How was I supposed to sleep like that? It was so disturbing, I just wanted to scream. I found a blanket in the closet and covered him with it. After that, I snuggled by his side, holding his frozen hand, and closed my eyes to wait for morning in the company of my demons.

***

It wasn't morning that woke me up, but a furious banging on the door. When I opened my eyes, I didn't even remember where I was, and I had to blink several times to understand why there was a glowing man lying next to me in a bed covered in soiled, sticky sheets.

"It's the hotel manager! Open the door!"

"What?" I mumbled, straightening my creased pink dress out of desperation, like that would make any difference in a room with the walls covered in blood splatters.

"Don't worry."

Francesca's voice startled me. She was sitting in an armchair in a corner of the room, calm and collected despite the stranger threatening to bust down the door at 4 AM.

"Open the door right now, madam," the hotel manager went on. "One of our guests heard screaming and yelling, and we saw you through the surveillance cameras, charging against the door with a chair. I'm really sorry for the inconvenience, but I need to make sure everything is in order. It will only take a minute."

Francesca bit her lip, pensive, then whispered, perhaps to herself, "Should I knock him out, or would you prefer to leave discreetly?"

The door-banging intensified.

"Please, madam, don't make me call the police!"

"So?" Francesca arched an eyebrow,

unfazed by the man's escalating threats. "What should I do?"

It took a herculean effort to restart my barely functioning brain and consider Francesca's question. Should we knock out an innocent man and use Francesca's talents to make him forget? Or was it better to flee as fast as possible and hope nobody followed us?

"I… I don't know…" I stammered.

"Madam, I have a key. I'm going to come in," the man's voice warned us from outside.

Francesca rolled her eyes and smacked her lips. "I'm not hungry anymore, but I guess I could do it for you," she murmured, throwing me a questioning glance.

"Okay, okay, let's get out." I sighed. "Can you make him forget before we leave?"

"I can, but do you expect me to clean up this mess too? Because if I don't, other people are going to see the state of the room sooner or later, after we're gone, and I won't stay here to make the whole town forget. Besides, I'm afraid I forgot my cleaning gloves and apron in The Cloister."

I took in the dark flecks covering all surfaces like abstract paintings and the inert vampire splayed in the middle of a ruined bed—hopefully, we would be able to remove that piece of evidence, at least. In any case, whoever came in was about to walk into a scene worthy of a horror movie.

"What about Alice?" I asked, hearing the key turn in the lock. "She's still in her room."

"I'll pick her up afterwards."

Francesca wrapped Clarence into a thick grey blanket, which made him look even more like a shrouded corpse. A gush of tears threatened to burn the corners of my eyes, but I held them back, concentrating on the search of an alternative exit instead.

He is going to be alright, I told myself. *One doesn't live for two-hundred years just to quit when things finally get interesting.*

Francesca threw Clarence over her shoulder, an odd sight to say the least, particularly when he was almost two heads taller than her, and took a leap to the window, ready to jump out once again.

"Wait!" I shouted, "What about me? How do I get out of here?"

"Just like me," Francesca said, her voice devoid of emotion as she assessed the street below us, perhaps making sure there weren't any witnesses. "Jump. I'll catch you. It's just a couple of feet."

Okay. What she had labeled a *couple of feet* was a *second story* window, to be precise.

Francesca disappeared just as the door of the room clicked open.

"Francesca! Help! I can't do it!" I cried, looking back and forth and digging my nails into my palms. I gathered my cheap skirts, holding onto the window frame, which in turn left me no free hands to pray and entrust myself to whatever god or goddess might be willing to listen.

Francesca was standing on the cobblestones

with her arms wide open, waiting for me. "Hurry up!" she mouthed.

My head started to spin as I stepped on the windowsill and looked down.

"I'm coming in, please cover yourself if you are not dressed," the hotel manager said as the door hinges squeaked.

"Jump!" Francesca growled with frustration. "Think less, trust more, remember?"

A man stepped into the room and turned on all the lights, his face gradually distorting as he assimilated the state of the place.

"Who are you?" he asked me with a terrified gulp, wiping his bloodied hands on his trousers.

"Just a crazy woman who thinks she can fly," I answered, closing my eyes.

And then, I jumped.

Chapter 31

Alba

Francesca caught me mid-air and set me kindly on the sidewalk, on the cobblestones of a narrow side street where the hotel manager would not be able to see us. A few seconds later, she repeated the process with Alice, who dropped out of the sky like a ripe apple.

"It's raining witches," Francesca said with a faint smile, kissing Alice as she placed her next to me on the ground and picked up Clarence again with one arm. "Fine, ladies. Where should we go now?"

I looked up to the hotel window. It wouldn't be long before someone came down looking for the crazy foreign woman who had jumped through a window and disappeared, leaving a bloodied room behind. "Let's go to my hotel. It's just a couple of hours till sunrise, and you two are going to need shelter soon," I suggested. "I'll just call Carlo to check if it's safe to go there."

Funnily enough, my phone was already

ringing when I got it out of my purse.

"I'm on my way," Carlo spat into the phone. "I just knocked out the guy who was trying to break in again, and he's hanging from the fire exit."

"What?" I shouted, rushing to follow Francesca to the edge of the village. "No, you can't come here!" I looked around, desperate to come up with a safe meeting point quickly. "Okay, let's meet at…"

"At the Sinner's Cemetery below the abbey," Francesca whispered, then grabbed my arm and dragged me into the woods at the edge of the village. I was about to point out that there was no way I could walk that much uphill in the darkness, when she added, "Don't worry, I'll take you."

***

The waning moon shone among fuzzy clouds when we reached the Sinners' Cemetery several hours past midnight. Carlo arrived riding a motocross bike which was definitely not his and probably woke up the whole town of Alcazar with its roaring engine.

"Very discreet," I commented as he got off his new ride with a smug smile. "I didn't know car dealers were open after 3:00 a.m."

"I'll return it," he drawled with a shrug. "But listen, I found out a few things. First of all, I caught the guy who stole your laptop, and I got it back." He opened his army backpack and presented me with my computer, which was neatly tucked inside. "Here, for you. He also confessed he had been hired by Natasha and was supposed to meet her in Spain. Have you heard of a place called Finis Terre? *The End of the Earth*?"

I stared at him blankly. "No, I haven't. But why would he tell you all that?"

"He and I had an interesting conversation while he was hanging upside down from the fire escape stairs of the hotel. I caught him while he was trying to run away after ransacking your room. Natasha has taken the other two vampires to a lighthouse in that place called Finis Terre, where she's also meeting a business partner. After that, she should head to London, not Paris as we first thought…"

Alice cleared her throat, glancing at her watch. "Speaking of which, we should really decide where to put the unconscious vampire we already have before sunrise toasts him. I know there's still a few hours, but we are out in the open, and the car is at the mechanic, and we can't go back to our hotels either."

"We'll bury him," Francesca said in a flat tone, and she ignored me as I nearly died on the spot. "Stop fussing. It has been done this way for centuries." She glanced at her nails with sorrow. "I'm just concerned it will ruin my manicure."

Carlo lifted a finger. "I have a folding shovel in my backpack, if it helps," he offered, scattering the contents of his rucksack on the ground. Two beers and a dozen miniature liquor bottles rolled on the grass, together with several bars of soap and tiny shampoo containers.

"You stole the whole minibar?" I said, shaking my head with disapproval. "Come on. Also pens? Towels! Hotel toiletries? What's wrong with you?"

"I stole the manager's motorbike too, so it's not going to make much difference if they catch me, is it?" He grabbed a bottle of beer and rummaged in his back pocket until he found a large silver object, then fumbled with it for a while until he managed to open it. "Here, drink. It will make you feel better."

I took a step back, glancing toward the abbey looming above us. The party was long over, and most lights had been turned off. "Thanks, you can have it. I need to be sober in order to find my way back to the crypt." All heads turned to me, and Alice closed her eyes as if dodging an invisible projectile. "Yes," I said as calmly as I could, "we must get this done tonight. We have nowhere to stay, and I'm sure the hotel called the police. They'll be trying to find us. I'm going back to the abbey, and I'll find a way to get in, even if it's the last thing I do."

"It will *probably* be the last thing you do," Alice said, horrified. "Nobody can get in without a Tyet key and the right incantation. The ghost knights will get hold of you and alert the witches."

"You said it was a simple incantation."

"Yes, but do you have a key? Nope. As far as I know, there are only twelve. Each of the witches has one, and they always wear them around their necks, even while they sleep. It's impossible to get hold of a sacred Tyet, unless you kidnap a member of the coven or…"

Carlo took a large swig of his beer and burped behind me. I turned around, rolling my eyes with disgust, but he just shrugged and picked a second bottle off the ground. "Sorry," he said. "It wasn't on purpose."

The bottle opener shone in the dim moonlight, and Carlo cursed as he tried to position it properly against the metal cap of yet another beer. "Stupid design, too narrow to fit," he complained.

"What the hell, Carlo?" I yelled, snatching the item from his hands and pressing it against my chest. "A bottle opener? Seriously?" The polished metal object was shaped like a human body with a hollow head and hung from a broken silver chain. "How did you get your hands on *this*?"

He stared at me, puzzled. "*Uh*… I was talking to that red-head… the one who almost turned me into a cockroach thanks to you, by the way," he said, "and I found this thing on the bar counter, next to a platter full of drinks. I used it to open a bottle while I waited for her to come back from the ladies' and—" He shrugged. "—it ended up in my pocket somehow."

"Almighty Goddess Diana," Alice gasped, examining the purported bottle opener with respect. It was just like Isadora's pendant, except a bit smaller. "Please don't tell me you have spent the night opening booze with a sacred Tyet!"

"Alice…" I said, tucking the Tyet into my purse and eyeing the steep path that led up to the gates of the abbey. "Would you come with me? I would feel so much better if I had you with me. But I'll understand if you refuse. I know it's a crazy idea, and…"

Alice blinked. "Yes, it *is* crazy. But you are talking to the person who allowed you to steal the most valuable piece in the museum she works for. Does that sound sane to you?"

"Is that a yes?"

Alice nodded slowly, and I ran to hug her, all the emotions of the day gushing out and turning into tears. "Thank you, Alice, thank you!"

She hugged me awkwardly, then pulled back. "But there is one condition," she warned me.

"Anything. Just name it."

"You must promise not to try any spells outside your level of expertise. We'll do our best, but if danger arises, we'll leave the grimoire behind and escape. Because fleeing is always better than dying, okay?"

"Yes, okay." I had to agree that her reasoning was rather sound.

Francesca and Carlo remained at the Sinners' Cemetery in order to find shelter for Clarence, while Alice and I started our uphill hike.

The path, though short, was frustrating and draining, particularly for someone dressed for a Carnival ball and not a hiking tour. I concentrated on the gorgeous view of the lights illuminating the sleeping village of Alcazar below, ignoring my painful, frozen feet. We were in the heart of the High Pyrenees, and the views were remarkably scenic. For a second, I imagined myself strolling up that path with Clarence on a sunny spring day, and the heart-warming fantasy made me smile.

I shook my head, the smile vanishing. *Never going to happen.*

Once we reached the abbey, climbing over the outer wall wasn't particularly hard. Thanks to Francesca, I had collected plenty of practice climbing graveyard fences; but also, the yellowish limestone had been eroded by centuries of wind and rain, creating a natural ladder which made the task fairly easy.

We found ourselves in the courtyard and made our way to the old refectory. The party was long over, and the door was locked, but Alice unlocked it with a hairpin.

"No spells?" I asked with surprise, following her down the stairs that led to the crypt.

"Energy conservation," she clarified. "Why use magic when a simple hairpin will do?"

"Makes sense."

Another lock fell, and we found ourselves facing the coffered door of the crypt. The ghostly suits of armor were still there, silent and menacing at the end of the hall.

"So… you know what to do?" I asked Alice. "You do remember the words, don't you?"

She nodded. "Oh yes. That won't be a

problem." She sat Indian style in front of the knights and started to hum.

"Are you sure that's the right way to do it?" I asked. I didn't remember Isadora doing any of that, and the last thing I wished was to end up dangling from a spear at the mercy of those French witches, all while Clarence remained buried like a… no, *concentrate on the now,* I scolded myself.

"I am a Witch of the Lake," Alice answered proudly. "Our ways are different. But they work, and that's what counts. Now, silence!"

While Alice concentrated on her humming, I took out my phone in case Carlo had texted me. There was no service, but I found a string of old-ish messages from Minnie which must have piled up during our hotel escape ordeal.

Minnie, 3:04 a.m.
We just landed in London! So exciting!
(Selfie of Minnie with Iris and Katie holding a neck pillow).

Minnie, 3:23 a.m.
Waiting for our suitcases! Yay!
(Blurry photo of an empty baggage carousel).

Minnie, 3:32 a.m.
Playing hide and seek while waiting for Daddy to get out of the bathroom!
(No photo).

I was evaluating Minnie's sanity levels, and my decision to leave my kids with someone who allowed them to play hide-and-seek in one of the largest airports in the world, when Alice interrupted my musings with an abrupt halt in her humming and the beginning of a muttered incantation.

"*Salve, fieles Caballeros de la Abadía*," she repeated three times.

A brief silence ensued, followed by a loud screech as the ghostly suits of armor came alive. I held my breath while they hit their halberds against the rock floor to greet us. My handbag slipped to the floor as we stood in front of them, terrified.

"Welcome, Keepers of the Abbey," a voice said inside my head. "You can pass."

"Shit," I said, picking up my things from the floor, "they startled me."

"*Shh.*" Alice seemed upset. "Don't swear. You must be respectful. The knights were the true lords of the abbey, and we are at their mercy right now. A false step, and we are doomed." I grinned nervously in apology, and she continued. "And now, unlock that damn door already!"

So much for not swearing.

I tried to fit the Tyet into the lock, but it was too large. After a couple of minutes of desperate fumbling, my hands got sweaty, and the silver key slipped off my fingers. "It doesn't work," I sobbed as I kneeled to retrieve it. "We came this far just to learn it was a bottle opener after all."

"You know that's no bottle opener," Alice replied with a clenched jaw. "You need to focus.

Magical keys don't work like ordinary ones. You must use the power of intention; otherwise yes, it's going to behave like a useless object. Tools are not supposed to do the work instead of you. You are supposed to *use them* the proper way. Or do you expect a hammer to assemble your furniture on its own?"

I took a deep breath and did as instructed. Holding the Tyet, I imagined it was an extension of my own hand, allowing my magic to flow. I had only tried this trick in order to blow things up, but this time, I had to use all my self-control to restrain the tingling without interrupting its flow. It was much harder to contain the magic than to set it free with a blast.

The Tyet slipped gently into the keyhole, and the door unlocked with a quiet click.

We waited for a couple of seconds, making sure we hadn't offended the ghostly knights with our disrespectful language or otherwise. They didn't seem to be bothered, so I threw one last look at their two ominous figures, now standing still and silent with their halberds pointing upwards, and followed Alice into the darkness of the crypt.

"Quick. I'll grab the grimoire, and we get out of here," I said. "I feel something's not right. This has been... I don't know, almost too easy."

Alice turned to me, her eyes saying clearly, *I know*.

The Alcazar Grimoire glowed softly on its podium with a white, faint light. I was about to seize it when Alice stopped me.

"It's probably secured to the pulpit with magic," she said, pushing me away. "I will scan the room for spells."

She closed her eyes and started her meditative humming once again. A loud thump resounded upstairs, followed by several more. It sounded like doors slamming closed and people running. Meanwhile, Alice carried on with her scanning, removed from the outside world.

"Alice, hurry up!" I nudged her. "I think someone is coming." Another bang, this time closer. "Alice. I'm freaking out. I'm going to grab the book, and we *run*, okay? Do you hear me?"

Alice was lost in her trance, and the steps were approaching, clear and unmistakable. "Alice!" I shook her arm, and she finally opened her eyes, a disconcerted look washing over her face. "We're leaving. Now!"

I grasped the heavy old volume and closed it, then secured it under my arm.

Horror distorted Alice's face as soon as she realized what I had just done.

"No!" she shouted. "Don't touch it! The whole crypt is hexed!"

But it was too late.

The book let out a piercing, continuous shriek which reminded me of an ambulance siren. The tome became hot under my arm, and its white glimmer started to turn red. It was too hot to hold it, and I dropped it; it crashed wide open to the floor, and a burst of flames enveloped it.

"Let's get out of here!" Alice yelled, yanking

me toward the exit, "Too dangerous! Remember your promise!"

I stood by the flaming grimoire, motionless. Tendrils of fire extended from its core, swirling, growing and creating a circle of scorching flames around us. We were imprisoned in the circle of flames, and there was no way to get out without crossing the growing barrier of fire.

The steps got closer, and several witches burst into the room, brandishing their wands in the air. As they raised them, the flames grew up to the ceiling, trapping us inside a sweltering prison with the grimoire at its center. The heat became suffocating, but the grimoire remained intact. The pages spun left and right, ancient spells flickering in front of our eyes with flashes of white and red light.

"I knew this would happen," Isadora growled. "Strays are a pest. They should be annihilated."

She drew a circle in the air with her wand, and the flames withdrew from the book and crawled toward me. Fire vines licked the bottom of my skirt, infusing the air with the foul smell of burnt synthetic fabric. I stepped on the charred rim of the dress before it burned me alive, but Isadora repeated her spell, making me jump and scream. I glanced at Alice in desperation, hoping she would find a way to appease the witch.

Alice held Isadora's gaze through the wall of flames, disregarding the pearls of sweat running down her reddened face.

"Please, sister," Alice said. Isadora's eyes glowed with fury at the moniker. "Have mercy. We were trying to help a friend."

"No mercy for thieves," Isadora declared, commanding the flames to climb up Alice's legs. Alice held her arms out and pushed back the fire, but the veins in her forehead bulged with the effort. "What do you say, sisters?" Isadora asked the others.

"I say burn the bad witches," one of them answered, and an ominous laugh blended with the crackling of the magical fire around us.

The witches joined the tips of their wands and directed the flames against us. I could smell the fine hairs on my arms singeing, blisters forming on my legs and bare shoulders. Alice held her arms in front of us, fighting the advance of the fire, but it was obvious she wouldn't be able to withhold the flames for much longer.

There were twelve witches against us. Hopeless.

"We're going to die," I cried, trying to mimic Alice's shielding spell. It didn't work.

"Then we can be roommates in hell," Alice muttered, a growl escaping her throat as she lost control of the fire. She tried to repeat the incantation but gave up, her energy depleted, and retreated toward the center of the circle, where I was standing. "That is, until Francesca joins. Then you'll have to move to your own dungeon."

I gave her a tight smile, appreciating she could still wield her sense of humor in such a hopeless situation.

"You said witches don't believe in hell," I muttered. "But they do believe in ghosts…"

"Yes. Say hi to the Angel of Death for me," Isadora cackled, and the smell of burnt hair—my hair—became asphyxiating.

Ghosts.

Of course.

"Laura!" I screamed, bracing myself against the implacable flames, "Laura, I accept your offer! Please, manifest yourself!"

Chapter 32

Alba

Heavy steps thundered into the crypt, and the enchanted armor guards appeared at the door. The witches turned around to look at the newcomers, and the flames followed their movements, receding just a couple of feet—enough to allow Alice and me to take a deep and very needed breath. My arms were blistered and in pain, and it was hard to establish how much of my hair was still attached to my scalp.

"Welcome, Knights," Isadora greeted them, "you can have the trespassers if you wish. Consider them a grateful gift from the Keepers."

The Knights bowed in agreement and hit their halberds against the floor three times, sealing our fate.

Isadora snapped her fingers, and a gap opened in the ring of flames, creating a narrow passage between them and us.

"Kill them," she commanded. "They are thieves and traitors. Don't leave any traces."

The ground started to shake, and a dozen knights came in, positioning themselves along the four walls of the crypt and pointing their halberds toward us. Isadora smiled with delight and raised a hand.

"On second thoughts, I'll kill the thieving stray myself, and you can have the Italian renegade," she said and pointed her wand at me. An orb of red light started to gather at the tip, and I closed my eyes, waiting for the impending blow.

I heard the explosion and felt the blinding flash of light coming out of Isadora's wand, but instead of pain, all I could feel was a cold, viscous kiss on my forehead.

"Don't worry, madam," said a little girl's voice, "we came on time, and the kind knights are our friends. They are specters, just like us! They will understand, won't they, *Maman*?" The ghostly girl looked at her mother's bodiless head, which she carried in one hand, clutching it by the hair. The head nodded, and the little girl kissed its ashy cheek. "I can't wait to hug Papa again."

The mother's head spun, dangling in the air from the girl's tiny, bluish fingers, and turned to the empty armor stationed along the crypt walls, "Honorable Knights, these two women owe us a magical debt. Keep them alive so they can repay it."

The knights bowed once and turned their halberds toward the Daughters of Isis, who screamed and started to flee, which caused the flames to go wild. Only Isadora and two of her sisters remained in the crypt, trying to control the fire and direct it against us. Meanwhile, a knight grabbed my arm, and another one did the same with Alice. I tried to escape his grip and reach for the grimoire, but Isadora saw me and opened a path through the flames to stop me.

"The book!" I said to the ghost girl. "We can't leave without it!"

The little ghost dove to the ground and picked up the grimoire, then dropped it into my hands. "There you go, madam. Now let's go; I miss Papa so much!"

I took the book, and as soon as I did, it started to scream again. Its screams blended with the shrieks of the witches, who were fighting against the knights, wand versus sword. Meanwhile, the fire crackled loudly, and the empty suits of armor crashed against each other in a deafening cacophony. The grimoire kept wailing when I threw it into my bag, but nobody cared among the reigning chaos.

One of the knights picked me up and dragged me toward the door, where Isadora was waiting for us, shooting fire orbs with her wand. The crimson orbs hit the knights, but they just bounced off their armor, and they kept walking. I, on the other hand, strove to dodge them the best I could. When we reached the door, Isadora had created a fire curtain to block the exit and was standing in front of it with her wand pointed against me.

"I defy you to cross this door and steal our sacred grimoire," she said calmly. "One more step, and I'll burn you alive. Give it back, or I'll retrieve it from your smoking ashes."

I wiggled in the knight's arm until he placed me back on my feet, and I opened the bag, holding Isadora's gaze. Alice stood next to me, inspecting the fire curtain with analytical eyes. Next to the grimoire sat Clarence's aged copy of *War and Peace*, almost the same size and thickness; both books were dark brown and leather bound. Swiftly, I slipped my hand inside the bag, grabbed Clarence's book and threw it as far from myself as I could, making it land on the other side of the crypt.

"Catch!" I shouted at Isadora.

Alice muttered a spell and lifted the fire curtain for a few inches, while Isadora hurried to the other side of the crypt to retrieve the false grimoire. We crawled out of the crypt under the curtain of fire, followed closely by Headless Laura and her ghostly daughter.

We reached the stairs and crossed the courtyard, escorted by two of the knights. Once we reached the cloister, they threw us over the fence in the most discourteous way and disappeared back into the abbey.

I lay on the frosty grass for a while, allowing the tiny particles of ice to cool the reddened skin of my arms and legs. I rolled on my back and made a frost angel, then sat up and washed my face with tiny snowflakes, taking a moment to ground myself despite the persistent screaming of the grimoire inside the bag.

"Will you make *him* shut up already?" Alice

complained, as if the book was a living creature. She had been standing against the wall and waiting, covering her ears with her hands. "Otherwise, the witches will find us as soon as they come outside. I would do it, but it's *you* who stole *him,* so I can't."

"I'd love to, but I don't know how."

"Try asking kindly."

I looked at the raging book, glowing red inside my handbag, and caressed the covers with gentleness. The grimoire slapped closed, pinching the tips of my fingers. "*Ouch!* Bad, bad book! It bit me!"

Alice rolled her eyes, "Just tell *him* what you want!"

The book started to shriek even louder than before, perhaps trying to alert its rightful owner.

"Hello, *book*," I said softly, raising my voice over the wailing, "Sorry we stole you, but we need your help. Would you please…*ehm*, turn down the volume?" My discourse worked, and the screaming turned into a quiet meowing. "Yes, very nice!" I encouraged it. "Now come with us, we have a mission for you."

***

Alice and I raced back to the graveyard, with the two ghosts following a few inches above our heads. The little girl kept asking me when she was going to see her papa, and I prayed there really was a spell to send ghosts to *The Other Side* in the grimoire because the last thing I needed was two angry ghosts following me around for the rest of my life.

My phone started to beep wildly. I took it out, in case Carlo was trying to warn us of some danger ahead, but found several messages from Minnie instead, their tone increasingly disturbing.

> *Minnie, 3:56 a.m.*
> *"Hello, Alba, no need to worry, but we can't find Iris and Katie. We've been searching for them for half an hour and they must have hidden really well while we were playing hide-and-seek at the arrival terminal. They are calling them over the loudspeakers so I think they'll come out soon."*

I reread that nightmare of a message to make sure I wasn't hallucinating again, then continued to the next one, dated fifteen minutes later, desperate for it to tell me my girls were fine.

> *Minnie, 4:12 a.m.*
> *"Okay, we haven't found them yet, but the police are here now. They said we must remain calm. For now, they have locked all the accesses to the terminal. Nobody can get in or out. They are checking the security cameras right now."*

Another message flew in as I was reading. This time a voice message, with lots of background noise, including whistling, weeping and offensively merry music.

> *"Hi, Alba… they are sending us to our hotel. The police say they will call us as soon as there's any news. I don't know how to tell you this but the girls… they have gotten lost, and nobody can't find them right now."*

I started to feel nauseous as I processed Minnie's messages and panic set in. Did she just say *gotten lost?* Because no. Katie and Iris hadn't *gotten lost*: my stupid ex-husband and his girlfriend *had lost them* due to sheer neglect. Interesting how calm Minnie's voice sounded despite the dreadful situation. I hit the call button, but Minnie had turned off her phone. *Incredible.* Mark's phone was off too. How could they do this to me?

Alice was standing behind me. I must have stopped walking without even noticing. I kept staring at the screen and pressing the call button compulsively, in my blind obsession to talk to Minnie, or Mark, or just about anyone who had seen my daughters in the last few hours.

"We must hurry, Alba. Isadora is probably searching for us right now," Alice said, tapping on my shoulder. "Is everything okay?"

I couldn't even answer. The massive knot in my throat didn't allow me to. Suddenly, the feat of retrieving the Alcazar Grimoire seemed mundane and inconsequential compared to my children being missing. My brain had stopped working. Nothing else mattered anymore.

"I don't… I don't know!" I gasped, breaking into sobs. My bag fell out of my hands, sinking into a muddy puddle. Alice retrieved it and rubbed my back with nervousness.

"Okay…" she said with a concerned grimace, "whatever it is, you'll have to tell me on the way. No time to waste crying here."

In the distance, I could see Francesca's silhouette, sitting somberly on the rim of a tomb. Her head was bent low, as if praying or sleeping. A faint, flickering glow was coming out of the open grave, turning on and off every few seconds.

"I'll be fine in a minute," I lied, squeezing Alice's hand in thanks as we ran toward the Sinners' Cemetery. "I don't want to talk about it now. Let's go."

Francesca heard us and rose to meet us, her eyes glossy with tears. Carlo must have returned to the village because he and his borrowed motorbike weren't there anymore.

"Glad you're back," Francesca muttered, then noticed the two ghosts hovering silently over our heads. "You have the strangest friends."

I tried to smile, but I couldn't. In front of us lay a half open grave. According to the tombstone, it had been once occupied by a monk who had committed suicide and didn't deserve to be buried inside the abbey. Francesca had slid the stone slab aside and placed Clarence inside it, covered with a blanket from head to toe. The blanket hid his features, and the blue flickering of the curse was becoming more and more infrequent.

Francesca leaned over Clarence, rearranging the blanket, then turned back to us and said, "Sit down please. I have some challenging news to convey."

Chapter 33

Alba

Darkness fell over the Sinners' Graveyard, our only companions the silence of the mountains and Francesca's muffled sobs as she spoke. A slight dusting of snow had started to cover the meadow, and snowflakes glittered under the moon like tiny, star-shaped pearls. Everything sparkled, but in the tomb where Clarence rested, the unnerving glow had come to a halt. Eerie as it was, the radiance meant there was still some energy for the curse to consume.

I sat by Francesca's side and uncovered Clarence's face under the blanket. His expression was serene, almost placid. He seemed almost relieved to be leaving this world forever. In my anguish, the idea of sleeping, forgetting everything and never waking up suddenly seemed quite appealing to me too.

"I'll leave you alone with him if you wish," Francesca whispered, caressing the crown of my head. "You two deserve a private farewell."

"No!" I snarled, directing my frustration toward her. "We have the grimoire, remember?" Francesca ignored my remark, dropped to her knees and started to pray in Latin, an ominous plea which reminded me too much of burial rites. "Can you please stop with the praying? It's making me nervous!" I pulled the stolen spellbook out of my bag and slammed it on the tombstone. "I'm going to cast that spell right now!"

I opened the grimoire and scanned the pages in search of what I needed. There were spells to make people fall in and out of love; to inflict magical revenge in several dozen ways or to call the elements and cause fires, floods and even plagues. There was no time to read them all. I clasped the Tyet in my fist, allowing the hard edges to dig into my skin. Physical pain brought me back to the moment and helped me calm my nerves. The pendant became strangely warm in my hand; its temperature fluctuated depending on the page I was looking at. Was the Tyet trying to guide me?

"Find me the counterspell for The Silver Cast," I demanded, not sure whether my command was aimed at the pendant, or the book, or whatever spirits might be watching over me and protecting me.

I flipped the pages and the polished surface of the Tyet turned warm against my fingers; warm, like Katie's peachy cheeks when she had been born; warm, like the summer apples in my grandma's orchard; warm, like Clarence's shoulder blades after lying naked in my arms for a whole night. The memories made me weep, sorrow bubbling up and out of my chest in salty, round, sincere tears.

So this is how losing everything feels.

If I were to lose my daughters, if I were to never see Clarence again… how was this any better than dying? How was this any different from ceasing to exist and becoming one with eternal oblivion?

Ultimately, I ran out of tears and collected myself, remembering there was still hope and not all was lost. But someone kept crying. At first, I thought it was Francesca, but she was sitting in silence by my side, her gaze lost in the faraway tombs. No, it was the grimoire that was letting out a soft, heartfelt lamentation. My sadness had spread to its pages like a contagious illness, and I cradled it against my chest, trying to appease its sorrow. When the book stopped crying, I placed it on top of Clarence's chest. It fell open at the right page, where a thorough scribe had added ten menacing skulls at the top, carefully traced in black ink next to a calligraphy title— *Silver Cast Curse Counterspell: to reverse mortal curses and death.*

Right under the title, a crimson warning preceded the main verses:

> *Defeat and agony fall upon those*
> *who the rules of sorcery dare forego:*
> *Twenty-five turns around the blazing sun*
> *your practice as healer must paramount;*

Procure the kindling of a waxing moon,
And never work this spell beyond the
tomb.

After this, someone had scribbled a few additional sentences in black pencil:

To be cast by at least five high witches.
Chant the incantation three times three
and channel the energy straight into the
subject's heart.
May Isis assist the healers and may
Osiris take them in their warmest
embrace if they do not succeed.

"The moon is still waning," Alice pointed out. She must have been reading the grimoire over my shoulder. "That's not good. Also, we need the power of more witches combined. I could get a few friends to come here. If I call them now, they could be here in a couple of days and…"

I glanced at Clarence's tomb, which had been dark since I started to read. The edges of his body had started to become translucent, not unlike a ghost's.

"I don't think we have time to wait for the next waxing moon or your friends," I said quietly.

"Probably true, but you can't cast this spell on your own. Call me crazy, but I'm not keen on joining you on a suicidal mission," Alice replied.

I took a deep breath. Yes, I knew what might happen if I did try to cast that spell alone—the many warnings had told me—and I would have never expected such an extreme favor from Alice.

"I understand," I told her. "Please step aside now because I'm about to begin."

"Alba, don't make me restrain you," Alice growled, standing up and towering above me with her hands on her hips. "No. Just no. I won't allow you to do it. It's stupid. You need five experienced witches, and even like that, it's extremely dangerous…"

Alice was lifted off the ground by an invisible force—actually, not invisible, just tiny. Francesca had grabbed her waist and was holding her tightly in the air, away from me and the grimoire.

"No," Francesca said, setting Alice behind herself, "this is not our battle to fight, Alice. Alba knows the risks and must make her own choice. Otherwise, her sorrow will be ours to carry when Clarence is gone. And I can't carry anyone else's grief. I have enough burdens of my own."

I muttered a quiet *thank you* to Francesca, my eyes turning misty again. Alice nodded in understanding and stepped aside. They both retreated to a safe distance, holding each other by the waist, expectant.

***

I knelt next to my beloved and lay my hands on his motionless chest while his body started to fade in front of my eyes.

If Jean-Pierre's description was correct, after the glow of the curse was gone, Clarence would turn translucent and then disappear forever, leaving behind a thin layer of dust the wind would have blown away by morning.

"Clarence," I pleaded, removing myself for a second from my self-imposed magical hypnosis, "I need you to stay with me. Please don't die on me now. Please stay here just for a little while longer."

Still as a statue. Colder than steel.

"Just a little… please. Do it for me. I'm going to read the spell now. Please."

No reaction. Just the stillness of the dead.

'Stay here for me… your Isolde… *you my only awareness, utmost rapture of love*… remember? I didn't forget. You said I would, but I didn't."

As I quoted Wagner in a desperate last attempt, a faint sigh left his lips.

The moonlight seeped into my bones, and a shudder passed through me.

I lay my hands on his immobile chest, my knees sinking mindlessly into the damp, frosty grass by the tomb.

> *"A life for a life,*
> *A curse for a curse,*
> *Gelid like silver,*
> *silver cast death*
> *The magic of Ra's*

Most secret names
Heal and destroy
The curse shall melt
Lighting strike
And dampened earth
Oh mighty Isis
Untie this spell…

Three times three I chanted the incantation.

Then I closed my eyes and let the moonlight course through my extended arms and into his heart. The energy the spell unleashed was like the tide: rising inexorably, like a stream of warm water gushing through my limbs, traveling from my heart to his, squeezing me from the inside, wringing me, emptying me of each living particle still residing in my being.

Finishing me.

But flowing, pumping, absolving.

Even though I knew where this spell was leading me, I didn't break it. It was unstoppable. Stronger than me, greater than life. A powerful lightning bolt that I was dissolving into.

The words in Tristan and Isolde's dramatic finale reverberated in my mind:

Unconscious—utmost bliss!

Clarence had asked me to remember them.

I nodded, finally understanding.

I, like Isolde, was ready to meet my destiny.

The last thing I saw of this world before I

died were those magical, brick-red eyes, open and alert, loving, concerned, disconcerted. His eyelids fluttered, and his lips cracked open, half-breathing, half-smiling, half… wincing as reality set in, his forehead covered in radiant snowflakes.

Then darkness enclosed me, and before the end became the end, I heard him whisper, "I love you."

Chapter 34

Clarence

London, 1836

The night my mother passed away, I confronted the quandary of turning a human for the second time in my vampire existence. Three times, I faced that choice in the course of my first year of unlife, but only once I went through with it, choosing the worst subject possible.

Obviously, it was not her.

Rose, unlike Harold, never asked me to turn her. She would have loathed such an existence; she knew my pain and sorrow too well to wish them upon herself. But I, in my selfishness, wanted to keep her by my side. I feared that once she was gone, I would lose the tiny part of myself that still remembered how to be human. For me, her wish posed a dire ethical dilemma: without her, I would soon be lost to the thirst, reduced to a predator with a reptilian brain. No more sorrow or guilt, just hunger and hunting, victims and stalking, prowling the streets in search of prey.

That night, as she coughed her lungs away into a bloody handkerchief, I told her my story. She listened stoically; she had known all that time. There were tears in her eyes as I spoke, but she remained quiet, encouraging me with silent nods, asking me to repeat the parts she had missed due to the pernicious, lethal cough. It was a long, heartfelt conversation, after which I tried to persuade her to remain by my side for the rest of eternity. She shook her head and squeezed my hand in reply, infusing me with motherly love and sorrow.

"No," she said softly, "I have had enough of this world, my dear child."

"Please, Mother," I pleaded, holding her as she nearly choked and a crimson rain sprinkled the white bed linens, "consider my offer."

Mother stared at me with an immense tiredness in her eyes. She paused to listen in, waiting for the maid's footsteps to fade away. "No, Clancy," she answered after a brief deliberation. "That would not be me anymore. I would be of no use to you, or me, or anyone, and you know that."

Indeed, I knew, but losing her… losing Rose… it was analogous to insanity. I couldn't even bear the thought. She was the last person I loved in the whole wide world, and she was about to vanish forever, right in front of my eyes, while I had a way to make her stay. Rose Auberon was my last shred of lucidity; the only remaining pillar in the crumbling universe I had been thrown into. Her demise would sever the last tie which prevented me from falling into the abyss; into the unbearable loneliness of the immortal. She was the last tie to my old life, save for Father, who was dead to me anyway. That night, I faced the reality of seeing the last person I loved with all my heart die.

"I fear myself without you," I told her, holding her feeble hand in mine. It was warm, small and bony, with dry and wrinkled skin and spidery veins protruding like the roots of an old tree.

"I will always be with you," she assured me, trying to sit up. I helped her up, and she kissed my forehead, leaving traces of blood on it. "Paint me, Clarence. So you will never forget me. But make it a beautiful painting, like those you used to draw for me when you were little, remember?" She beamed, lost in her fond memories. "Give me long lashes and a happy smile… and only nice, bright colors. Will you do that for me?"

I nodded, glancing away so she would not see my tears.

"Promise me, Clarence."

"I will paint you," I assured her, "bright and kind. Like the angel you are." Like the angel she *had been*. "You have my word."

She smiled the last of her smiles and whispered, "I would really like that."

Chapter 35

Alba

The blanket was too heavy, and it covered my face. I couldn't breathe. I kicked it off, revealing where I was. It was the bed I used to share with Mark in our house in Emberbury, and confusion washed over me as I studied all the items scattered around the otherwise tidy space. Everything was just how I remembered it: the half-read romance novel on my nightstand, with a receipt as a marker. It was still on the page where I had stopped reading because my sobs were bothering Mark, who was trying to sleep. Mark's black suit, resting on the wooden valet, and my black mourning dress next to it, over the armchair, were both freshly ironed and ready to be worn.

"When is the babysitter supposed to come?" Mark yelled from the bathroom, and he peeked through the doorway, his face partially covered in shaving foam.

"Babysitter?" I asked, trying to dispel the thick fog muddling my thoughts. I pinched myself, just like in the movies. Was I awake or dreaming? How had I ended up in Mark's bed if the last thing I remembered was kneeling over Clarence's unconscious body in France? "What babysitter?"

Mark huffed. "Seriously, Alba? When do you intend to get your shit together? You said you would call a nanny to take care of the kids during the funeral, didn't you? Or did you forget that too?"

Funeral…

Yes, I remembered.

Mark's mother's funeral.

It was today.

"Mark, what's the date?" I asked, feeling weak. But he just rolled his eyes and started to button up his shirt, ignoring the question.

I got dressed, moving like a robot, unable to ignore the tight gold band on my finger, and the engagement ring next to it. Was I still married to Mark? I was tempted to ask him, but I decided against it, knowing my inquiries would be met with more sneers and few helpful answers.

The nanny came, and we drove to Emberbury Central Cemetery in a tense silence. Mark was moody, which was understandable for someone whose mother had passed just a couple of days ago. But he was always moody around me, no matter what.

We arrived early and were received by dozens of wreaths, sprays and baskets full of flowers, sent from the four corners of the world in memory of Mark's mother and tastefully arranged around the expensive mahogany casket. Work colleagues, old friends, teammates: everyone adored Mark. Mark's mother had been sick for years, and her death had been more a relief than a shock for the family; those people were there for him, not her.

Soon, Mark was hopping from one attendee to the next, unfolding his social butterfly side and charming everyone with his natural allure. It was hard not to love that version of my husband. I knew it well because I had been the recipient of those charms once upon a time. Those days were long gone now.

Knowing nobody would mind my absence, I walked away into the foggy pathways, wandering among the oldest tombs. I had at least half an hour before the service began, and I desperately needed some peace and quiet to put my thoughts in order.

As I strolled aimlessly among the graves, I admired the statues which adorned the mausolea of the richest families of Emberbury, trying to clear my mind. Pleading souls. Lamenting Madonnas. All mournful, or praying, or sleeping the sleep of the dead. All except for one: an angel statue which happened to be my favorite, erected in a secluded spot under a weeping willow. I remembered visiting it often. It was sculpted in white marble, his weight resting on one knee, with wide shoulders bearing the sprouts of torn wings, which lay at his feet. A fallen angel. His face was tilted down, as if wondering how he lost those wings. I had to crouch myself to look at his face. I had forgotten that detail. When I stared into the fallen angel's eyes, time stopped. My heart was pierced by an invisible silver bullet.

It was him, and there was no doubt: the angular jaw, framed by unruly, wavy hair, all illuminated by a soft, roguish smile, which contrasted with dark, sorrowful eyes.

It was him.

Clarence.

I held my breath, trying to ascertain what was real, and what was the dream. If Clarence was a statue, and I was still married to Mark, there was only one answer to my question.

I started to cry at the feet of the fallen angel. I remained there, lost in my grief, until a lady passed by and asked me whether I needed help.

"I'm okay, thanks," I lied, wiping off the tears. "I just need a minute. My mother-in-law just died."

And the man I thought I loved.

And the part of me which still knew hope.

"My condolences," she said with sympathy before resuming her stroll. "I know how much it hurts, losing someone you love."

I thanked her again, although I didn't think she knew *how much it hurt*. Had she ever lost someone who never existed?

Had she ever woken up to realize her whole present had been a dream, and she was still a prisoner in a previous life she thought extinct, while the future had never even happened?

I sat on the ground, dry leaves sticking to

my expensive coat. My expensive suede heels sunk into the mud, and I couldn't care less.

There had been no Clarence.

No Francesca.

No vampires, no witches.

Just a statue I used to pass by, which my mind had recycled as a real person in an extremely long and vivid dream to shield myself from reality.

The sadness of this realization was so devastating that it felt like being crushed under a mountain of rocks, then chopped into tiny pieces and scattered into the wind. Was it possible to die from a broken heart? The pain was unbearable, and I tried to make myself hollow to avoid it, in a vain attempt to detach from a heart which only brought me suffering and sorrow.

I could not breathe. I tried to call the kind lady, but she had disappeared already. I must be really dying, and it hurt, and I was alone… and lonely. They must have been wrong because there was no tunnel, and no light at the end to follow. Only pain, and loneliness, and the shadow of a fallen angel.

***

Night had darkened the graveyard, and a man approached me from the other side of the path. He had long, raven hair, which contrasted with his sparkling maroon eyes, and carried himself with the gracefulness of a lion and the lightness of a leaf dancing in the wind.

"Clarence?"

Was that even possible?

Where did the nightmare end and reality start?

He opened his arms and embraced me. He was so warm. Warmer than he had ever been.

"I thought I was lost," he said, then smiled, "but I'm not anymore."

"I'm lost too," I agreed. "And so confused."

"You know what they say…" He smiled fondly. "*Not all who wander are lost*… but I was lost without you."

I squeezed his hand, but it felt odd, unlike him. How was he warmer than I? Something was wrong, very wrong, and it wasn't just his presence at my mother-in-law's funeral, three years before I had even met him at The Cloister.

Looking around, I realized that Emberbury was no longer the graveyard I was standing in. It was a different place… an abandoned sinners' graveyard in France, at the foot of an abbey once owned by the Knights Templar.

Shaken by the flickering flashes of hallucinations and reality, I took a deep, steadying breath and gathered the courage to pose the question I had been dreading to ask, even though I already knew the answer.

"Am I dead, Clarence?"

He nodded warmly, his eyes pools of sadness and compassion. "Yes. Yes, you are." His voice broke, the last word almost inaudible as I nestled in his chest and started to weep.

"But…" I wept, inhaling his rusty, pinewood scent, "but I don't want to be dead," I cried, and he nodded again and kissed me, allowing me to continue. "The sun... I'll never see the sun again…"

"The sun is but a star, my dear," he whispered. "And now they are all yours. For all eternity."

He let me weep in his arms for a very long time, and after that, we remained under the willow, hugging each other in a silence full of questions, promises, and hope.

"What do we do now?" I asked weakly.

Clarence smiled, a slight hint of mischief lightening his gaze, and he said, "Let's just stay dead together for a little while longer, shall we?"

Chapter 36

Clarence

I found myself inside an open tomb in the Sinner's Cemetery of Alcazar, unable to remember how I had ended up there but relieved to feel the ice inside my heart magically gone. Alba lay over my chest with her arms limp around my neck and her eyes half open, her pupils riveted on the faint lights of the faraway abbey. Her breaths were choppy, sparse; her skin cool and pale. We must have been lying that way for a long time because a thin layer of snowflakes had made her bare shoulders glitter, partially melted under the veiled moonlight.

My first, half-conscious thought was how she was the loveliest creature I had ever encountered. Exquisite in her glorious imperfection: enticing, alluring, generous… *mine*. But perplexed as to how I was awake again, and in the most unexpected place, I failed to comprehend what unearthly power could have aroused me from my doomed slumber. I nudged her, but she remained still. A heartbeat, then silence. Another one. Then a longer silence.

A lightning bolt illuminated the sky, revealing the most distant peaks of the Pyrenees, and realization struck me just the same: she should not be here now, on the verge of death, with her hair spilling like a silken cobweb down the stone slabs and to the damp, cold earth I should have returned to. Wild briars were tangled in her skirts, and an open book lay at her feet, glowing menacingly.

I knew exactly what she had done, and fury started to boil inside me. Stifling a howl, I sat up and cradled her head in my lap, rocking her side to side. I tried to muffle my anger by taking it out on the briars around us. I uprooted them with my bare hands and threw them as far away as I could. My hand bled under the hardy spines, and my blood stained her dress, but to my frustration, the wounds healed as quickly as they had appeared.

A fresh, leafy briar grew again from the ground, sparked by a faint glow emerging from Alba's chest. The briar started to bloom, and I growled as I tore it down again and again. But it kept growing, springing from one side of the grave and disappearing into the other one, mimicking the enchanted briars that had joined Tristan's and Isolde's tombs after their death; the ones nobody had ever been able to cut down.

After a while, I gave up and allowed the implacable briars to grow at will. They built a canopy over us, sheltering us from the light snow while the North Star shone through the gaps in their abundant pink blossoms.

When the canopy was finished and completely covered with wild roses, Alba took her last breath.

I shook her in despair. Why? Why her? Why now? I had accepted that she would be gone before me, but... but not this soon. *Not like this.* I hadn't deserved that woman's presence in my life. She should have never been mine in the first place.

It should have been me turning to dust among the briars.

Not her.

My Isolde, my savior, my wings.

Just like Harold, just like Rose, just like so many others before her, I beheld a loved one marching to her demise, and once more, it was because of me. History repeated itself, mocking me with a devilish sneer. Only I was the devil. And she was my willing victim, sacrificing herself, even though I had lived too much, and I didn't really deserve—or even *wish*—to live any longer.

I howled like a wounded wolf, and my fierce, enraged yell alerted Francesca, who materialized out of nowhere, holding a white handkerchief against her delicate face. She had been crying, but for whom? For Alba? For me? For the love we would never have?

"Why?" I growled at her, holding Alba's limp body against mine. "She should live, and I should be dead."

Francesca watched me in silence, nodding.

She agreed, but she also knew what I was thinking. And I knew what she would have done in my place, but I? I did not know. How to be sure she would not hate me?

Our eyes rested upon Alba's neck, where a faint blue vein still pulsed sluggishly under her skin, the last sliver of a life bound to end too soon.

"You did it once before," Francesca said. She opened a gap among the briars to kiss my forehead, then inhaled deeply behind Alba's ear. "If you don't do it, I will," she added in a quiet whisper. "But I think it should be you."

***

I had only turned one human into a vampire in my whole, long, troubled existence. On that occasion, I had acted out of impulse, imbued with hatred and revenge for a man who now called himself Vlad. I would pay for that selfish urge for the rest of my darkness-filled days, or until I managed to right my wrong and end our centuries-long cat-and-mouse game. But that time, many decades ago, I had wanted to hurt him. *I had wanted it to hurt.*

Yet this time... this time was different.

Could you create a monster out of love?

Was my stone-cold heart capable of such sentiment, or did I just want to redeem the guilt I felt after her extreme sacrifice?

Francesca cleared her throat and nuzzled me softly with her nose, then backed off, expectant.

Alice appeared behind her, watching us in concerned silence. Francesca hugged her, and her fangs glistened under the moon. She had meant what she said: if I didn't do it, she would. She had always been braver than I, that little one.

The memory of Alba's blood was enough for my fangs to descend. I kissed her listless lips, pausing at the corner of her mouth, which didn't respond to my kisses anymore. Desperate, I let the tips of my fangs slide along her neck, feeling the delicate skin, still warm but barely alive... I was reluctant to break it, aware that doing so would break my heart, one way or another. How I wanted that moment to last forever, as I grieved in advance the loss of her warmth, the touch of her living hands, and everything that made her mortal, delicate, and warm. All those things would be gone forever... and perhaps *all of her* would be lost to death, one way or another, spent by a spell she was never supposed to cast, or consumed by unrestrained magic and newborn bloodlust. Turning witches was hazardous, and there were a thousand reasons not to do it. But did I have a choice, if I wanted to remain sane? I had let Rose go... and I still regretted that choice every day, two-hundred years later.

"Whatever happens now, know that I'll love you forever," I whispered into her hair.

But would she ever look into my eyes again after what I was about to do?

Tears rolled down my cheeks as I sank my fangs into her skin, and her sweet blood flowed freely, like a river of fire; a slow streaming farewell leaving her feeble heart forever. Her body quivered in my arms, and I had to force myself to keep going, not to stop now, just go through with it and finish what I had started.

A soft moan, then a sigh, and then… she was gone.

Dead.

"I'm sorry, I'm sorry… I'm sorry," I hummed against her broken skin, kissing, and crying and screaming inside as my heart shattered with guilt. Dead, like Rose. Dead, like Harold. Dead, like so many others I had loved and lost.

The briars started to swarm with worms. No. Not worms. *Caterpillars.* They crawled over the pink blossoms, then knitted a thousand silken cocoons around us, and they shone like goldthread beads. I closed my fist over the branches, relishing the piercing pain, allowing the thorns to drive into the skin of my palms and wrists. My blood started to flow, and I brushed my fingers against her blue lips to make her drink. She didn't react to my urgings at first, but I kept trying. She had to drink. She must. Otherwise, I would lose her forever.

Francesca and her witch stared with joined hands, holding their breath as I tried to make Alba drink. Francesca nodded, her eyes saying, *Insist. Don't quit now.*

The golden cocoons exploded like fiery lanterns, and Alba took a deep breath, her eyes staring at me in shock.

"Drink, my love," I said, hugging her with

relief.

A thousand butterflies emerged from the cocoons, and a gust of erratic winds propelled them in all directions, carrying a heavy snowfall with them. Alba kept drinking from me, avid and alien, her eyes showing no recognition of me or her surroundings, just unending thirst... and terror. The snow storm turned into a hurricane whirling around us, but it didn't touch the inside of our briar chrysalis. We remained in our bubble of blood, death and rebirth, until the ritual was complete, and she fell unconscious once more, her body jerking as she dropped onto my chest.

Silence fell over the Sinners' Cemetery. This silence was different though, and it buzzed with the hum of a hundred cursed souls anticipating the birth of a new sinner.

The snowstorm abated, and the briars started to wilt and crumble until our cocoon burst open, and the world around us became visible and real once again.

Francesca stepped closer, glancing at the sky with apprehension. Sunrise was looming, but we had to wait for Alba to wake up, if she ever did.

"You did well," Francesca said, placing a hand on my shoulder. I might have started to cry then, or perhaps I hadn't stopped at all. She caressed my head, motherly and calming, letting me know that it was fine. That I had the right to mourn. To cry.

"I don't know," I growled. "Did I?"

"You did, and she's one of us now,"

Francesca reassured me, and I joined her in a tortured embrace, waiting for the woman I loved, who would never be the same, to wake up and abhor me for the rest of her cursed, immortal days.

Chapter 37

Clarence

One hour to sunrise, and she still lay rigid and lifeless in my arms. Her body had cooled off, all rosiness gone forever from her cheeks.

A tremor shook the frosty blades of grass, and they tinkled like bells as they brushed against each other, a fairylike sound only detectable by immortal ears. It wasn't until minutes later that the roar of a motorcycle approached up the mountain path, and strong white headlights washed over the Sinners' Cemetery, carrying Carlo Lombardi's smug rear. The corrupt policeman parked his motorcycle with a cocky pirouette and clambered down, his hands full of foul-smelling, heavy-looking bags.

"Seems nothing can quite kill him for good…" he said to Alice, referring to me. I took a deep breath and ignored the sneering. "Here, I brought the supplies as agreed. For the trip." He gave one of the bags to Alice, who studied its contents with skepticism.

"I thought you were buying only essential

goods," she said, lifting a large, transparent bottle.

"Yeah, the vodka is *essential*. I need to keep my cool while traveling with two witches and two vampires. I think I could do much worse than vodka." He looked around, as if searching for something. "Where's Alba, by the way?"

"Oh, she's…" Alice's voice trailed away, interrupted by Francesca.

"She's fine," Francesca stated in a daring tone, hands on her hips. "She fell… *asleep* while you were gone, but if I were you, I would let her rest. Maybe go to the train station and wait for us there. Use the opportunity to return that…" she searched for the word, then gave up, "*velocycle*, or whatever you call it." Lombardi squinted and took two strides toward us. Francesca allowed him to pass, a look of curiosity growing on her face. "Good, as you wish," she said with a shrug. "But don't say I didn't warn you."

"What's *that*?" Lombardi gasped, pointing at the spot above our heads where the two ghostly entities were still hovering with impatience. I had been wondering why they wouldn't go away too. They didn't seem to belong to the Sinners' Cemetery, but it was hard to guess, as they refused to talk to me or Francesca. Ghosts were often envious of vampires, condemned to an incorporeal unlife as they were.

"Oh, that's just Laura… and her daughter," Alice explained. "They are waiting for Alba to wake up and send them to the afterlife."

"The Angel of Death is gone, madam," the

child ghost said in a hiss, looking at the witch. "Can we go home now too?"

"Well…" Alice picked up the grimoire, which was still lying on the ground, and sat down on a nearby grave. "Maybe I should try and do it because Alba might be a bit disoriented when she wakes up." She turned to Carlo and added in a whisper, "We don't need two angry ghosts haunting us, on top of everything else."

Lombardi grimaced, studying the specters with animosity, while Alice tuned out the world and immersed herself in the antique spellbook. After a few minutes, Lombardi recovered his composure, but it didn't last long because his eyes fell on Alba, still lying inert and pale in my arms.

"Oh, fuck." He made the sign of the cross and brushed the back of his trembling hand against Alba's bare shoulders. "She's… freezing." His hand found her chest, hesitating over her unbeating heart. "Oh… fuck, no, no, no… she's…" He swallowed, glowering at me. "Dead! She's fucking dead, Auberon! What did you do to her?" He grabbed her shoulders and tried to shake her, in an attempt to wake her up. I growled at him and forced him to step back. The man remained paralyzed, staring at Alba, motionless. I could smell the anger growing inside him, waiting for a spark to make it blast. As much as I loathed that mortal, I could empathize with him for once; I felt the same myself.

"I told you to leave," Francesca reminded him, standing beside him with her arms crossed.

"You did not listen."

"You two are sick!" he spat, his voice quivering with barely controlled anger. "How could I ever trust you! Vampires! Monsters! I was right all along!"

"You have no idea what you are talking about, *human*," Francesca scoffed.

Alba stirred on my chest, her eyelids fluttering for a second before she fell limp once again. Francesca hushed Lombardi with a wave of her hand and hurried to kneel beside us. "She's coming to," she observed, holding Alba's hand.

Alba's eyes popped open, an eerie green glow sparkling behind her lashes. She sat up abruptly and turned her head left and right, a startled expression on her face.

We remained silent. Breathless.

Francesca got up again and inched closer to Lombardi, peering at stirring Alba with wariness.

Newborn vampire.

Helpless human.

Bad combination.

"Oh, no," Carlo gasped, finally understanding the situation.

Within fractions of a second, Alba leapt out of the grave like a missile, knocking Carlo down and perching on his chest with a vicious grimace.

"Francesca!" I yelled, rushing after Alba before she killed Lombardi in her craze. "Stop her!"

Alba sank a glistening pair of new fangs into the human's neck, pinning him to the ground like a rag doll. The man screamed, then froze with shock as she fed from him, unable to match the brutal thirst of a new vampire.

"Alba!" I shouted, striving to detach her from the man and bring her back to her senses, "Alba, stop, please! You will kill him!"

I tore her off him, and she turned to face me with her eyes glowing. Sharp, virgin claws emerged from her delicate fingers, tearing at my skin like a tiger and leaving deep, bleeding marks all over my chest. She scratched and bit as I tried to restrain her clumsy but reckless attacks; all the while, she kept growling like a wild beast, ready to kill me if she had to. My wounds closed as soon as she withdrew her claws, and a disconcerted look formed in her now emerald-glowing eyes. In her madness, she didn't understand why I was healing, nor did she seem to remember what I was, if she remembered me at all. It was typical for newborn vampires to wake up thirsty, but aggression toward their own maker was extremely rare and invariably punished with a swift execution—which was out of the question in our case.

She paused her attack, studying me with half-closed eyes, surely devising a new strategy to pounce on me from a different angle.

A group of teenagers passed by, drinking cheap wine and singing obscene songs, burning the last hours of a long night and jesting about chasing witches, ghosts, and the other *imaginary* creatures which loomed over the abbey. They seemed young; yesterday's children. Alba's nostrils flared, and I prayed to all gods I didn't believe in for her to stay put where she was and not lunge at the children, as it was bound to be a massacre.

She would never forgive me for that, if she ever came back to her senses.

"Do not move," I said softly, but baring my fangs. She noticed them and snarled like a cornered beast.

Grief clasped my core as I stood in front of her, watching the creature she had become... all because of me.

Who was this devil holding my gaze?

What had she done to the woman I loved?

And most important of all, were there any traces of kindness in that vicious shell of a human?

Turning witches was forbidden. Turning witches was hazardous. Turning witches wasn't supposed to be done because it often brought doom upon them and those close to them. It often unleashed madness and reckless magic, destroying everyone within reach until the witch, and her loved ones, were consumed by a mixture of rage, thirst and unbridled powers.

But *I* wasn't going to stand and watch her self-destruct. Not as long as I had two hands to stop her.

Ignoring her aggressive stance, I opened my arms and took a step forward. When she saw me approaching, she crouched, ready for a new assault.

I held her gaze, admiring the new hue of her eyes: dark, enigmatic and green, and as deep as the oldest ferns of the Amazon rainforest, with golden speckles where before they had been sprinkled with brown. She had been beautiful and lovely before; now she was terrifying too.

A flicker of vulnerability crossed her face—perhaps her sanity flashing back—and she faltered. Losing no time, I gripped her tight. It felt so out of place, using force on her. I had to remind myself that this was not her. Not anymore. Or at least, not yet.

She resisted and squirmed in my arms, but I used all my strength to hold her, until she gave up and remained still; a predator devising a new escape strategy.

Slowly, I loosened my grip, turning my clasp into a hesitant embrace.

"You are safe," I whispered into her hair. "You are safe with me. I will take care of you."

She lay her head on my shoulder, and a sigh of relief escaped my lungs.

She was coming back… she was…

A horrible agony shook my whole body as she sank her fangs into my neck with a rage I wouldn't have employed even on my worst enemy. It hurt like hell, even for a vampire, but I allowed her to drink while Lombardi ran to safety on his motorcycle, taking the Italian witch with him.

As Alba fed, she started to calm down. She drank for several minutes, and bit by bit, her kicking and scratching diminished, her thirst slowly quenched. We would need to find her a human, but it was nearly morning, and she was too dangerous to feed in the open and unsupervised.

"Alba, my lovely, look at me," I said, trying to steer her face toward me. I was getting weaker with all the blood loss, and I would need to stop her. "Who am I?"

Her eyes flickered to my face, her fangs tearing my flesh, and she squinted at me in silence. I flinched with pain but kept my voice calm.

"You are going to be fine," I assured her, even though I didn't believe my own words.

She licked her lips of the last drop of blood, then closed her eyes and started to weep in silence, collapsing against me and relinquishing all resistance.

"*Shh*," I comforted her, caressing her hair. "It's fine. I understand how you feel. Just come here. Come. Come home."

She threaded her fingers behind my neck and rested her cheek against my shoulder. I relished the softness of her skin against mine, and the sound of her choppy sobs as the rational part of her brain finally started to wake up. I planted a feathery kiss on her forehead and leaned back. Her eyes glimmered, but this time with curiosity, devoid of all previous threats. She tilted her head, and her lips parted, barely an inch from mine. My whole body responded to her invitation, and she smiled.

Alba pulled me against her with the force of a tidal wave pushing me into the ocean, fierce and unstoppable, compelling me to drown in the most passionate kiss we had ever shared.

Snowflakes faded and melted, then turned gold, and red, and blue, flashing like rainbows as we kissed inside an anonymous sinner's grave. She opened her eyes again and freed me from her grasp to admire the shifting colors around us. Meanwhile, I let my hands drop to her waist, pushing her against me and running the tip of my tongue down her chin, exploring all the way down to her cleavage. Her skin was firmer and colder but still as delicious as it used to be. Her hands delved beneath my torn shirt, and she moaned softly, whispering my name into my ear.

She remembered it.

Francesca cleared her throat, dragging us back to the present moment, and we parted abruptly with a frustrated gasp, our bodies already mourning the unwelcome separation.

"You two could benefit from the privacy of a hotel room," Francesca reproached, "if only you hadn't ravaged the one we had."

Alba smiled at her with discomfort, her true self bubbling back to the surface. "I'm sorry," she muttered, shaking her head and holding it with both hands. Her voice sounded like her, just like her kiss had felt like her. She turned to me, with her arms extended in front of her, and examined them with puzzlement. "Clarence…" she said. "Why do I feel so strange?"

Epilogue

Alba

Cape Finisterre

Finisterre or *The End of the Earth*, was a long granite finger at the end of the Bay of Biscay, dipping into the vast Atlantic Ocean and covered in a tapestry of green, mossy grass and grey stone. Once upon a time, this place was believed to be the very last place on Earth. If you dared to keep walking, or decided to swim for a while too long, you might fall into the void and be lost into nothingness forever.

Today, the world was known to be round, which meant that far, far away, there must be my old home in Emberbury, and The Cloister, and all the memories that kept coming back in painful ripples since waking up at the Sinners' Cemetery a couple of nights earlier.

I stood under the moonlight at the very edge of this rocky cape on *Costa de la Muerte*, an ominous toponymic—though well-fitting— which translated to *The Coast of Death*. No better place for someone like me, after dying and rising from the dead, as I held my undead lover's hand under the expectant gaze of two ghosts: one headless, one not so much.

Clarence and I had followed the clues Carlo had coaxed from the hotel burglar all the way to a lighthouse, where Natasha was supposed to meet one of her business partners. But we had been late. We hadn't been able to locate Julia or Ludovic either. The hunters had been gone before we had arrived, perhaps alerted by one of Natasha's contacts in Alcazar. Francesca was on her way to The Cloister, although we still hadn't decided what she would tell Elizabeth about me. She would probably meet Alice and Carlo back in Emberbury.

Now it was just Clarence and me, and the ocean extending before us, full of possibilities, doubts… and choices.

To the right, the chance of finding my daughters, still lost despite their father's reported efforts to find them. Clashing with this need was the horrible fear of harming them when we met again, unable to control myself around humans as I was. Panic took hold of me when I remembered how I had almost slaughtered a group of teenagers two nights earlier. Who knew what I might do to my own offspring if the bloodlust clouded my mind, as it seemed to do at nightfall?

And then, to the left, Emberbury, and the promise of freedom and justice for someone who had helped me when I needed it most: Julia, the previous witch of The Cloister, captured by hunters together with her husband, Ludovic. According to the burglar, both were still alive but suffering under Natasha's imprisonment.

Clarence's hand squeezed my shoulder, and he leaned against my side to comfort me. He probably knew what I was thinking, and I was grateful for his rare silence. I turned toward him to find him staring at me with a sweet expression of longing.

"What is it?" I asked, watching my arms like they were someone else's. I wasn't used yet to the transparency and pallor of my skin, which made the blue veins under it clearly visible.

"Nothing," he said. "You are so beautiful."

I exhaled, seeking my reflection in the puddles left by a late-night rain, but it wasn't there anymore.

"I wish I could see what I look like," I whined.

"I know." He nodded. "But you can trust me. You are as beautiful as ever. Even more than before, if that's even possible."

I thanked him with a playful nudge, and he staggered back, taken by surprise. I still forgot I was stronger than I used to be. "Okay. I think I've made up my mind."

"So? Where are we going first?"

"I can't help anyone else until my children are safe. I'm not sure I can trust myself around them right now, but I trust you to be at my side if I lose control."

"Good choice," he said. "Even though London is the last place on Earth I would like to visit, I applaud your decision."

"You don't want to go to London? Why? I thought you liked it."

"Yes, I do indeed. But there is someone there I would rather not meet."

"Really? And who's that?"

He shuffled his feet, pensive. "His name is…" he hesitated, his eyes scanning my face, "Vlad. Some distant relative of mine. He would like to see me dead, and vice-versa. The usual family squabbles."

"Oh, I see. But London is a big city."

Clarence let out a broody rumble, which could have meant just about anything, though mostly nothing good.

"What?" I asked.

"Nothing. Look at this," he said, waving his arm in the air as a faint smile crept back. Performing one of his favorite tricks, he produced a ring out of his sleeve with an exaggerated flourish, and he presented it to me on the palm of his hand. "For you."

"Isn't that Francesca's ring?"

"I'd like you to have it now. She approves."

I blinked, my hand hovering over his but unsure of what I was supposed to do with his offering. "Are you trying to tell me something?"

He laughed, shaking his head. "No, of course not. We already discussed that when we first met, remember?"

I sighed with relief. Yes, I remembered that. *Vampires live too long for that kind of commitment.* "Good," I said, "because I already did that once, and I don't think I ever want to do it again."

"Not even with me?" His eyes glinted, maroon with red sparkles of hope and mischief.

I smiled. "Sorry, but…" I muttered, although my heart whispered, *Maybe one day.*

He hugged me and bent down to slip the ring on my finger, brushing his lips over the back of my hand before standing up again. "I don't blame you." He bumped his nose against mine and stepped back to watch me. "But no, no need to fuss. This is just an enchanted trinket, meant to bring you luck and hopefully keep you safe. If you get lost on the way, hold it and think of me so we can find each other again."

I took off my shoes and relished the coolness of the grass on the soles of my feet. I could feel each tiny blade. I could even tell whether they were pointing left or right or straight upwards and whether they were fresh or dry. Not only were all those new sensations fascinating, they were a great way to avoid thinking about the hundreds of things I was terrified of dealing with.

"So?" he said, cocking an eyebrow and nodding toward the ocean. "Shall we?"

"I guess I need to shift if we are to cross the sea, don't I? Will you teach me how?"

All the way here, I had been trying to shift but never succeeded. Because of that, we had run for two days to reach Finisterre, but running wouldn't do in order to reach London.

"It's easy," he explained. "Just jump, and it will happen. Your body will know what to do, once it has no other option."

God, he was handsome. Now that my senses could catch so many more details, I marveled at all the little things I had missed before, and it was hard to concentrate on anything. I could have sat and stared at a drop of water for hours, gaping at the rainbows and shapes inside it. Perhaps one day, I would just stay in bed and stare at Clarence for a whole week, listening to the nuances of his voice and investigating his body and its wonders up to the very last inch.

A large wave splashed and sprayed my face, waking me up from my sensual reverie.

"Let's go," Clarence said, glancing at the sky. The sun was about to rise. I threw him a helpless look, too embarrassed to reiterate my worries for the hundredth time. "You can do this. I believe in you." He framed my face with his hands and kissed me, making all my doubts and fears evaporate. "See you in London."

Clarence jumped off the cliff and disappeared into a grey mist, fusing with the stormy clouds for a few seconds until his raven form materialized and soared over Finisterre, gliding over my head and waiting for me to take a leap after him.

Standing on the edge of the cliff, I opened my arms, delighting in the soft caress of the fabric on my skin as my dress billowed in the wind. With my eyes closed, I imagined how flying would feel.

Being weightless…

Opening my wings and shooting into a starry sky…

Clarence's words from many months ago echoed in my mind: *Taking off is always scary, but once you are airborne, all troubles become so much smaller.*

The rock I was standing on crumbled under my toes and gravel tumbled down to disappear into the hungry black waves.

My turn.

I swallowed, closed my eyes and took a leap into the night sky, jumping as far and high as I could. It felt like flying.

Clarence had said my body would know what to do, but as I plunged toward the raging ocean, doubt started to creep in. I flailed my arms and legs, time slowing down, and as I was about to crash to the surface of the water, my hands turned dark and small. Still, I sank into the ocean, unable to fly. I tried to call to Clarence, but the waves muffled my screams. Finally, I managed to start swimming using my new, foreign body, and I wondered what might have gone wrong as I reached for the surface.

Clarence descended in soft spirals, spreading his wings over me as I paddled furiously in the water, trying to figure out how to use my new, alien shape. *Trust,* his eyes said, *trust like the caterpillar trusts in its rebirth. Trust when you have no other choice, and the tide is dragging you to the high seas.*

"Clarence... what happened?" I wanted to speak. I wanted him to help me, or at least to tell me what had gone wrong, but all that came out of my throat was a deep, hoarse growl. Yet looking at Clarence, I saw no concern—only fondness and... *admiration?*

The first ray of morning sun peeked among the clouds, finally revealing the answer to my question.

I hadn't turned into a raven; I had no feathers at all. Instead, ebony fur covered my arms; arms that ended in soft, delicate pads, which hid deadly black panther claws behind them.

Astounded and delighted, I swam, releasing my fears and expectations into the salty water. I swam into the unknown, trusting like the caterpillar, ready to open my butterfly wings and fly into a new, exciting adventure.

The End

This story continues in the 4ᵗʰ book of the series.

The Vampires of Emberbury

"Taking off is always scary, but once you are airborne, all troubles become so much smaller."

About the author

*My name is Eva and I have always lived in a world of magic.
Tales of fantasy and sorcery have haunted me since I was a child,
which has caused much tripping on my own feet while walking
around absorbed in yet another story.*

Scan the code to stay in touch:

Acknowledgments

I finished this book during a very stressful period of my life, and I am certain it wouldn't have been published on time, if it hadn't been for the people who stood by my side, helped me with the editing and rewriting and above all, believed in me and my story.

So, to all of them:

thank you from the bottom of my heart.

You know who you are.

A big hug to my beta readers:

Charlie, *Queen of the Forest Fairies;* **Helen,** *Demon Empress,* and **Ksenija,** *Knight of the Sharpest Pen and Eye.* Your comments helped make this book better. Also, to **Wendy**, Georgian and Victorian era expert, who knows Clarence's times better than him (he was too busy biting people to pay attention).

To the ladies of *The Coven*, as always.

And to **Bori,** for the unicorns, chocolate and supersonic preliminary editing. One day we'll celebrate the end of this series—with a proper Roman party! Also to **Elizabeth**, for taking care of the final edits.

And of course, thanks to you,
who are reading this book,
for following Alba and Clarence's adventures and
giving me a reason to keep writing them.